When Somebody Loves You Back

Patriece

When Somebody Loves You Back

Cover Art by TakynmiAzziz

Printing by Falcon Books

San Ramon, California

ISBN 10: 0-9778096-0-9
ISBN 13: 978-0-9778096-0-8

Published by
Pressin On Publications
P.O. Box 2304
Oakland, CA 94614-0304

www.PressinOnPublications.com

PRINTED IN THE UNITED STATES OF AMERICA

Acknowledgements

I acknowledge my entire family, my host of friends and acquaintances who encouraged me throughout the years it took me to publish this book. I appreciate you all, Thank you!

Finally, thank you to the ones that believed in me so much—our parents Mattie and Larry and Connie.

Dedication

This book is dedicated to my beloved who are dear to my heart and always will be.

Marco Dante Sutton, whose death inspired me to live 3/21/75—11/17/90

Roger Fitzgerald Aragon my first true friend 04/01/67—05/28/03

My biggest fan, cheerleader and best friend Joe, my beloved family—and my daughters Yanni and Ari, especially.

Thank you Jesus!

We couldn't have done it without you!

Preface

When Somebody Loves You Back is about life and love and romance. Not a fairytale kind of romance, but the everyday appreciation of love.

The kind of romance when your lover passes you toilet paper while you're sitting in the bathroom or a lover that uses your toothbrush while on vacation because he forgot his. It's the time he bought you a rose out of the gas station to make up before your long ride to the fishing hole. You know it's that day that you let him listen to "his" song on the radio, the one you hate.

When Somebody Loves You Back is about people easing their guards down at their own pace and finding themselves standing before one another clothed in only their love, simultaneously.

It's that wonderful warm feeling you get when you realize that...*Somebody Loves You Back.*

1

In every life there is a day when coping is hard. That day for Nicole Collier was today. This morning she lost the tears she had been determined to keep. They simply slid from her like water from ice. She cried for every wrong in her life, from her bastard birth to her present homelessness.

Living in this apartment was surviving—nothing more. Grandma's house had been home. Nicole had no choice, but to let it go. There was no way she could afford a mortgage. The flowers for Grandma's casket depleted her life's savings.

It was hard to believe that the woman that never loved *anybody* had taken a second mortgage against their home for rehabilitation treatment for anyone, including her daughter.

Nicole stood on her head to please Grandma and nothing warranted a word of praise, or a hug of approval, not even a *pretentious* gesture of endearment. Yet, at this moment she longed for even that cold love. If Grandma were there at least she would have gotten the 'Happy Birthday' due her this morning, despite its lack of warmth.

Nicole felt like twenty years ago to date she entered this world and no one even cared. Not even the woman that labored to bring her here. Reflecting on her relationships platonic and romantic none of them were authentic. She had let go of all that wore the label of "friend" when she moved from Grandma's. Those people weren't her friends. Her supposed to be girlfriends only wanted to use her to attract a man of their own or borrow her clothes etc, the men in her life had only wanted to lay down with her, even the man she gave her virginity to. That wound was so deep, the spot in her heart was tender to even a thought.

All I want is a normal life...A man, child, two-car garage and someone to love me. What's so wrong with that?

The tears taking over her face forced Nicole to the bathroom. She looked into the mirror, all her life people ranted and raved over how beautiful she was. Nicole didn't want to be pretty; she wanted to be loved. Just to feel it for even a brief moment. Her tears were coming as fast as she could wipe them. Nicole was tired. Tired of hurting. Tired of being alone. Especially tired of yearning. She wanted to do something other than drift. She wanted to take a chance, satisfy a dare or accept a challenge. She wanted to feel alive. As she stood there a quiet determination claimed her. Slowly, her faith was restored.

She stepped into the shower tearless. Crying had done her some good. The plan for today was to wash clothes, rent a movie, polish her toes and have a glass of wine. She slipped into a pair of jeans and an old T-shirt then went back into the bathroom to sort the clothes. In checking her pockets she ran across a piece of paper…a receipt…a phone number. She tossed her head back in disbelief. The ugliest man she had ever seen, with a pulse, had given it to her. She had slipped it into her pocket not to be rude. He asked her to call him if she was interested in a free meal and some compliments.

There was something attractive about him, though it wasn't his face. Something that was gnawing at her this very moment. He had style. A confidence that was graceful. It was the reason she dropped the garment she held in her hand and paged him.

♣♣♣

Champ got the page. It couldn't have been timelier. Denise was really starting to get on his nerves. If she didn't lay so well, he wouldn't have been there this long. Her house was a mess. All she ever did was smoke weed and beg. If she wasn't doing one of those she was complaining just as she was doing right now.

Champ walked out of the room into the kitchen so he could respond to the page. The number was unfamiliar to him and he didn't want whomever it was to hear Denise's loud mouth. As he dialed he made a mental note to find somewhere else to live because he was tired of all this arguing. When he was with Nita the loving was better and there was no arguing.

"Hello, someone paged?"

"Yes, I am trying to reach Champ?" Nicole stumbled on the name. It was quite unusual.

"Who is this?"

"Nicole. I met you at the grocery store a few days ago."

"Oh!...How you doing? This is me."

"I'm fine. I finally got a minute to call."

"So, what's up? You wanna get into something?"

Nicole wasn't expecting him to be free tonight. "Yes, I would love to go out. It's my birthday and I was planning to watch a movie and polish my toes."

"Well, don't. I'm taking you out. Is seven good?" Champ was already planning what he was going to do for her. He was a master at wining and dining. He picked up on the fact that on her birthday, Nicole was calling a complete stranger to spend time with her.

"Seven's fine." Nicole hung up feeling very much alive.

Champ turned around just in time to stop Denise from hitting him in the back of his head.

"You bett' not be talking to no bitch on my phone!" She was struggling to free her hand and strike him.

"No! You better sit yo' ass down 'fore you get knocked down. You gon' make me hurt you." He slung her, by the wrist, to the floor. Stepping over her he went into the bedroom and tossed a hunter green silk shirt on the bed. Denise charged into the room and struck him across the face. With one punch Champ knocked her out cold, stepped over her again then took his shower. When Denise came to he was completely dressed.

"You betta' not ever bring yo' ass back here! I hate you! I hate you! You bastard!" Denise's face was swelling and she was crying.

Champ ignored her totally. After he was dressed he walked out the door without a goodbye.

♣♣♣

Nicole opened the door at exactly 7:00 pm. Champ looked nice. Even his face had improved somehow. He stepped around Nicole without being invited, and entered her apartment. She closed the door behind him. It was that confidence that turned her on. He wanted to come in so he did.

"I'm ready." She whispered.

"Alright let's go."

He doubled-checked the lock on her door as they started down the steps. Nicole smiled. She had been looking for that type of concern for herself all of her life.

After dinner they walked along the bay. Champ unknowingly filling her life's voids one after another. When he stopped to kiss her she let him. She could feel him against her. Immediately she returned to her senses. When he felt her pull back he let her go.

"I apologize if I offend or frighten you. I didn't mean to. It's one of those things that a man cannot prevent. Every time I'm with a beautiful woman this happens." He smiled. He had a nice smile. Nicole had not noticed it before.

"I'm not offended or afraid I'm just not ready."

"Ready for what? I was just kissing you. I wasn't trying to get you into bed." Champ knew then that she was hungry for love.

Innocence shone through her like sunlight through a window. Champ was intrigued. She was not just innocent looking—she was innocent. He had to respect that.

"So how long has it been?"

"Longer than I care to admit. I'm tired of meaningless lovemaking. I have had three lovers and not one of them really loved me. I promised my body that I would not share it with anyone who wasn't willing to marry me." She never meant to share all of that as she smiled nervously and somewhat embarrassed.

"I guess, I'm the marrying type. My Grandmother certainly wanted that for me. She died when I was eighteen, and I've been on my own ever since. My mother died having me." Champ had not intended to share that, but it was so easy talking to this girl. She was soothing. She had the kind of honesty that made a liar forget to lie. He had never talked to anyone like this before. Especially bringing up his mother.

"I'm sorry about your mother. My mother is alive but she's a drug addict, so it's as if she isn't. I haven't seen her in months. I don't even know how to get in touch with her, where she lives or anything." Nicole started to cry. Champ eased his arm around her and let her cry. She was so beautiful to him. He thought about Denise while he was holding her—he was going to have to hurry up and get out of that situation. Remembering Nicole's apartment he smiled. Everything was so clean. Even now as he held her he could smell the shampoo in her hair. Again he felt himself rising. Out of respect for her he shifted his thoughts and allowed himself to relax.

Nicole was grateful for his shoulder. She thanked him and they went back to the car. Champ took her to a spot in the Oakland Hills where they had a magnificent view of San Francisco. They talked all night. At dawn Nicole told Champ she had to go to work at 1:00 pm and needed to head home. Champ pulled up in front of her apartment, walked her to the door then kissed her goodnight. Nicole went in the house and crawled into bed. She could not sleep. She felt too good. Taking charge of her life for one day was the best birthday present she could have ever given herself.

♣♣♣

Champ returned to Denise's and went straight to the bedroom. Denise was already in bed.

"Denise? Denise? Babe? I'm home." He laid down next to her. He knew he had no place to go, so he had to be nice to Denise. He was going to make the best of the situation until he got it together with Nicole.

Denise turned over. "Where have you been?"

"I went for a ride. I needed to think, about us. We need to try to work this out. I'm sorry 'bout hitting you, but you brought that on yourself."

"I know. I'm sorry too. I know I should stop nagging you so much."

Champ could tell by her cuddle that she wanted to make love. He did too just not with her. Nicole was all he could think about, so he had to keep his eyes closed as he made love to Denise.

2

Nicole received compliments like a toddler in a frilly dress and silk hair ribbons. Everyone that laid eyes on her found it difficult to turn away. She was smitten by love and her joy was showing.

In the past three weeks that ugly man had given Nicole immeasurable joy. Champ was the answer to her prayers. She was being spoiled and loving it! He picked her up from work everyday and they always did something special. She felt feminine, loved and beautiful whenever she was with him, lately all the time.

Nicole was finally happy. She had what her mother had denied her and what her grandmother had withheld from her. In her heart she knew that Champ didn't have to care about her because the two that were supposed to didn't. It was for this reason she loved him.

Unbeknownst to her, he was securing himself a place to live. If that gained him a place in her heart, so be it. As early as day four he knew his presence was making her happy. It was all over her face. Showing up was all he had to do, and that was easy. So easy, he was putting a stop to all the wining and dining.

"Champ, I don't want to go out tonight. Let's go to my apartment and I'll cook."

"I don't know. I have a few runs to make and then I was gonna take you to grab a bite to eat." He was lying. He was going to suggest the same thing, but since she beat him to the punch, he couldn't pass up the opportunity to shine. That's how highly he regarded himself. As long as she kept appreciating him, making him feel like a king and her demands remained low, everything would be ok.

"Just drop me off. I'll cook. Go do what you have to do, dinner will be ready when you come back."

"Alright." He agreed adding just enough hesitance in his voice to make her feel she was irresistible.

Nicole got out of the car a little short of skipping.

Mesmerized by her innocence Champ sat there for a minute.

Nicole thought it sweet of him to wait for her to get inside during broad daylight.

♣♣♣

Champ walked in the door and Denise started in on him.

"For the past month you've been coming and going like you want to! Now I was trying to be cooperative and work it out like we said, but the more patient and understanding I be, the more disrespectful you be so, if you leave tonight take all yo' shit with you." Denise had never been more serious.

Champ knew his time had run out. What he didn't know was how close he was to moving into Nicole's apartment. It was too soon for him to disappoint her. More importantly he didn't want to. He really cared about her despite his ulterior motive.

"Shut up girl! I ain't going nowhere. I know I've been gone a lot, but I been making money so don't trip." Reaching into his pocket he handed Denise a small wad of money, about three hundred dollars in 20's and 10's figuring that would satisfy her. He had been promising her something on the bills for two months. The $800 in his wallet, he kept for himself. Part of that was going to buy his way into Nicole's place.

Denise took the money and smiled. When she tried to kiss him he held his lips together tightly preventing her tongue from entering his mouth, and pulled away quickly. She was a sloppy kisser and lately he didn't care for nothing or no one other than Nicole.

♣♣♣

Grandma's old furniture had been resurrected. Removing the knitted and crocheted throws had modernized it a great deal.

Nicole polished the cherry wood trimming on the couch and chair, then the coffee table before them. She changed the water in her almost fresh flowers and placed them back on the coffee table.

In the corner sat the cherry wood chest that used to sit in Grandma's room. In the drawers Nicole stored her videos, while the 19" TV sat on top. As she stood there, she looked across the room at the brass-trimmed mirror that occupied the wall near the door and then at the treelike plant beneath it. This was her favorite corner in the house. The way the brass plant holder shone against the hardwood floor. Often she sat on the couch focusing on that image as if it were a dancing fire on a winter night. It gave her a serene feeling, a healing, sometimes even hope. With that feeling she walked into her bedroom, which contained all of Grandma's old furniture save a new spread and mini blinds. Nicole's perfumes were lined neatly across the dresser. Aside from a few African pieces that she'd picked up at a moving sale, the walls were bare, but it was enough.

There were two steaks and two potatoes in the oven and a salad in the fridge. All she needed to do was get dressed. She wasn't going to rest this one on pretty. Champ was a keeper and that's what she intended to do. Keep him. She'd do whatever it took to keep him in her life. His presence had become a necessity.

♣♣♣

Champ knew he needed to get going. Nicole was waiting, but Denise's threat was on his mind. If everything had been in place with Nicole he would've told Denise what she could do, but since it wasn't and he wasn't positive on how close he was to getting into Nicole's apartment, he couldn't chance it.

The telephone rang. It was one of Denise's friends. Two minutes later she was out the door. A minute after that Champ was too.

♣♣♣

"Hi Baby." He stepped in.

Nicole was attempting to pout, but couldn't. It didn't matter anymore that he was late just that he was there. She was setting the table as Champ came behind her. He embraced her from behind, inhaled her hair and kissed her behind the ear.

"I didn't know your hair was this long. It's beautiful. I can't keep my hands off of you."

Blushing, Nicole turned in the circle of his arms. "Then don't." She had been suppressing the urge to be physically loved by Champ for as long as she could. Today's tardiness jolted fear of his disappearance. Fear that forced her to remember that before him she was alone, and she wasn't going back to that. Ever.

With everything perfect and the memory of their first date fresh on her mind, *'I guess I'm the marrying type'* Nicole shared herself with Champ in Grandma's old bed. It was more than she could ever have anticipated. Champ was a superb lover. His pace was perfect, his technique chilling and his expression of passion weakening.

Nicole had been made love to before and it had been good, but it was carnal. What Champ did to her body affected her emotions as well. He rested atop her and looked at her. Then traced her facial features like he was reading Braille.

Then he closed his eyes, pulled his bottom lip into his mouth and bit it.

Nicole pushed back.

They exchanged passion until both were exhausted.

"Champ what's your real name?"

"Leslie Andrews." He opened his eyes and looked at her. She was tucked neatly under his arm. Her leg resting across his. He wanted to see her reaction to his name. He hated it. It was so feminine. "I was named after my mother. I guess my Gramps thought it was a way of holding on to her only child."

Champ turned away from Nicole because he couldn't let her see his pain. Secretly, he felt like he had murdered his mother. Sometime he felt guilty about even wanting to know her after that.

Snuggling closer, Nicole offered him her comfort. She wanted to give him what he'd given her. "Babe, it's ok. We may not have parents or family, but we have each other."

"I have family. I have a play brother. We call him Black. His name is Andre. We've been friends since fifth grade. He's the one started calling me Champ. His whole family adopted me. They're good people. Matter-of-fact, Black and Feather, that's his woman, her real name is Maya, are having a Superbowl party. You can meet them then."

"Black? And Feather?" Nicole wondered how they got their nicknames.

"Nicole when you meet them you will understand." He inhaled her hair again. He loved how clean she smelled even after making love.

That feeling of aloneness crept upon Nicole again. No one had adopted her. This man she had fallen for with so much in common, had just shown indifference. Pain was registering.

"Nikki let's eat."

Dismissing that pain was easy. Nicole was weak for affection. Often she had wished to use the informal Nikki, but Grandma had forbid it.

She sprang to her feet, slipped into her gown, prepared and heated their plates, with perfect timing Champ, in his drawers, sat down at the table like he was appropriately dressed.

"Babe you like this antique look huh?"

"Well, yes and no. After Grandma died, I kept what I could and salvaged the rest. All of this belonged to her."

"It's nice though. I ain't knocking you. You did good with it. You know…updating it and all."

"Thanks. So where do you live?"

"Right now I'm staying with a friend. They needed a roommate, but it's not working out, so I'm about to move. I'm paying everything anyway. I'm trying to be out by the first of the month."

Gut instinct told him she would be ready by then.

"Have you been looking for a place?"

"No. I been with you, I'm gonna start tomorrow." Remembering Denise's threat Champ grew uneasy. What if she had come home and changed the locks?

Nicole was tempted to ask him to stay with her, but she couldn't get it out. She didn't want to scare him away.

Champ walked back to the bedroom.

As Nicole put away the dishes, she turned around to see Champ completely dressed.

"Babe are you leaving?" Masking the feeling of being used, Nicole stood composed.

"Oh yeah. I gotta get up early. I got lots to do tomorrow; I'll still make time to see you." He walked over to her and kissed her.

Nicole was unable to deny his passion. When he let go she felt the weight of loneliness and it was settled. He could stay with her. She would tell him tomorrow.

Denise had not changed the locks. Nor had she returned. Champ sat down relieved. He thought about almost blowing it with Nikki. He was so used to coming and going as he chose, but he saw the pain that Nikki was feeling. Standing there wide-eyed and disappointed, her hair hanging lovely around her shoulders, the white gown making her look angelic.

He picked up the phone. "Hey Nikki, I made it."

"Hi baby, I'm glad you called. I was missing you."

"I'm missing you too. I was tempted to tell you we should find a place together, but I didn't want to rush you." He laughed.

"I'm not rushed. I'm ready."

Champ relaxed. "We'll talk tomorrow."

Nicole was beside herself with fear. She wanted this relationship so bad. "There's nothing to talk about. You can stay here."

Champ smiled. "You're sweet."

"No, I'm serious." Nikki was relieved. It wasn't a 'yes' , but it wasn't a 'no' either.

"Goodnight baby."

"Goodnight."

Champ heard Denise coming as he hung up. He ran to the bedroom and slipped into bed pretending to be asleep.

With her presence came the aroma of alcohol, weed and cigarette smoke. She got in the bed.

"Babe?"

Champ ignored her.

"Babe? I know you hear me. That damned fool Lisa was with done stole her paycheck and her VCR. I told her he was smoking crack."

Champ ignored her still. Denise talked and cursed until she fell asleep.

3

The day Champ moved in Nikki's glow was as the sun. Sitting on the sofa staring into her favorite corner of the house, a serene feeling of wholeness evolved within her. The reflection of the brass pot against the shining wooden floor represented the beauty she felt within. It was such a perfect image—exactly how she wanted her loving to be.

Every stitch of clothing that Champ owned was already put away. Nikki put them away as he dropped them off. He was gone to pick up his furniture; this was his last trip. Nikki hoped it wasn't too much. The house was fully furnished already, but for Champ she would squeeze a whole 'nother household into it. She loved this man.

Never had life been this good to her. Never. She was happier than a spoiled child on Christmas morning. Walking into the bedroom, over to the chest of drawers, she pulled open one of the drawers. Looking at all the new garments she thought...*These belong to My man* she picked up a piece of Champ's clothing and inhaled the dying scent of detergent.

Nikki's worth suddenly increased. She was needed. She was loved.

Champ walked in with a 19" television in his arms and the cord swinging dangerously close to his feet.

"Babe, toss that cord up here. I almost broke my neck on those stairs."

Nicole trotted over to help.

Champ placed the television in the bedroom on top of the chest of drawers, and went back to the car, returning with a stereo system. It fit perfectly in Nikki's apartment too.

After everything was settled they made love. Nicole went straight to sleep. Champ eased out of bed, peeked into every room and admired their cleanliness. He felt like he had won the lottery. This was the best place he'd ever lucked up on. Excited, he called Black.

"Hey man. I called to give you my new number."

"What's up? When I didn't hear from you for a while I knew I should've been praying for somebody's daughter." Black laughed.

"Yeah boy. I had to leave Denise. She bitched too much. , but shorty I'm with now is a real woman. She reminds me of Feather."

"Oh yeah. You bringing her tomorrow?"

"Yep."

Black was impressed. Champ had never actually taken his women around his friends. They just kind of bumped into them at the store or somewhere. "You serious huh boy? It's about time."

"Yeah. This is the right one. She works, gotta nice place, no kids, don't smoke and she's *fffiiiinneee.*" Champ was sincerely expressing himself, surprising himself too. What he was feeling was real. He relaxed. He was going to love her and not fight it.

"Wait 'til I tell Feather. I can't believe you finally fell for someone."

Champ didn't comment. "Man, what do you want us to bring?"

"Aw hell naw! You're gonna bring something too? I gotta meet this woman!" Black turned to Feather, "Babe, Champ got a new woman."

Feather was not surprised. She knew at first glance that Denise wasn't going to last. She kept walking.

"Wait, he's bringing her tomorrow."

Feather stopped. Looking quizzically at Black as she sat the bag of goodies, for tomorrow, down.

"He also wants to know what they can bring."

Champ sat on the other end feeling like a kid. He'd never felt like this before. Excited. Afraid. Overwhelmed. Simply wonderful.

Unpacking the bags, Feather sarcastically tossed her reply. "Tell them to bring soda." She smiled. That was something she already had plenty of and if they didn't bring it, it wouldn't be a problem.

"Alright. Man, I'll see you tomorrow."

"Alright."

♣♣♣

I'm in love...I can remember wishing I had what him and Feather got. Damn, I got it.

Champ thought back to his ex-girlfriend Nita. He loved her as best he could until she started talking that baby mess. The whole idea scared him. He started dreaming about her dying and stuff. He hated to leave her especially like that, but fear won. Sometimes he regretted not being able to tell

Nita the truth. He wasn't running from her or his responsibility, he was scared. The bigger her belly got so did his fear.

Nita had a little girl. He'd seen them around town a couple of times and she looked just like him. They never spoke, and neither did he.

Returning to the room he looked at Nikki, her legs curled, one hand tucked neatly between her knees and the other between the pillow and her cheek. For her he'd at least try to dissolve his fear.

As she lay before him he realized that she was actually beautiful. Her features were perfect. Perfect skin. The width of her lips, the length of her eyelashes and the shape of her mouth everything was perfect. Her fingernails were perfect, even her nose lay in exact proportion to her other features. Everything complimented each other. Even her voice sounded like it was especially made for her.

Impulse drew a kiss from him and he planted it on her cheek.

Her eyes opened like the clinched fist of an infant. She smiled.

"I've been waiting to tell you this."

"Tell me what Babe?"

Nicole crossed her fingers under the cover. All kinds of "what ifs" had run through her mind the past week. It was so soon. Maybe she should have said something before he moved in. "I think…I think…well, I know...I'm p-p pregnant."

"You're what?"

"Having a baby." Nikki's tears were already formed.

Champ's heart was beating with fear. He had the urge to run. To leave, then he looked at her, by the time he realized what was really happening his heart spoke through his mouth as if it was going to be ok. "Well, why you crying?"

"I'm scared. Scared of what you feel. Or that you're gonna leave. We've talked about a lot of things, but we ain't talked about no baby."

"Oh." All Champ could think about was how he was going to get out of this one. He didn't want to go through this now. Yeah, he had just told himself he was ready a minute ago, but that was because it wasn't real. Then he looked at her face and his heart fluttered. He loved her. He surrendered. "I'm not leaving, but I'm scared too."

"I think we can do it." Nikki offered with relaxed fear and a fresh focus. "He ain't gon put no mo' on us than we can bear."

Her smile comforted him.

"Ok. I hope you're right. And it's a boy."

"Guess what else?"

Nikki could tell by his expression that perhaps she'd better just tell him. "I brought home a pregnancy test. Let's do it."

Before he could answer Nikki was out of the bed and in the bathroom. It took a minute before he went, carrying with him a little hope and even beginning a prayer. Suddenly, reality was inching up from his heart to his mind.

The five minutes were not even up and the + sign appeared. Nikki's heart raced. She was going to be a mother. She was going to be what her mother was not. Someone, two people, needed and loved her. Nikki was the member of a family.

Champ pulled her into him. He understood. Yet, he was still scared.

♣♣♣

When Feather met Nikki she was perplexed. Nicole was definitely not Champ's usual choice of woman. Normally, he dealt with the kind of woman that Feather hated to even share her gender with.

Feather approached her carefully. "Hi. I'm Maya. Most people call me Feather. You can too."

Nicole leaned into her warmly. As they exchanged a cordial hug the way women do. "I'm Nicole and you may call me Nikki." She smiled a genuine smile.

Feather swallowed her whole. Taking in her well-manicured nails, not sculptured her own. She was golden toned, like a piece of white bread after it's been toasted. She had orange, yellow, and brown hues perfectly blended all over her face. Her hair was down her back and around her shoulders. Her eyes were slanted almost to the degree that Feather wondered if she was also of oriental persuasion. She stood about 5'3", and like Feather, was ethnically built. Very well proportioned. Her attire was simple and tasteful.

"You watch football too?" Feather asked trying not to stare. Taking the bag of sodas from Champ. She smiled her approval and hugged him too.

"Girl no. I just came to get out the house and to meet Champ's brother."

"Get used to it. They hang something tough. I'm always telling Black, when we do get married, I'm gon' have to marry'em both." They laughed.

Black entered the kitchen. "Hi." He extended his hand to Nicole and shared his dimple. "I'm Black."

Nicole thought he was very handsome. He was a brown so deep Hershey or Crayola would kill to patent it. He was 6'4" tall, muscular build; with the most sensitive eyes a man could possess and still maintain a masculine look. Nicole glanced over at Feather and she could tell instantly why Feather had chosen him and he her. They were absolute opposites. She was a soft brown, short, tiny, baby-faced, delicate woman. They complimented each other well.

"I'm Nicole." She shook his hand. Champ pointed to Black and then to Feather. "Babe, this is my brother! This the man and that's my girl too. These good people."

Black grabbed the two beers he'd come in to get and they left.

The girls went back to talking. "This is a nice place, and you have it fixed up so cute and comfy. You know some homes don't have that cozy feeling. This is cozy."

The men in the living room burst into a roar. Some stood up and shook their fist, in applause. Some slapped high five. Everybody cheered.

Feather knew what she meant. Her house was well lived in and she enjoyed it. "Add a football game, a bunch of men and some food it will always feel homey".

Feather didn't say so, but she felt an acceptance of Nicole. A kinship. The other guests' mates lacked warmth. April was snobbish. Connie was immature. Bridgette was phony. Nicole was well balanced—on her level.

"Girl how did you meet Champ?"

"I met him at work. I work at the Albertson's grocery store on High Street. He was in there one day and I was his checker. It was real sweet. He picked up his bag then asked if I could fit him into my schedule for dinner or a movie or both, but before I could answer, he wrote his phone number on the back of his receipt and said 'that's alright, if one day you want a free meal and some compliments call me.' So, I called and we've been inseparable ever since."

"You both certainly seem happy. I'm especially happy for him. He's never chosen anyone of your caliber. You should have seen some of his other women. The kind that walk on the back of their shoes, wear headrags to the store and refer to themselves as 'who's."

Nikki understood now why he stared at her. She smiled. It made her feel desired and appreciated.

Feather noticed that the men were drifting off into their own conversation. The game was either boring or almost over. She wondered which as she pulled two cast iron skillets from the cabinet.

"Well, I guess we better feed these hungry Negroes. I'm gonna fry the two bags of Party wings I seasoned earlier, they are sitting in the sink."

Nikki nodded in agreement. Noticing the loose chicken parts swimming in seasonings waiting to be fried, Feather turned the fire on under her two skillets.

"Usually, we have spaghetti, but this time I made some red beans and I'm going to cook rice."

"I'll cook the rice." Nikki offered.

Normally, Feather would object. She was particular about who fumbled around in her kitchen.

Nikki left the kitchen briefly. She returned with empty beer cans and requests. She went to the refrigerator and grabbed a six-pack.

Feather was amazed at how comfortable she was with Nikki. She felt familiar like an old trusted friend. Feather knew that she had a kind spirit. Besides that she was domestic, so that was a plus.

"I'll get it." Nikki buzzed by Feather.

"Feather do you know April?" She asked from the door.

"Yes! Let her in. That's Tony's girlfriend." For a minute Feather thought they weren't coming.

Nikki embraced them all. April, Bridgette and Connie.

"I'm Nicole, Champ's girlfriend. It's nice to meet you all."

They introduced themselves to Nikki and proceeded to the dining room. The chicken was frying, as Feather turned to greet her other guest. There was some beauty in that kitchen. Black women tall, short, thin, thick, bald, blessed, sheer beauty in every shade of brown imaginable. The new arriving guests went to their usual resting spot, the dining room. They nestled in and began to play spades, gossip, swap recipes, make announcements and discoveries, even told a few lies.

Nikki and Feather stayed in the kitchen. They bonded. Each woman admired the other's beauty. After the game, they came together as a group. They played cards, ate, drank, embraced and listened to music.

"Babe we didn't come over here to cry all night." Champ complained halfheartedly. The other men agreed as Nikki put on one love ballad after another.

"That's what I'm talking 'bout "D" said with Bridgette riding his knee. "Them brotha's whipped and they want everyone else to be too."

"You doing a good job." Black teased, pointing at Bridgette on his lap. "But you right. These new artists are crazy. Paying bills, cooking dinner, washing clothes soon as he get home from work. Hell, if I went to work I ain't doing nothing else."

Everyone laughed. Even Feather, who knew him to do it all, but she let him joke. That was just his way.

The night was filled with laughter, good cheer and just the right touch of nostalgia. When it ended everyone was in love.

Champ and Nikki were the last to leave. Nikki and Feather cleaned the kitchen. Champ and Black lounged in the living room, talking quietly. When they finally did leave, almost in harmony the women said 'It was a pleasure meeting you.' Both men were pleased that they meant it. It had been a good day. Good people. Good food. Good loving. A good time.

♣♣♣

Champ and Nikki walked into their place a little after 10:00 pm. They both felt complete. In his own eyes, tonight Champ stood tall. Usually he felt out of place. He was always weighed down with maintaining the role of *player* instead of man. Tonight he was a man. He had his woman with him. Looking good, smelling good and loving him.

Nikki was floating on the cloud of happiness. She had made a friend. A real friend. Feather was so warm and genuine that it was almost necessary to pinch her to make sure she was real. Nikki had truly enjoyed herself. Her love for Champ was intense. If it were able, Love would have stepped right out of her and stood boldly before him, simply to let him know it was really real. He had given Nicole more than himself. Because of him she had a lover, a child, some friends, and all the love her little heart desired.

"Did you tell Feather about the baby?"

"No."

"I figured you would so I told Black."

"Well, I didn't. I wanted too, but I guess I figured she wouldn't care. She doesn't know me."

"She would've been happy for us anyway; she's like that. It's going to be her family too. She's my brother's wife or might as well be."

Nikki knew he was right and went to bed regretting not telling her.

♣♣♣

"I really like Champ's girlfriend. She's too sweet, especially for him. I hope he don't hurt her. She really cares about him." Feather sat on the couch and Black sat on the floor between her legs while she rubbed his shoulders.

"I like her too. I feel sorry for her though. She's pregnant."

"What?" Feather stopped massaging him. "She just meet him about three months ago, and she's pregnant already?" Feather was shocked.

"She's about two months. He's excited though. He wants a boy. He's staying home and stuff. Talking about settling down like me." Black looked up, over his head, at Feather.

"Don't be trying to score no brownie points off of Champ's statement. You ain't settled you're settling." She kissed his forehead. "Wanna shower with me?"

"Yeah." They headed for the bathroom.

4

The image of Nikki's beauty had remained with Feather since the day they'd met. It was nearing six weeks since that meeting and still Feather could see a vivid mirage of her gorgeous face, the way the warmth of her person shone all over it, adding to what was already perfect.

Feather calculated her pregnancy to be at three and a half months now. Wondering how she was doing she smiled as she signed off her computer. *Nikki's the kind of woman who is going to look good pregnant. Hair flowing, belly bulging with life, smile bright. She's such a pretty girl.* Feather had been praying for her.

Grabbing her purse to go stand out front and wait for Black, he was to pick her up any minute, she saw a young girl going into the airport walking on a pair of Birkenstock sandals that soles were clearly worn away. A toe polished here, one polished there, a pair of jeans that were unbuttoned and revealing of her baby that was near delivery; she wore a man's shirt that reeked his musk. Feather shook her head. *That is not what Nikki is going to look like when she's that far into her pregnancy and me either.* At that exact moment Feather felt the first strike of her maternal clock. Shaking it off she thought. *Before I even think about any babies I need to get a car. This sharing with Black ain't gon' get it.*

As quickly as the pleasant thoughts of Nikki entered her mind the fear of her relationship replaced them. She knew of Champ's so called love and its destruction.

She thought of Nikki again. *Lord please bless Nicole with a halfway decent looking child.* Champ was literally the ugliest man Feather had ever seen. It hurt for her mind to wonder how Nikki let him touch her, let alone make love to her. He was a decent height; he had beautiful skin, and an attractive demeanor. To notice him from behind was to want to get a good look at him. Surely a man that possessed such a stride had to be delicious to look at. WRONG!! Champ was the exception to that rule. As soon as he turned around the urge to apologize for assuming he was going to be a delight engulfed the onlooker.

Feather was always grateful to have Black when she had these thoughts. Black was a good man. He loved her as a best he could, and it was the effort that she loved about him. He was even romantic in his own sort of way. For him romance was helping clean up when he could be playing basketball. Even now Feather smiled. He reminded her so much of her father that she loved him some, because of that too.

Michael Ford was the man that could do no wrong in the eyes of Feather. He was the reason she was attracted to Black in the first place. Michael was dark, not as dark as Black but dark. He was the kind of man that would pick his woman up and twirl her around in excitement. That held her when she was hurt. That kissed her when she cooked and let her warm her feet under his buttocks while they watched movies. The difference was that Michael had good intentions only. Black's intent became action, always.

Feather was a happy woman. Life had been kind to her and she knew it. Out of all of Black's friends she had gotten the cream of the crop. Good men were hard to find, so finding him in tenth grade was a Godsend. Keeping him for four years while still feeling the newness of their love was a blessing.

Feather stood there loving her man, praying for her new friend and planning her dinner menu for tonight.

♣♣♣

"Big Mama I'm gone. You know I gotta pick up Feather."

"Ok Baby. Be careful hear?"

Black smiled to himself. He loved his grandmother so. When his parents first separated and they moved in with her he thought Tee (Theresa), his little sister, was going to die. She hated the way Big Mama fussed over her. Putting all that Vaseline on her face and tucking her in bed at night. Tee was five going on twenty-five. Black was eight and glad to be there. He loved the fussing personally. Big Mama had nine grandchildren. Black was the only boy.

She was molding him into her dream lover. Adding a little bit from a lover she loved and the good of a lover she was glad to be rid of. Big Mama and her daughter had known some heartache in their lifetimes and she was not going to have a child of hers putting women through that mess. She was grooming her grandson to be a man. Teaching him that the sensitive side of a man is to be shared—that there is more strength in love than in pride. Black had learned his lessons well. Not only because his teacher was great, but because of his personal observations. He had seen his mother, Patricia, go in and out of relationships, for the past fourteen years like they were doors. He had vowed that he was never going to treat his woman like that as a boy. He was holding true to his promise in the manner that he loved Feather. She was truly the love of his life. He looked forward to seeing her face at the close of each day and the opening of each new one.

He pulled up at the moment that she was beginning to weave her brows together in wonderment of his whereabouts.

"Hi baby, I stopped by Big Mama's for a minute. She was coming home from the grocery store so I helped her in. And well, you know Big Mama she was trying to talk me to death."

"I know you too. You probably was over there getting on her nerves." Feather leaned over and kissed him on the lips. She loved the way he loved his grandmother.

Black smiled to himself; she did know him, recalling when he had asked Big Mama about her love life and how she had shooed him away.

"Babe, I've been meaning to ask you about Champ and Nikki, how are they?"

"I guess they're cool. I talked to Champ the other day and we were talking 'bout hooking up this weekend."

Feather smiled. She wanted to see Nikki. To know how she was doing. Then she noticed that Black had gotten quiet on her. "Babe what's wrong?"

"Nothing. I just think that Champ is starting to get scared. His voice sounded kind of shaky. And when I asked about Nikki he just said 'she's fine.' I wasn't comfortable with his tone."

"He better not be mistreating her. When we get home give me their number. I'm gonna call her." Feather looked out the window disgusted.

Black loved her. Her feistiness always turned him on.

♣♣♣

Champ rose and pulled his pants on. He sat on the side of the bed and looked at the young lady lying next to him. *Tina? Trina?* He couldn't even remember her name. He had gone to buy some weed and ended up with her too. She was throwing herself at him from the moment he entered his supplier's house. Sitting wide legged and backward in a chair with no drawers on. She kept winking and so when she asked if she could go too, of course the answer was yes.

Besides, he missed freaks. Nikki was a woman to the fullest meaning of the word. She fed him as a form of foreplay. She bathed him. She massaged him. She made love by candlelight. She cuddled afterwards. She was careful and generous with her loving. It was good love, but sometimes he liked to fuck.

That's what he had done today. With Tina he could be rough, inconsiderate and as freaky as he wanted to be. He was not comfortable that way with Nicole, especially not now.

Oh shit I was supposed to pick Nikki up from the doctor. "Hey, you staying here or you want me to take you back?"

"You can take me back where you got me from and my name ain't 'Hey it's Tina."

Champ looked at her and smiled. Ignorance always made him feel intelligent.

"Whatever, get yo' ass up I gotta get home."

"Get home? You talk like you got a woman."

"I do."

"Well, what the hell you doing here with me?" Tina stood up with such force that her breasts were swinging.

Champ grew excited at the hardening of her nipples. "Accepting an invitation." He smiled. He knew he had her. He was truly there because she asked to go with him and this is where he wanted to go.

Tina snatched up her clothes and finished getting dressed. She could not believe his arrogance.

Champ finished getting dressed and hit his joint. They rode back in silence. When she got out of the car he slapped her on her butt hard. She smiled. Then he knew he could see her again if he wanted to.

In the last six weeks he committed to loving Nikki. Tina was stress relief—that's all. He was trying to overcome his phobia about her death and the pregnancy. He didn't want Nikki to die. Didn't want his child to know his pain. The time spent with Tina released some of the pressure.

♣♣♣

Nikki lay on the bed watching a Colombo re-run. She loved how perfectly he worked people's nerves.

Champ walked in guilt ridden as soon as he saw her. She looked so adorable on the bed with a spoon turned backward in her mouth and intense interest on her face. She was covered in her mass of hair and had not yet noticed him.

"Should you be laying on your stomach?"

Nikki smiled. She loved it when Champ showed an interest in the pregnancy. She put the spoon in the empty pint of ice cream box and looked at him.

"I'm not laying on my stomach. I'm lying on my side. I wouldn't do anything to hurt your baby."

"You mean my son." Champ eased in and laid next to her. Then he pulled her gown up and circled her navel as she eased over on her back to allow him to. He planted a kiss on her lips and she smiled.

"You act like a man that has missed his woman."

"I have. I'm sorry I couldn't pick you up from the doctor. I got tied up."

"In what?"

"In this." He reached in his pocket and handed her a wad of money.

Nikki smiled. "Thank you baby. I do so love a man that takes care of his home."

"Then we're a perfect match because I love a woman that manages one well."

Nikki looked at him with hungry eyes. She wanted him. For her there was nothing better than a clean house, a balanced checkbook, a good meal and a fine man with good loving all over her. She had to drop off *fine,* but three out of four wasn't bad.

Champ eased down her panties and caressed her there, all the time undressing himself.

Nikki arched her back. Still he kept his same seductive pace. She tugged at his loin still he kept his pace.

"Baby please."

It was the lowest scream he'd ever heard. No one had ever responded to his touch that way. When Champ finally entered Nikki she relaxed every muscle in her body and allowed him to have his way.

One-hour forty-something minutes later they lay together exhausted.

Nikki was tucked neatly in the corner of Champ's frame. He lay there starring at the ceiling.

"I love you, Champ."

"I love you too."

"I'm glad we met."

"Me too."

"Thanks for our baby." She whispered inhaling the masculine spices of his deodorant and kissing his armpit. Just barely missing the bush of hair living there.

"You're welcome. I wanted it too. I'm glad it's you." Feeling less afraid today, he reached over and touched her stomach.

"I can't wait to see him. I love'em already. Leslie Andrews Jr."

"Naw!" Champ rose up. "Enough with that Leslie shit! I don't want my son taking on my identity. Let him identify with himself. That would be like traditionalizing pain and for what?"

Nikki was shocked. He'd never shown her this side of himself. Part of her was afraid.

Champ realized he was tripping by her expression. He had decided that he wasn't going to act like that with her. Nikki was the prettiest and best thing that had ever happened to him. That day at the store he'd felt she was out of his league and wouldn't give him the time of day and now her womb was full with his seed. He calmed himself.

"Babe, I'm sorry. I just never wanted nothing like I want you and this baby. I want this child to have a mother. You know how you want your kids to have all the things you didn't have? Well, all I ever wanted was a mother."

Nikki felt for him. "Well you got your wish, I'm going to be a mother to our baby."

"Wait 'til you have it. If you're still alive I'm going to hold you to it." He smiled.

She did not. That was a horrible thing to say. It was ok, though, when he reached over and stroked her hair until she fell asleep.

Champ rose once he realized she was fully asleep. He went into the kitchen and got a beer. Then back into the room and sat on the bed still naked. He watched Nikki sleep.

There was an envelope on the nightstand. He picked it up and wrote a poem, then laid it back down, lit his joint in the ashtray next to him and took a hard hit. When he looked at Nikki again he wondered if what he was feeling was really love. It was definitely something. He hadn't written any poetry in years.

5

Nikki had been assigned the 10items or Less lane until after the baby. She was a huge six months. As Feather predicted she was beautiful. She made pregnancy look enjoyable, the slight waddle and all. Her nails and hair had grown to record lengths. She was living the dream of every expectant mother.

Even tired she was a treat to look at. And she was tired. Her last customer approached. *Thank God.*

"Hi. How are you?" Nikki pulled the customer's items across the scanner without making eye contact. She wanted to go home. Pull-Ups, baby Tylenol, Apple juice. Nikki looked up. She had to see the little owner of these products.

Her mouth fell open. It was Champ. He was sitting in the cart with four little ponytails. She had his eyes and his lips. His complexion…everything. This was Champ's baby. Had to be. She looked too much like him to belong to anyone other than him. Nikki's baby kicked inside her. Her stomach moved.

"I really miss that. A miracle in the works." Nita smiled.

Nikki returned a nervous smile. She couldn't see any features of this lady in that baby at all. Not one. She wanted to ask her if Champ had fathered her child, but she didn't have the courage. Her heart told her that this was Champ's baby. Then relief swept over her as a man approached and began to take the baby out of the cart. Nicole relaxed without even looking at him. "Twenty-one, sixty-two."

The man handed the baby to Nita and reached for his wallet. Taking his money, Nikki looked at him. The little girl didn't look like him either. *That's Champ's baby. Why did he not tell me? I know that's his baby* Nikki's own baby kicked again.

Champ walked in as she gave the couple their change.

Nita's expression soured from friendly to hatred. Nicole followed her glare, looking over her shoulder, there he was...Champ, standing there looking like a shit eating opossum.

I was right. That is his baby. Nikki's baby was really kicking, a knot of pain had formed in her throat and tears stung her eyes. She was hurt. *He could have told me. What kind of man lies about his children? The kind that will lie about anything.*

The tension between Champ and Nita spoke aloud.

Finally, Nita looked at Nicole in her face, then at her stomach, then back in her face. "Be careful Miss, he's got some serious hang-ups."

Nicole held on to her tears. She had had lots of practice, so she was successful at pretending that she was not hurt. She nodded at Nita, as if she understood and appreciated the warning then turned to her drawer and cashed out.

Nita looked at Champ, flipped him off with her eyes and followed her man and her baby out of the store.

Champ said nothing. In his mind he was hoping Nicole's feelings weren't as soft as her skin. *Damn. I should have told her.* Then he grew angry. *That was before her time.*

Nicole passed him on her way to turn in her till.

"Babe, I'll be in the car."

Again Nicole nodded and pushed her tears back down her throat.

The ride home was silent, for the most part. Champ couldn't take it anymore. The silence was killing him. He knew she wanted to talk. He knew she was hurting. Her silence was speaking for her.

"Nikki, that ain't my baby."

"Well, I wonder why she looks so much like you?"

"Let me put it to you like this, when me and Nita were together she was sleeping with other people, so when she came up with that 'I'm pregnant mess' I wasn't gonna be the one to pay for someone else's nut. Anyway we got into it big time and I moved."

"So, you left before the baby?"

"Yes."

Nikki knew he was lying. The lady in the store seemed as levelheaded as her. Nikki remembered her warning. "Well, Champ now that you know that the baby is yours, don't you feel like you should help her?"

"Look, that don't pertain to you. Nita has a father for her baby. And you have a father for yours." He touched her stomach. "All I'm saying is that is my past. You are my future. I need to move on. Please let me!" Champ knew he was pulling on her heartstring.

Nikki got out of the car. Her pain had dissolved. That night Champ had a run to make. It was just as well because Nikki needed some time to herself. Regardless to how stupid she looked, she wasn't stupid at all. She was in love, actually in need.

♣♣♣

Champ pulled away from the curb. *I don't know why Nikki's tripping off that baby. That ain't got nothing to do with her. She needs to be worrying about me. She ain't one time asked me how I'm doing with all of this. Man this shit is killing me. This the last baby!"* He parked the car. As he entered his supplier's house, Tina walked up.

"Hey girl. What's up with you?" Champ hit her on her butt.

"What you want to be up?" Tina was looking at his zipper area.

"Girl, you somethin' else, but you on the money. Let me run in here and get my weed. I'll be right out." Champ got the weed. He needed it like yesterday. First of all his hustle was off. He'd lost at craps, got in on a Sega hustle; lost at that. Came out of his potna's house, and car on a flat. Went to pick Nikki up and there was Nita and his daughter. He was having a rough day. What he needed was some rough sex. Nikki was too delicate, and pregnant.

Champ shook all negativity as Tina removed her clothes and lay out on the bed as if she were his own personal sexual feast.

♣♣♣

Nita's warning was haunting Nikki. *'Be careful, he got some serious hang-ups'*. Nikki was hurting. She was also praying. She knew that her life was changing again. She wasn't ready to start the war again. Why couldn't Champ tell her from the beginning? Her baby moved. She smiled. It no longer mattered. She was his woman, this was his baby, they were happy. The phone rang.

"Hello?"

They hung up.

The phone rang.

"Hello?"

They hung up.

Women's intuition whispered in Nikki's ear. *You need to stop ignoring that itch.*

Nikki pushed the thought aside and took a shower. She had been taking them a lot more lately. She was trying to rid herself of that itch. She kept washing herself. It kept itching. Today was the worst.

The phone rang. "Hello?" They hung up. *That ain't the wrong number. That's a girl, but Champ wouldn't do that. He loves me. I love him too good for him to do that. He ain't got no reason to cheat… 'Be careful he got some serious hang-ups.'*

Nikki laid down; she felt the spin of confusion. It was 9:30 pm. The itching had ceased. She was tired emotionally, as well as physically. The baby had been kicking a lot today. Now that it was still she was going to lie down because she had noticed that whenever she was still it was moving. Sleeping good was a thing of the past. She was going to get this rest while the getting was good.

At 1:00 am the phone rang. "Hello?" (She noticed that Champ was not home.)

"It's one o'clock in the morning. Do you know where your man is?"

This time Nikki hung up. The answer was no. She did not know where Champ was, but she was going to find out. She was going to know exactly what time he walked through the door. Once women started calling the house, it was definitely time to talk. Sitting on the couch she decided to call the advice nurse about the itch.

"Are you experiencing a discharge?"

"Yes."

"Is it odorous or yellowish in color?"

"No. Neither."

"Does it burn when you urinate?"

"No. It just itches."

"Have you looked at the tissue after cleaning?"

"Yes." Nikki started to cry.

"Does it look like cottage cheese?"

"Yes." Nikki's heart was beating. She could hold her pain no longer.

"Oh Honey, no need to cry. It sounds like a yeast infection. It's real easy to treat. You don't even need to come in. You can purchase over the counter medicine for it."

"I'm pregnant. How is this medicine going to effect my baby?"

"Ms. Collier, yeast is very common during pregnancy. The added moisture and warmth sometimes induces yeast production. Your baby is very well protected. The medicine is not even going to reach the baby."

"Ok." Nikki stopped crying. "Does this mean my partner is being unfaithful?"

"Not necessarily, but having multiple partners can also produce yeast activity."

"Ok. I'll try the over the counter medicine. Thank you."

♣♣♣

It was a new day when Champ walked in. As the door opened, it startled Nikki. She was still on the couch. Rumpled and hurt and angry.

"Hey Babe." Champ was touched. She looked cute, mad.

"Where were you Champ?" Nikki could feel the baby kick. She neglected to eat last night.

Champ was also impressed to find that underneath the softness was a callused layer. "I went out. I had something to do. I got caught up in a dice game and here I am. I lost all my money and I don't need this shit." Champ could tell he had her by the heart. Tears welled up in her eyes. "What's up Nikk? You want me to leave? You puttin' me out for tryin' to feed you?" He threw his hands up as if to suggest his surrender.

Tears spilled from her eyes as she realized her defeat. "No." It was a whisper. She walked past him into the bedroom. He slapped her butt as she passed, but much gentler than he would have if she were Tina.

Nikki plopped down on the bed crying. She ignored her kicking baby and her vaginal itch. She was hurt.

Champ fumbled around in the kitchen. He checked the microwave in case Nikki had cooked. She usually left him a plate of food in there if he hadn't made it home by the time she went to bed. There it was. Pork chops, macaroni and cheese, green beans and corn on the cob just waiting to be nuked and eaten. For an instant Champ felt bad. No one had ever been this good to him. Then he reminded himself that despite his spending time with Tina he was really in love with Nikki. *Let me chill on that thing with Tina. I ain't goin' risk all this over her trampy ass.*

Nikki couldn't ignore her baby anymore. The scent of Champ's food hit her nose hard and went straight to her womb. She wiped her eyes.

Champ was going back into the kitchen. "You alright Nikk?" He asked without looking her in the face. He couldn't stand to see the tracks of tears on her face.

"Fine." Her tone was stable and firm. It took Champ by surprise.

Reaching for another heartstring he pulled her into him. "Y'all hungry too?"

He held her tighter. "Nikki I'm sorry. I was trying to win my money back baby." He kissed her lips then her cheek, her neck, her shoulder, one breast and last her belly. When he looked up, it was into her smile. She was whole again and so was he.

"I love you Champ. Don't do that again." Nikki had not forgotten about the hang-ups and especially about that question at 1:00 am, but she didn't say anything. She didn't want to ruin the mood.

"I love you too, baby."

The phone rang.

"Hello?" Nikki answered.

"Hey girl, where's that man of yours? This man of mine and I were wondering if y'all wanted to play some spades later?"

"He's right here. Let me see. I do. I need to get out of here."

"Champ, Feather wants to know if you wanna play spades over there later?… He said yeah. How you been?"

"Girl, fine. I've been thinking about you. I keep saying I'm gonna call and never get around to it."

"I would call you, but I never did get your number and Champ ain't never home, we on two different schedules. All we do is sleep together."

"Well, let me give it to you. I don't be doing nothin' girl. Every once in a while I shop."

"I love to shop."

"Well, honey we must hook up. How's the pregnancy?"

"It's ok. I'm tired. It's a lot of work."

"Well, you ain't gonna work tonight. I'll have dinner ready when you get here so you can just kick back and let somebody wait on you for a change."

"That's so sweet." Nikki was sincerely touched. Before Champ came into her life, didn't nobody care to wait on her. Didn't nobody care about her. Her love for Champ was renewed. If it was a girl on the phone, so what he loved her. He was hers, giving her the family she never had and for that she loved him.

"Ok. Well I'll see you in a little bit."

"Ok-bye."

"Bye."

6

Feather was pleased to hear the joy present in Nikki's voice. Dealing with Champ required a special kind of strength. Feather prayed that Nikki had it or at least enough sense to know if she didn't.

They arrived about 6:00 pm. Nikki was as beautiful as Feather remembered her. She leaned into her giving her a one armed hug while gently placing her free hand on Nikki's stomach.

"Congratulations." Then leaning into her belly she whispered, so that everyone could hear, "Hi baby, it's Auntie."

Nikki smiled. It was great to feel love.

"So what do you want?" Feather ignored the strike of her maternal clock.

"I don't really care…I'm lying I sort of want a boy."

Black and Champ stood in the doorway to the kitchen in a halo of marijuana smoke. Nikki and Feather sat in the kitchen. Before them, sat a meat tray, a tablet and a pitcher of lemonade. Feather had really gone all out for them.

"You hungry?" Feather was already on her feet and pouring Nikki some lemonade.

"No. Not really."

"We playing partners, couples, boys against the girls or what?" Black joked.

No one answered him.

"Hey that's the jam right there." Champ walked out of the doorway of the kitchen into the living room and turned up the radio. He sang along.

He danced back into the kitchen and pulled Nikki to her feet. Dancing all around her as she blushed. Feather and Black smiled. Never had Champ been so happy, so normal. Whatever Nikki was doing was agreeing with him. Black smiled deeper than anyone did because he always knew that Champ was a decent person who had gotten off to a bad start in life. They remained friends when everyone else abandoned their friendship with him for that very reason. At times, Champ showed some good qualities. For one he was a hell of a poet, and anyone who could write about beautiful things had to know something about them.

"Nikki what did you do to Champ? I have never seen my brother so relaxed."

"Man, she loving me good. You know what I'm talking about?" Champ winked at Black.

"Yeah, I know all about that." Black boasted, grabbing Feather by her waist and pulling her into him.

The radio disc jockey was in perfect tune to their mood. He played one jam after another, easing into ballads.

Feather had prepared a pot roast, potatoes, carrots, cabbage and cornbread. It was delicious.

"What's the stupidest thing that entertained your thoughts? Something so stupid you were ashamed to even think it?" Feather threw the question out there. She no longer wanted to play cards. No one answered. "Black?" She assigned the question.

He knew how to play, even though they had never played before. They had that kind of telepathy.

Black leaned his head to the left and looked at the ceiling. Finally, he spoke putting on a serious mask. The gang sat up, waiting for Black's response, peaked their interests.

"Have you ever noticed that if you fart in the tub it stinks worse than a regular fart?"

Champ dropped the cards; (He had been shuffling them from one hand to the other the whole time.) threw his head back with laughter, while the girls laughed in their own feminine way.

"Boy you crazy." Champ laughed.

"Naw, he stupid."

"Uh-huh he need help." The girls commented.

"Ok. Ok...Seriously. I guess that I can't die mostly because I don't know anything about it. No one in my family has died. I've actually never had to deal with death. Even my goldfish lived until I out grew them."

The atmosphere was serious again. It was Black's turn to ask the question.

"Nikki, what's the thing you fear most?"

Nikki didn't have to think long. She knew it was going back to where she had come from. "Loneliness. I would hate to be the last man alive. I saw a Twilight Zone episode once where this man woke up and was the only man on the planet. I've been afraid ever since...well, actually, more afraid. I've never wanted to be alone even before watching that program." She looked at Feather and directed her question. Passing between them was a silent understanding as to how she had become the woman in Champ's life.

"If you could have anything you wanted, but you could only have one thing what would it be?"

Feather was confused instantly. She wanted *sooo* many things in life. She wanted Black, her parents, a better relationship with her mother, kids, a car, a job, money, happiness and peace of mind. "Black." In her heart Feather believed Black to be the connecting link to all her desires.

It was Champ's turn. Feather caught his eye. He was serious. She'd never seen this side of him. He looked intelligent, even to her.

"Champ if you could make a, as in ONE wish and it were guaranteed to come true what would you wish fo-?"

"I'd wish for one thing." He started to answer before she completed the question.

"For what?" Black asked anxiously.

Nikki and Feather waited anxiously. The baby even kicked.

"I'd wish for a…conversation."

While he paused everyone filled in the space in their own minds. Black had filled in *Mother* before he even said the word conversation.

"With God." The room grew hauntingly still. No one could imagine Champ approaching anything from a religious perspective.

Speaking in a melancholy voice, "Yeah, I'd like to meet my Mother. I'd like to find out if I will ever experience unconditional love?" as he stared off into space as though he were in a trance. When he blinked he looked at Black. It was his turn again. Champ had missed the pledge of unconditional love that Nikki willed to him with her eyes, but Black and Feather saw it. Both were touched.

"If your whole family. Meaning your wife and kids were trapped in a fire; dying, but you could only save one of them, which would you save?"

"Both." Black didn't even hesitate.

"Man you can only save one." Champ responded.

"I know, but I'd save both or just die trying. I wouldn't leave either of them. I couldn't. In a situation like that I'm already dead."

There was a growing respect around the table as each of them learned the other. Fondness was like vine; love was spreading like shade under a tree. It was evident the feelings shared by each couple were genuine. They talked until morning. They listened to music and even danced.

At 2:00 am Feather called in an order to Nation's Giant Burger restaurant. The guys went to pick up the order of food.

Nikki fell asleep while waiting.

Feather admired her pregnancy. Again, she felt her maternal instincts.

7

The visit to Black and Feather's strengthened the bond between Champ and Nikki. Champ had become a new person. He was staying home all day everyday. He had even made her a key, well allowed her to make a key to his car. Nikki was driving herself to and from work. Nikki was not aware of her rank at the time, but it was high. No woman had ever driven his Lexus.

Champ was not smoking as much weed either because every time he went to get it he ended up in bed with Tina. After seeing the honest loving exchanged between Black and Feather he decided to do right by Nikki because he did love her.

Nikki was cooking and cleaning. She was happy. Happy, happy. She and Feather had gone shopping for the baby. She drove her car.

Champ and Black had picked up a baby crib.

The two couples were growing closer and closer. Everything was going smooth.

Then Champ's fear returned.

"Champ!! Champ!! Help me!!" Nikki was lying in the bed screaming. The baby was due in three weeks, which really meant any day.

"Champ!!"

Champ was in the kitchen frozen in place. He could not respond. All he kept thinking about was that she was dying. He wanted to go see about her. He wanted to call 9-1-1. He could not move.

"Champ! I got a cramp in my legg!! Help me!!!"

It took a minute to register that it was *just* a cramp. *Move…It's a cramp. Go. Move your feet. Go see about her. It must be a hell of a cramp to have her screaming like that. Oh shit!! If she can't handle a cramp. She ain't having this baby. She gon' die."*

"Champ!" Nikki was lying in the bed, too big to move good enough to help herself. She wanted Champ to help her get out of the bed so she could try to walk it off.

Champ finally came in the bedroom. He could see the knot of the Charlie Horse in her thigh. He rushed over to her and started massaging it. At first she looked at him with hatred as he pressed on the knotted cramp in her leg. As it began to dissolve, so did her disposition.

"Thank you baby." Nikki was near tears. That was the most excruciating pain she had ever felt in her life.

Champ sat on the bed relieved that it was only a cramp. Fear crept up on him again. Tina also came to mind. He needed to get out. His adrenaline was pumping, his heart was racing. He wanted to run. He wanted to go away until after the baby was born. Then he would come back and be a father, but right now he couldn't handle it.

"Babe, I'm 'bout to go get some weed. Yo gon' be alright?"

"Yeah, I guess so. That cramp almost killed me. This lady at my job told me that during her pregnancy she got bad leg cramps all the time. I shared with her that I had never had one and I'm almost due. That's what I get for bragging." She smiled a tired smile. That cramp had really rocked her.

"Ok. Well, I'm going to get some weed. I'll be right back."

"Ok." Nikki puckered for a kiss.

Champ touched her lips with his so lightly that the impact of his breath was stronger than the kiss. He was scared to touch her. He was nervous about the whole thing.

Champ got the weed and a piece of Tina too. This time he gave Tina his cellular number. She was fussing about him being available on his schedule only. So, he gave up his cellular number and told her to call when she wanted to see him, but he reminded her that he had a woman.

Champ's fear was getting the best of him. Nikki was on maternity leave and home all day, therefore, Champ was not. He was lying up under Tina for the most part. Taking her to movies, dinner and the motel. She was keeping him broke.

Nikki was not complaining yet, but she was getting tired. All the utilities were riding on arrangements the kind that her disability checks could handle. Lately, every time she asked Champ for some money he said he had 'an off day'.

Whenever she was still a whisper of doubt spoke to her. *Nikki what's wrong with you? Are you crazy? So, you really think that this man loves you? He sitting back watching you struggle like this. He doesn't even come home at night. You are exactly where you never wanted to be.*

Champ came home that night at 12:15 am with $143.00. He'd managed to help keep her arrangements. She was happy—happy enough to offer herself and crushed when he refused her.

At two o'clock in the morning the phone rang. When she answered it there was no one on the other end. Immediately after that Champ's cellular vibrated off the nightstand onto the floor. He left it there pretending not to hear it.

8

I need a car. I hate to call Mama. Every time I ask her for something she remind me that I didn't have to move out.

Feather sighed. "Hi Mama. Can you pick me up from work tonight? Black has to work overtime."

Lillian pulled up at ten minutes to five. Feather was off at 5 o'clock.

They got along pretty much. Lil's biggest hang up was Black. When she looked at him and Feather she saw her and Michael. She wanted to protect Feather. Feather was so trusting.

Sometimes, Lillian looked at Feather and her beauty and she knew her daughter could have won the heart of a doctor or a lawyer. It upset her that she chose a mail sorter.

Feather knew her mother felt Black's job wasn't prestigious enough. She didn't let it bother her, she was a Customer Service Representative at the airport and that didn't exactly warrant the hand of the President.

Feather got in. "Hi Mama."

"Hi baby. Now, you know y'all need two cars. Every time Andre work's late I can't pick you up."

"Mama, we'll get another one. We're just barely making it now."

"Barely making it now? You need someone with more potential Feather. I don't understand why you haven't gotten a car yet. I tried to tell you living on your own wasn't easy. I think y'all think it's a game."

Lillian was going to buy Feather a car until Feather moved out. Lillian was so hurt. She decided to let Andre get her a car, since that's whom she wanted to be with. Truth is Lillian was more scared than hurt. Feather had been her everything. She had passed up many dates because she didn't want to set a bad example for her daughter. Looking back she realized that was an excuse too, to try and protect her own heart from being broken.

Lillian knew in her heart that Feather and Black were going to make it. It had been four years and the most they had asked her for was a ride from time to time. That made her proud but sad at the same time.

"Mama come on. I'd be struggling if I were with a doctor. I don't want a doctor. I want Black."

"Why Maya? Why him? He's never going to be anything more than a mail sorter." Lillian wasn't trying to give Feather a hard time. She just didn't want to see her baby go through the same mess she went through with her Daddy. She had married Michael under the same terms—love. Then came the struggling. And as soon as they made it through the struggle, they grew apart. It was the struggles that kept them together, and when it was over so were they. They learned that they weren't good company to one another, friends or anything else. They were two people that complimented each other in an organized way. There was love and good sex, there was no passion. Loyalty was the basis for their marriage. The awkwardness brought on distance and boredom, which lead to divorce. From Lil's point of view, Feather's relationship with Black was the same thing. She had no idea that Feather and Black were riding high on the waves of passion, but there are some things that a mother will simply never know.

"I chose Black Mama because we love each other. Happiness is more important than finances."

"Girl, please. You can only keep your head above water for so long."

Feather did not respond. She was tired of the conversation.

Lillian stopped in front of Feather's apartment.

"Call me when you get home Mama."

"Ok. Do you need anything? I got a few bucks."

"No thank you." Feather's pride spoke without hesitation.

"Alright see ya later." Lillian drove off when Feather got inside. Feather changed into her sweats, hit the cassette button on the radio on her way to the kitchen. *Now I understand why Daddy left. She's so damned difficult. Not to mention hard to please. Most mothers would be glad that their daughter found someone to treat them right. Not mine* Gladys sang "Midnight Train to Georgia" Feather sang with her.

The phone rang.

"Hi April...Yes we're going over to Champ's tomorrow. Y'all?"

"Ok. See ya there." Feather hadn't talked to April since the Superbowl.

♣♣♣

The visit at Champ's was cool at first. Then he started clowning Nikki for no reason at all. It was like he was trying to impress everybody. No one was impressed. "D" was downright disgusted. He and Bridgette left soon as Champ started his mess.

First he complained about how big Nikki was. Then he complained that she over seasoned the food. Nikki's demeanor visibly changed from joy to embarrassment.

By nights end Black had pulled him into the kitchen and told him to chill, like a big brother does his kid brother. Feather had taken Nikki into the bathroom to console her.

Champ had called her a 'stupid ass bitch' in front of everyone. He wasn't real loud with it but loud enough for everyone to hear.

On the way home Black expressed his disappointment of Champ's behavior. Feather was quiet. She wondered if Champ and Black's friendship dissolved how it would effect her relationship with Nikki.

♣♣♣

Nikki was devastated. She had gotten excited about this event to be disrespected by Champ like that.

Making it through the night was hard for her. She was embarrassed and felt like everyone was looking at her.

When the evening was over and everyone was gone, she straightened the house to avoid Champ. She was so angry with him.

Finally he eased over to her and kissed her neck. "Babe I'm sorry. I had a hard day. You know how I am when I'm broke."

Nikki wasn't ok until later when he apologized physically. He had his face in the place and her pleasure peak reaching new heights. *Apology accepted* she thought.

9

Black sat in the car. He wore Burberry jeans. A whiteT-shirt. A navy, burgundy and gray sweater vest and stark white tennis shoes. His dimple was accenting like jewelry. He wore a gold link bracelet and a small hoop in his left ear. His skin was like flawless leather, but smooth and soft as mink. His mustache was thin and well groomed.

Feather was inside rushing. They were on their way to Big Mama's for Tee's 17th birthday party.

Black honked the horn. *Feather is a typical woman. Even if I don't start getting dressed until she's dressed, I still end up waiting on her.*

Feather came running out. She wore jeans too. A white T-shirt and soft leather black clogs. On her shoulder was a huge purse. Feather had been carrying huge purses since high school. She wouldn't even look like herself without an enormous purse swinging from her shoulder. She jumped in the car.

"Did you get the potato salad?" He asked.

"Yeah…You don't need to be so pushy. I ain't gonna keep you from getting to your Big Mama." Feather teased Black.

♣♣♣

Black and Feather walked in minutes before expected. He pointed, with his head, at Feather to let everybody know she was the reason they were late. Actually they had done well, because Big Mama expected them to be a lot later than what they were.

They were smiled upon. The older people were envious, wishing they could keep their wisdom and go back. The younger people were proud and hopeful that they'd travel the same path. Everyone took his or her places.

Surpriisssee!!!

Tee was touched. She knew they were going to do something, but a surprise party? She had no idea.

♣♣♣

Big Mama had sat out candy dishes. Helium balloons were dangling from the ceiling. The countertops were full of paper plates, napkins, and utensils etc…Party paraphernalia was everywhere.

Black looked at the door every time it opened. He had personally invited Lillian.

He had a picture in his heart of how he wanted his family life to be and it included maintaining a healthy relationship with his in laws. That meant Lillian.

Lillian was nice, cordial-like, but something was missing. He had talked to Big Mama about it and she advised him to keep being himself; 'Either Mrs. Ford will accept you or she won't, don't matter you are loved.' Black relaxed.

He was also going to put more effort into meeting Michael. On several occasions they had scheduled meetings and each time one or the other became unavailable at the last minute. For four years they have been trying to meet. They spoke on the phone, but never met physically.

Lillian was pleasantly surprised at the location of the house. Malcolm Street was located in Oakland hills. *Maybe there is some hope for Andre. He has been exposed to some nice things. Lord, I don't want my baby to struggle all of her life.*

Pat greeted Lillian at the door, "Hi, I'm Bla—Andre's mother." Taking Lillian's coat, she introduced her to the rest of the family. Big Mama called Lillian "Lil" like her own family did. Adding natural warmth to her pleasant surprise. Lillian was pleased that Feather would enter this family eventually. They were a personable group and their love was genuine.

Lillian was a very attractive woman. She looked as though she should run a corporation, but she sold real estate. She was petite like Feather, but about two inches taller. It looked as though she had started the old age spread, but stopped short of spreading too thick. Her hips were eye catching, her breast greeting and her stomach rather flat. She had long hair and it rested on her shoulders. Every thing about her screamed class.

Feather was proud. So was Black. They both were admiring her when the door opened again. It was Champ and Nikki. Nikki was what pregnancy was meant to be. There wasn't a piece of lent on her. Her toes were polished even though, you knew she couldn't reach them. She wore a metallic blue silk dress with large silver hoop earrings, a silver locket and a silver bracelet. Her sandals were white. Her face was free of make-up, but naturally radiant. It was hard not to stare. She was breath taking. Champ was her only flaw. He stood next to her with a "Hey Kool Aid" grin on his unattractive face.

Big Mama peeked out the room and saw Nikki. *Lord please watch over your child. I've been where she's headed. Poor baby, looking—needing loving and it ain't there. Champ ain't the one. And Father bless that baby with some of his mother's looks if not all of them. He really shouldn't inherit anything from his Daddy…hmph...even Champ's ways are ugly.* She smiled to herself at her private little joke.

Big Mama had accepted Champ because of her love for Black, but she knew the first time he came over, in fifth grade, that he was the kind of person that was never going to be happy. She had prayed that he didn't corrupt her baby.

Black and Tee reached them at the same time. Tee was obviously taken by Nikki's beauty. She had that *'what are you doing with him?'* expression on her face.

"Hi. I'm Nicole. You must be the birthday girl…oops lady. Happy birthday." Nikki embraced her as best she could with her protruding stomach.

"Yes. I'm Tee. Hey Champ."

"Hey what's up?"

"Tee where are you putting your gifts?"

"Over there by Big Mama." She pointed.

"Oh, I see Feather. I'm going to talk to her. She'll show me."

Nikki and Feather had gone shopping the week before and bought Tee's gifts. Feather bought her an anklet and Nikki bought her a tennis style outfit. Something she would've liked for herself except she was nine months pregnant.

"Hey girl." Feather greeted Nikki. "My mother's here. I want you to meet her." They started towards the kitchen. There was Lillian and Pat talking to some other women.

"Mama this is Nikki, Champ's girlfriend."

Lillian knew better, but her mouth dropped open, her eyes widened with shock. "Hi baby." She tried to regain her composure. *This girl is gorgeous.* She extended her hand. Nikki smiled and embraced her.

"This is Pat, Black's mother." Feather continued. Nikki leaned into her too.

"You sure are pretty." Pat couldn't hold it anymore. Nikki was angelic. She reminded Pat of a diaper commercial; she was simply adorable.

"She sure is." Lillian agreed. "Just as pretty as she wanna be. Most young folks don't even wear maternity clothes any more. They walk around wearing big ole T-shirts and unbuttoned jeans. You really look nice baby." Pat and Lillian nodded in agreement.

"Who is this. I know Feather ain't brought nobody in here and act like she didn't see me. I'm Big Mama baby." Big Mama pulled Nikki into her bosom and gave her a little squeeze. Then she pinched her cheek and patted her belly. She sensed that Nikki had not been touched with a mother's hand before. She looked like she needed it. As always, Big Mama adopted, silently, another of Black's friends.

The party was starting to move. The music rose two octaves. You could hear the popping of fingers from the living room. And a few shouts of "Heeeyyy!!" as people recognized the beat.

"You remember this?" Pat popped her fingers and rolled her big hips around from one side to the other with an exaggerated pause, doing the Four Corners. Lillian joined her.

Black looked on from the living room. *My mother and mother-in-law dancing.* He smiled. This is all he ever wanted.

Feather caught a glimpse of him. Looking back at her he winked. She winked back. They both smiled and went back to their circles.

♣♣♣

The party was finding its groove when Big Mama started to serve the food.

Bo, Black's uncle, was staring at Lillian. The weight of his stare finally got too heavy for Lillian, she acknowledged him with a smile. He smiled back. His eyes said 'Hello, I'd like to know you better' He said nothing. Lillian pretended not to understand the message. It was all she could do. She wasn't about to get hurt again. Wasn't about to spend anytime with a dog. This man was so handsome it would be foolish to think that he was not married, involved or something.

On the other side of the room Black was falling in love with Feather all over again. He wanted to make love to her. He could imagine how good it was going to be, because whenever she drank...it relaxed her into total cooperation. He made a mental note to fix her another drink.

Nikki was comfortable. It wasn't the attention it was the atmosphere. These people loved each other. It even felt like they loved her and her baby. Finally, she tasted what she knew existed all of her life. Grandma was supposed to stroke her the way Big Mama did. Her mother was supposed to pat her belly and talk to her stomach the way Pat and Lillian did.

Nikki peeked at Big Mama all evening. Her beauty moved her. The cold black hair and soft as cotton hands with the raised veins. Big Mama was the essence of Grandmotherhood. Big Mama knew Nikki loved her, so she tried to be the Grandmother figure she knew to be.

When Bo put on the Blues even Big Mama's feet caught the beat. The room was full of laughter as she did her thang; the way Grandmama's do.

"Go Big Mama, Go Big Mama, Go Big Mama." Black started the chant. Everybody joined in.

♣♣♣

Lillian and Pat had become friends. Possibly sisters-in-law. Bo had finally eased over to Lil and expressed his interest. He made himself plainly clear concerning his availability. He was available.

Big Mama and Nikki bonded. "You better take it easy. If your bag ain't packed you better pack it. You gon' have this baby soon."

Pat overheard the conversation. "You better listen Nikk, Mama don' predicted all the babies in this family and she ain't missed a one."

Lillian looked at Nikki then. "Ooohh she has dropped."

Champ checked his phone. It was Tina. He called her and made arrangements to stop by after his sister's party. All these festivities made him want to make love. He hung up and went to tell Nikki they had to go.

After they left they became the topic of conversation. No one could believe that Nikki was actually with Champ. Big Mama knew Nikki was quenching a thirst and that he was filling a need but she kept quiet.

The party ended at 1:00 am. Overall it was a pleasant evening.

♣♣♣

Lillian crawled into bed humming. Her phone rang as soon as she laid down. It was Uncle Bo.

Black was surprised to find Feather in the mood, as he forgot to make her that drink. She fondled him all the way home.

Nikki was disgusted. Champ dropped her off and kept on going. He didn't even wait until she was inside. He just drove off. Talking about he had a run to make.

♣♣♣

Thank God it was Saturday. If Feather had had to go to work today she would've called in sick. The party last night had exhausted her. They didn't get home 'til about 2:00 am, but they didn't get to bed until about 5:00 am. They made love from the front door to the bedroom. Feather didn't realize how vigorous until this morning/afternoon. It was 11:00 am. Her entire body ached. She had cramps. Not the kind that are related to her menses. She had rough sex cramps.

Black rolled over, in his sleep, and dropped his arm across her stomach. Feather almost hit him back. Sometimes it was dangerous to be so tiny in comparison to him. Soon as he eased back into a rhythmic breathing pattern, she eased from under his arm. She got up, showered, brushed her teeth and put the same gown back on. This shower was just to remove the feeling of sex from her body.

While she prepared breakfast she chitchatted on the phone with her mother.

"So, how do you like Pat?"

"I like her. I like her mother too. She reminds me of Muddeah. I could sit back and watch her all day. You probably don't remember Muddeah. She died when you were a tot."

"I don't. I do remember you flirting last night."

Lillian blushed. "I was not. I was being sociable."

"Yeah right. Uncle Bo was flirting. Did you notice that?"

"Yes I did. Maya you need to quit." Lillian waited a while. "I did talk to him last night. We're supposed to be getting together today."

Feather flipped the last piece of French toast. "Is that right? Go Mama, Go Mama, Go Mama." Feather was glad to hear that Lillian was going on a date. As pretty as she was she hadn't been out in about five years.

Lillian blushed. "I'm going. Let me call you back. You know getting ready is an all day thing with me."

"Ok bye."

Black walked into the kitchen.

"Good morning."

"Good morning." He sat in his boxers and a T-shirt.

Feather sat his plate in front of him.

The phone rang. She lost a sigh.

Black answered. "Hello?"

"Hi Andre. This is Lil, can I speak to Maya?"

"Good morning. Just a minute."

Feather took the phone with questioning eyes.

Black mouthed "Your mother".

She nodded. "Hello?"

"Feather do you have some black jeans? He wants to play miniature golf. And girl my one pair of jeans are too faded, you know I've had them forever."

"I have some, but mine are old too. You can come take a look at them but I wouldn't wear them on a first date. He'd have to be an old friend."

"Alright. I guess I'll run to the mall. I told you it was gonna be an all day thing, me getting ready."

"I got some dark blue jeans. If you don't find any black ones. They're pretty new."

"Alright. I'll call you when I get back. Unless, you wanna go with me?"

"Naw. We're in for the day. Black's on graveyard shift starting next week."

"Ok. Bye."

"Bye."

Feather put their plates in the sink and got back in the bed. Black crawled in next to her.

The phone rang. They looked at each other. Neither wanting to be bothered. There was overcast. So, the room was dark. The temperature was perfect. The best part was the series of classic Black films on special program. It was definitely a day to enjoy some stress free living.

"Hello?" Black handed the phone to Feather.

"Hello?"

It was Nikki. "Hey what you doing?"

"Nuthin, laying here with Black."

"Oh."

"What's the matter?" Feather could hear the tears in her voice.

"I'm tired, Feather. Champ don't love me. He just...I don't know what he's doing. I'm tired though. Last night he left. Girl, he didn't even park. He stopped the car. I got out, I thought he was parking and coming in. He leaned over and said he had a run to make. Then drove off. It's twelve and I ain't heard from him since."

Feather rolled her eyes towards the ceiling. She wanted to tell her to wise up and leave him. After that incident the other night, she was crazy to still be dealing with him. "Did you page him?"

"No. I get tired of hearing the lies. 'I must've turned it off accidentally...It has a low battery...it was in my coat and my coat was in the car.'"

Nikki felt helpless. She couldn't do anything about whatever Champ was doing. She just needed him to show up at night, be that warm hard body in her life. She needed someone to check that thump in the night. A man to reach the upper cabinets without use of a chair she needed a man. She needed him. Champ.

"Well, do you wanna come over here until he get home, so you don't have to be alone?" Feather remembered her feelings on being alone.

Black elbowed her.

Feather drew a line from her eyes to her chin to let him know that she was crying. He nodded and pouted like a little boy.

"No. I don't want to disrupt your day. I guess I should just wait. He'll be here if ain't nothing happened to him. I'll call you back if he's not here by evening."

"Ok. Bye."

"Bye."

Nikki heard Champ enter the house. She eased the phone back down and laid back in the bed, closing her eyes she pretended to be asleep. He came in and kissed her forehead. She could hear him fumbling around the room. Hearing noises in the kitchen she peeked open one eye. Staring her in the face was a single red rose. Her anger was erased.

♣♣♣

"Babe, I'm about to turn the ringer off." Black whispered returning the phone to its cradle. Snuggling closer Feather nodded. She enjoyed lying up under him. He was so big and strong feeling. His arm was a little smaller than her thigh. That turned her on. She fondled him.

He smiled. "You are a energetic little bunny." He kissed her and moved her hand to his chest. Snuggled up they fell asleep. Missing the entire tribute to Black Film Makers.

♣♣♣

Nikki fell asleep for real.

Champ was in a frightening good mood when she woke up.

"Babe did you get your rose?"

"Yes. Thank you."

"You want to go to dinner tonight?"

"Yes." Nikki wanted to go, but she also wanted him to help her pay some of the bills.

Dinner is a nice treat, but he needed to be taking me to the grocery store. She thought, but didn't rock the boat.

"Ok. Go slip into something nice."

While waiting for her to get dressed Champ put his feet up on the coffee table. His joint ash burned a tiny hole in the ivory antique sofa. Looking around the room he appreciated Nikki. Everything was so neat and orderly. *Fuck Tina. I got a woman. A real woman. That's why I gave Nikki her rose. Now who's laughing. Gon' give me a rose and then get on the phone with a niggah. I'm glad I left my phone. Now, I know how she is.*

Nikki walked into the room. She was gorgeous. Her hair was pulled into a knot. She wore black pants and a black and white maternity top. Her stomach had dropped some more.

Champ noticed the lowness of the baby. At dinner his phone rang six times in two hours. He smiled. He wasn't going by there tonight at all. Tonight he was loving who loved him.

10

Nikki had been on the phone for a few minutes trying to find Champ. She paged him over and over again. He never answered her page. She called over to Black's.

"Hello?"

"Hey Nikki. What's up?"

"Hi Feather. Is Champ over there?"

"No. Black left me a note saying that he was at "D's'."

"Girl, I've been paging Champ and he hasn't returned any of my phone calls."

"Are you in labor?"

"No." She paused. Tears were spilling into her voice. "This girl called here talking about her and Champ have a relationship and she ain't giving him up and she gonna knock my baby outta me."

The phone signaled that Nikki had an incoming call waiting.

"Hello?"

"Yeah tramp. I'm gon' whip yo' ass! Get ready, I'm on my way."

Nikki clicked back over to Feather. Her hands were trembling with fear. She was not this kind of person. She had never had a fight in her life.

"Feather that was her. She said she was coming over. I could hear her friends in the background." Hearing the fear in her own voice Nikki felt embarrassed. She knew if the shoe were on the other foot Feather would probably react differently.

Feather was pissed. *I knew it. I knew that bastard wasn't going to do right by Nikki. I wanted to believe that he was ok, but Champ ain't shit. And I bet this girl he dealing with is a disease-breeding tramp.* "Do you have anything to protect yourself?"

"No not really. Plus, girl I can't hurt nobody." Nikki was crying tears of frustration through her voice, but she was holding the tears in her eyes well. The baby was pressing down like it was ready, but this being her first child she didn't know.

"Girl, some people will make you hurt them. Boil some water 'til I get there and if she come over there acting stupid douse her ass." Feather hoped she didn't come across too ghetto, but self preservation brought out the worst in her. Then she grew slightly angry with Nikki. *How can you be scared at home?*

"Ok."

Before they could hang up the phone there was a pounding on the door.

"Hold on Feather. Someone's beating on the door right now." She put the phone down and started towards the door, but stopped by the kitchen to set the water to boiling. The person continued to bang so loud, the holding Feather could hear.

Nikki peeked out the peephole and saw three girls. None of which she knew. They all looked intimidating and violent. The one in front spoke. She had a deep, unfeminine voice her tone was dripping with malice.

"Open up bitch! I got something for you!" Tina was referring to the ass whipping that she had promised Nikki over the phone.

They all started to laugh. Then quickly they all turned to look behind them. That's when Champ came into view.

"What you doing at my house? HUH?!!" He slapped Tina, the one talking all the mess before she could respond. Her friends stepped back in fear. "Get off my porch and don't ever come back here again harassing my woman. She's pregnant and if she so much as tell me she lost her appetite, therefore my baby didn't eat, I'm a whip yo' ass! You hear me?!" He relaxed his nostrils then turned to enter the house.

"She ain't no better than me. I'm pregnant too!" Tina screamed, through her tears, at the back of his head.

"So what it ain't mine." Champ closed the door in her face knowing good and well that the baby in her womb was just as much his as the one in Nikki's. Tina remained outside screaming obscenities and threatening to abort their baby.

Do what you gotta do. Champ thought reaching for Nikki.

"Nikk, you alright?"

"Yes. Let me tell Feather, she's holding." She picked up the receiver, told Feather she was ok and hung up.

Champ walked to her. Touched her stomach and kissed her forehead. (Tina was still outside screaming profanities and threatening abortion.) Nikki was touched by his gesture. They held each other for a minute.

Nikki was relieved beyond words. She heard every word Tina spoke, even about the baby, but she believed only the words 'It ain't mine'. Champ had stood up for her. For the moment she was going to enjoy his love.

♣♣♣

Feather sat on her bed dumbfounded. *Now I guess everything is fine. Yesterday ya go spend the evening and most of the morning with yo' woman. Then the next day she comes to the house. Thank you Jesus because it could have been my story.* Appreciating her relationship and loving Black Feather started to undress.

He walked in when she was down to her underwear and loving him forced a smile.

"Hi honey." She greeted.

He looked at her and walked out. Then right back in.

"Hi honey!!" Running and jumping into his arms, he lifted her off the ground.

"That's mo' like it. If you're going to be happy to see me then act like it."

She playfully punched him in the upper part of his arm. "You so crazy. I was loving you so, I was glad to see you."

"I don't believe you." He said looking at her with lust filled eyes.

"Well, too Baadd!!" She teased and trotted away from him.

Black went into the living room and started watching a basketball game.

Feather couldn't pinpoint why, but she was aching for affection. Sex actually. She was just playing when she said 'too bad', hoping he would pursue her.

There he sat in the living room on the couch with his eyes pasted to the TV.

Feather came out of the bathroom wet. She didn't even bother to dry off. Whenever they watched porno movies and water was involved Black was extremely interested.

"Babe what you watching?" She moved into view.

"The game." He said, glancing in her direction then doing a double take.

"Babe, what's up?"

"What does it look like?" She dried her back revealing her front.

"It looks like you're in the mood for some Mr. Goodbar."

Feather lost interest. That smirk on his face and hand on his thang just turned her off.

"I was." She walked out of the room. Mentally she lost interest, but her body was screaming 'it's just a joke' as she entered the bedroom she was rocked by a cramp. It all made sense now. She had the kind of body that got horny right at the time of her period. She was going to be out of commission for about a week real soon. She threw on a spaghetti strapped T-shirt and walked back into the living room.

Black turned around to find her sitting Indian Style next to him with her entire bottom half staring at him.

A commercial started.

"Come here." Feather invited.

The phone rang as it was getting good.

"Don't answer it." Black panted.

Feather moaned. "What if it's important?"

"It ain't."

"How do you know?"

"This is priority."

"But Babe." She whispered with pleasure.

He did something that made her remove her hand from the receiver. The answering machine picked up.

Black finished as the message began to record on the machine.

"Feather, come home as soon as you get this message. It's Mama."

Feather picked up. "Mama?" She could tell she was crying. Tears welled up in Feather's eyes. She couldn't stand to see her loved ones hurt.

"Just come."

"I'm on my way." She jumped. It was serious. Lil never needed her.

Feather pulled on her panties and some jeans. She slid a button down shirt over her spaghetti strapped T-shirt, slid her feet into her sandals, grabbed her big purse and was ready. Black was already at the door, fully dressed and ready to go.

They got to Lil's in ten minutes.

Feather used her key.

"Mama?!"

Lillian stood in the doorframe of the kitchen on wobbling knees with tear filled eyes. Black rushed to her.

"Mama!!" Feather's adrenaline was pumping. She ran to her too. "What's wrong?" They eased her to the sofa.

"Baby…I have some terrible news for you." Lil was visibly shaking.

"Your...uh.you...You lost your Daddy today."

"What?" Feather let go of her. Lil reached to her. Feather shook her off. Black went to her. Feather screamed.

"AH…AAHHH! Aaahhh!!! No!! No!! No Mmaama Not my Daddy!! Not my Daddy... I NEED MY DADDY...Mamma I love my daddy." Feather was shaking her head no.

Black embraced her. He rocked her.

Lil was wrenched with pain. She loved her ex-husband too, but not like Feather. Feather had loved him through each broken promise, each lie told, each excuse and disappointment. Even though she had not spoken to him in three months, pretending she had had enough. Lil knew that without a doubt that she was still a Daddy's girl.

Lillian wanted to help her, but couldn't. It was killing her to witness her baby's pain the same way it killed Feather to hear her message.

Feather fell asleep somewhere between "ooohh Daddy and not my daddy..." in Black's arms.

Lillian made coffee. As she came back with two cups she noticed Black had some pain in his heart too. He'd never even met Michael. Knowing his pain was coming from his love for Feather she loved him too.

For the longest time she felt like he was taking her baby, today she realized he was sharing her baby. *Thank you Lord for this good man in Maya's life.* She appreciated finally, Feather's choice.

11

The day of Michael's funeral Feather woke before Black dressed and sat waiting on him to get dressed. *I have never been on time for anything in my life. I can't believe I'm going to be on time to my Daddy's funeral. I can't believe he's gone. I can remember him plain as day. I can remember his scent, touch, mannerism, the sound of his laughter and voice, but it's true…there was a Quiet Hour yesterday and he was there…lying there.* She began to cry, but only on the inside. The pain was knotted and twisting on her insides. She was running in her mind. Running to a place where she could find her way back to, at least, the day before. She needed to see him again, to have him hug her; she needed him to do anything. Oh how she needed that, she wanted to be angry with him. She was angry with him. He was too young to die. He was much too strong to die. He had overcome so much in his life why not the aneurysm? Why did he give in to it? Why did he leave her at this young age in both their lives?

Feather was sitting on the couch crumbling. Black entered the room. He wore a black suit, a grayish tie and a sad pain inflicted expression. Feather looked at him tenderly. She was glad to have him in her life.

"Ready?" Black spoke to her as if she had a choice.

"Yes." Feather was giving the illusion that she was fine.

Black needed her to be so he accepted the illusion. For the past three days their house was silent the kind of silence that can be heard. He didn't know whether to hold her or leave her alone. It was killing him to see her walk around all day without a smile, laughter and warmth. She never spoke. She hadn't even turned on the radio. Her tenacity enhanced her beauty somehow, but Black wanted his baby back.

Lillian rode to the funeral with Uncle Bo. She was not comfortable riding in the family car and didn't want to overshadow Michael's girlfriend.

Feather didn't seem to notice that her mother wasn't with her. Nor did she notice that Nikki wasn't present. Nikki stayed at Feather's house. She made sure that the guest coming straight there could get in and that the food was set out for those arriving after the funeral.

Her cramps were really rocking her now. There was some pressure and some paralyzing moments before everyone arrived.

Feather was a mess. A well glued mess. It was clear that she didn't really understand what had just happened to her. Nikki knew her pain. Big Mama did too. They both knew that she was going to break down one day and hoped to be there for her when she did.

Things appeared to be normal. The next day Feather cooked, cleaned the house and lay on Black for the first time since they'd gotten the news. The next morning she spoke to Black about going back to work. Black was glad. He had simply wanted to touch her through all of this but it had become laboring, watching her hold tears that were straining to get out.

That night Black heard Feather snoring lightly. She had not slept in days. He was hopeful that she had returned to herself.

♣♣♣

Champ had left Tina completely alone. When he got the phone call that Feather's Dad had passed away it tickled something deep inside of him, changing the value of life in his eyes. He was going to put more effort into living right, loving right and being a good father. He even thought about his daughter briefly.

Nikki had reached the nesting stage of pregnancy. She cleaned everything in the house even stuff that wasn't dirty. She changed the color scheme in the bathroom and refolded the baby's clothes for the hundredth time.

Champ sat there watching her buzz around. She had that little waddle down pat.

"Babe you want something from the store? I'm 'bout to go get some zigzags. I'll be right back."

"No thank you. I'm gon' lay down I'm tired." She called from their bedroom. As soon as the door closed pain unknown to Nikki's imagination ripped through her body. She thought its mission was to shred her apart with the dullest of blades. For the first time in a long time she wanted her mother. The thought passed quickly, as another contraction stole her attention. At that point fear swallowed her. She inched her way from the hallway entrance in effort to make it to the door.

For the first time Champ, returned home as promised.

"Champ it hurts!!" She moaned. One hand was palming her vagina the other was reaching to him.

He saw his mother. He didn't move.

Nikki didn't know why. Didn't care either. She needed him to move.

"Help Mee!!!" She screamed.

"Ok. Oh-kay!!" He trotted to the kitchen. Grabbed the phone and dialed Black's number. He hated to call under the circumstances, but he couldn't do it alone. He needed his brother.

"Hello?" Feather was not sleep.

"Feather, I'm sorry to call so late, but um...um..."

"CHAMP!!"

"Nikki's in labor and I was wondering if y'all could come."

"Yeah, we'll meet you there."

"Alright." Neither said good bye. Feather woke Black and they headed out the door. Nikki was down the steps and tugging on the locked car door.

Black and Feather arrived to find Champ in the lobby drenched with sweat and a confused look on his face.

"What did she have?"

"She ain't had it yet. She's still in there. I...I—uh forgot the bag. Black let's go get it." He was pulling Black out of the door with such force Black found himself walking with him. "Feather stay with her."

He was nervous and obviously running from the situation.

How could he leave? She thought watching the back of their heads. She went to the nurse's station and was directed to Nikki. Nikki's hair was wet and matted to her head. Her lips were ashy white and her eyes were pleading.

"It's ok Nikk." Feather cooed.

Her face contorted. Another contraction pierced her stomach. Feather thought to go get the nurse. Like osmosis she appeared. She was an older, grandmotherly, type woman with loving soothing eyes. Feather had to suppress the urge to crawl into her arms and lay her burdens down.

The nurse checked Nikki then turned to Feather.

"It's time. Are you the coach?"

Feather wasn't sure how to respond at first. One glance at Nikki is all it took. "Yes."

By the time the guys returned Feather had cut the cord of Nikki and Champ's firstborn. It was a beautiful, beautiful experience. Feather held on to her tears until Nikki asked her if she could give him her Dad's name as his middle name.

Feather blinked back a tear. "Thank you." It did her heart good to see this baby enter the world. She felt like she had a lot to live for. She wanted a baby.

Nikki was terribly saddened by Champ's disappearance. She always dreamed the man whose children she bore would be there. Champ hadn't even looked like he wanted to be there. *Thank God for Feather.* Nikki had grown to love her.

The nurse came back in. "You were wonderful baby." She praised. "And so was your friend."

"Sister…this is my sister Fea–"

"Maya." Feather interrupted. "Thank you." Feather smiled in Nikki's direction; accepting the change in their friendship.

As the nurse left the room Champ and Black walked in.

"It's a boy" Feather whispered.

Nikki was falling asleep.

Champ stood there. No expression. Not joy. Not even sadness. He was in a blank stupor.

Nikki lay in the bed drained and pale. She almost looked lifeless.

"Let's go to the nursery and see him." Feather was talking only to Black, but Champ came too. He couldn't bear looking at Nikki.

Between Feather and Black passed the silent acknowledgement that Champ was tripping. Neither spoke. They didn't have to. They knew each other well enough to know they were on one accord.

12

Everybody dropped by Nikki's to see the baby. Countless people had prayed that this baby look like his mother and their prayers had been answered.

Johnathan was so pretty and so full of hair he had to have a train, football—something on every garment he owned; it was easy to assume he was a girl.

Champ was putting an effort into being home at a decent, respectful hour every night and his hustle, as he put it, was good also. It was so good that he'd told Nikki she didn't have to go back to work in six weeks. The gesture was nice and she was touched, but too often in the past she had waited on Champ's income and it didn't come.

Nikki thought she was near death when Champ went to Mrs. Harris', the lady that was going to keep Johnny when she returned to work, in exactly six weeks. She didn't want to go back, she didn't want to leave her child. Johnny was the best thing that had come into her life ever. He was better, even, than Champ.

She didn't have to deal with any hang-ups over the phone because the number had been changed. Everything in Nikki's life was good again.

When Champ requested some loving from her she gave herself willingly, bleeding and all. He deserved it. Besides, his track record reminded her that because she didn't give it to him didn't mean he wouldn't get it. She didn't want to run that risk. They finally resembled something of a family.

Making love that night was as painful as giving birth. Champ had no consideration for the changes her body had gone through. He pounded inside of her with a vengeance. She took three Advil's before going to sleep.

♣♣♣

Feather was withdrawn for about a month after Johnny was born. She had her moments when she felt normal, but quickly returned to her grief. She felt guilty about smiling, relaxing and that sort of everyday thing while her poor father lay six feet underground.

Black was becoming concerned. Silence was returning. They were careful not to touch one another in bed at night. He had learned how to successfully distract himself when becoming erect knowing she wasn't going to allow him to touch her. He went to Big Mama with his problem.

She explained. "Baby, Feather will be fine once she let it out. One day the dam is going to break, just hold on baby. You're a man now. When you start dealing with life and death you can truly say you are grown. I'm proud of you baby…You hang in there she'll be all right. She needs for you to be silent, talking, holding, staying out of her way and whatever else it might take without asking you. Listen to her gestures it's as loud as her voice can get right now."

A couple of nights later Feather wanted her Daddy. She wanted his smile, his laughter, a promise…a lie even. She wanted to see him again.

Black had gone somewhere with Champ. So, she couldn't lean on him. She didn't feel her mother was strong enough to help her. Lillian would only start crying with her. She didn't want to cry she wanted to understand.

She dialed Big Mama.

"Big Mama…this is Feather."

This time it was Big Mama's maternal instincts that stood attention. "I know Baby. Come on. I've been expecting yo' call. Black tole me 'bout how you cried real good that one time. Well, do that now. Cry 'til you get here. Cry all the way. Mama'll be here. I can help ya, but not over 'dis phone. I needs to give ya something."

"Ok." Feather choked on that two-letter word and hung up.

Big Mama turned over the fried chicken and peeked at the rolls in the oven.

Pat and Theresa would be home any minute. Pat walked in, tossed her coat on the couch and looked up into the stern face of her mother.

"I'm gonna hang it up."

"You need to. Feather's on her way over here now. She sounded real bad. Po' baby."

Big Mama shook her head and began a silent prayer.

A knock bounced off of the door. It was Feather. The car had actually driven her there. She'd done just as Big Mama told her. She cried all the way there. Her eyes were swollen. Her hair was all over her head, but she still looked like Feather. Just as pretty as she could be, looking like a precious sparkle in the eye of infant. Big Mama, Pat and Tee simply adored her.

"Hi baby." Pat opened the door.

"Hi, Mom." Feather evaded eye contact.

Pat lifted her chin, looked in her eyes and whispered "It's gonna be all right." Then kissed her forehead.

Pat was 5'6". Big Mama was 5'8". Tee was 5'5". Feather was a mere 5'0". She felt like a real feather amongst them. They were all close together in a group hug. Then, Big Mama eased Feather into her bosom and that was it. A sob rose from the bottom of her feet and sprang into Big Mama's chest.

"Ssshh…It's ok." Big Mama's moan sounded like a soothing gospel hymn. She held and stroked Feather for nearly forty-five minutes right there at the door. Big Mama knew she had to get Feather to talk. She eased over to the couch and sat down with Feather still in her embrace. Feather hadn't even realized that they had moved. "Tell Mama baby. Tell me what you miss about him?"

Feather couldn't/wouldn't talk.

"Feather Mama wanna know. I wanna miss it too. I wanna know your Daddy too. Who is he?"

"My Da-daa...daddy's a man...uh...He had a beautiful smile. It was so irresistible. Even when he was lying and you knew it you still believed. He was charming that way. When I was little he used to call me his lil' feather weight baby. Over the years I became Feather. That was always special to me. When people used to laugh at my nickname I wasn't even hurt because my Daddy gave it to me…He picked me up until I was thirteen. My Daddy was a big man, just like Black. He had a dimple in his chin and hated it so he grew a beard. I can't believe he's gone. I can't never touch him again."

Tears were rolling down her cheeks again. Big Mama was pleased.

"Yes Baby, I know. You gon' be all right. You know some of that stuff you said was true, but not all of it." Big Mama had begun to rock Feather in her arms to a motion that was persuasively soothing. Her voice was as low as a whisper, but could be heard perfectly clear. She paused between her words to let the impact of them fully register.

"You can touch him. You can touch him with your mind, any time...you want to. You know something I did? I kept everything I could of my Mama and Daddy's after they passed. Then one day my house burnt down with everything I owned in it. 'Cluding Mama and Daddy's stuff. That hurt me to my heart. I mourned a long time 'hind dat, but one night I dreamed of Mama. She said *'I'm still here...I'm still here.'* I knew then I was gonna be ok. Now, I didn't have her coat and wedding ring and a few dishes, but I had my memories and feelings and love. Those are my treasures. Make'em yours. That's what I had to give you, the gift of wisdom and peace. The know how of coping. You'll never fully understand death until you meet it so don't bother trying. Trust in the Lord. Feel your pain, baby it's healing. To hurt is to heal. Remember your Daddy. Treasure your memories. You're gonna be fine."

Feather was mesmerized by the feeling of peace and actual understanding that flowed from this woman into her.

Her tears fell continuously. She fell asleep in Big Mama's arms to the humming of a gospel tune.

Big Mama knew her baby was going to be all right. She would continue to have bad days throughout her life, but at least now she could cry and love her way through them.

♣♣♣

Black walked in the house. He hadn't seen the car in the driveway, which meant Feather was not home. It was an hour before he started to worry. He checked the answering machine.

"Hi baby, this is Mama. Feather was having a rough time, so she came over here. Call me when you get there. I'll pick you up if she's not up to it."

Black called.

"Mama is she all right?" He asked as Pat picked up the phone.

"Yes. She's sleep. You want me to come get you?"

"Yeah. I'll be outside."

"Black she's fine. Mama's been talking to her. And anyway it's 10:00 pm. Do you always stay out this late?"

"Mama, I've been here. I just didn't check the messages." Black was a little perturbed that his mother would even come at him like that. He had been by Feather's side through this whole thing. When she was silent, even if he wanted to talk he was silent. When she wanted to be alone he pretended like he wasn't home. If she didn't cook, he didn't bother her about it; he bought something and if she didn't eat it he threw it out. Today he needed to get out of the house, to feel normal again, just for a little while. And his mother was not going to put him through a guilt trip for taking a mental health break.

Walking into Big Mama's room, after he grabbed a piece of chicken, he spotted Feather. She was curled up in Big Mama's king-size bed looking like a piece of lent. He wanted to touch her, but Big Mama gave him the evil eye. She'd crept alongside him.

"She's gonna be fine baby. She was a little lost, but Mama put her on the right track."

She whispered to him in that same soothing tone that had put Feather to sleep. "You love her don't you baby?"

"Yes Mam."

"Then be good to her."

Black knew she was referring to his leaving her alone and they both knew it without it being said.

That night Black slept on the couch.

Feather woke during the night to find herself in Big Mama's bed and Big Mama lying on the other side. She smiled. She rose to go to the bathroom. "Black?" He woke as she neared.

"Hi baby."

"Hey, Are you ok?"

"Now I am. I love you. And I know why you love Big Mama the way you do." She smiled sincerely.

Black was pleased. "I love you too." Things were getting back to normal. "You better get back in there 'for she wake up."

'Ain't nobody sleeping with nobody less they's married.' They sang in unison. Feather leaned into Black and kissed him

tenderly. He rubbed her thigh, wishing he could make love to her. She went to the bathroom and back to Big Mama's bed and back to sleep.

Big Mama's eyes were closed, but her ears were open; she heard her children and she prayed for them. She was pleased with their love for one another.

When Feather woke the next morning she was better. Much better. She didn't understand how her 48-year-old father had a fatal aneurysm. She didn't need to anymore. This was their fate. She had to accept it.

♣♣♣

Feather was truly feeling better. At Big Mama's she came to understand that it was ok to laugh, and live in Michael's absence. She placed her Daddy in a spot in her heart where he would remain dear.

"You know Babe I keep remembering Johnny's birth. It was so beautiful…made me want a baby."

"Oh yeah?" Black wanted a baby too, sometimes. More so since Johnny arrived, but he didn't feel like now was good time. He wanted Feather to be more of herself first.

"I think I want to do it, but I'm scared. Plus I don't want to get pregnant because my best friend just had a baby, but it was his birth that made me realize that I want a child. And if it's a boy we could name him Michael after Daddy." She was vibrant with hope. This time she spoke his name without that cloud of pain.

"Ok. It's ok with me. We can have a baby but…you need a car first. Let's work on that. I ain't having you and 'Michael' on the bus." He smiled. The trip to the hospital for Johnny's arrival had had a paternal effect on him too.

"Thanks Babe. I'm going to stop taking my pills now because I heard it takes a couple of months to get them out of your system."

13

Dressing for her six-week appointment Nikki regretted sleeping with Champ. *What if I'm pregnant? God I'm sorry. If you let me out of this jam I will do better.*

Champ was tripping again. This week he stayed out all night, twice. The first night Nikki called the hospitals and jails, cried 'til morning and he walked in talking about he was trying to win his money back. The second time Nikki prayed, nursed her baby and went on to sleep. Loving a man didn't have to be this hard.

She knew she needed him and wasn't going anywhere for there was too much to lose. Feather, Black and Big Mama. (These people had become dear to her.) These were Champ's people. They belonged to him. To lose him was to lose them. Nikki needed this family.

Feather knocked on the door. She was taking Nikki to the doctor.

"Hey girl, you know you early." Nikki smiled at Feather.

"I know. I had to see that baby again." Feather confessed. Since she and Black decided to try to have a baby she was being open about her maternal feelings.

Nikki noticed the way Feather looked at Johnny.

"I can't believe it either. I'm somebody's Mama. It feels weird."

"Girl I know. Just the other day we were becoming friends, now we're sisters and I'm an Auntie. Life is a trip."

Feather picked Johnny up off the bed. He was lying there falling in and out of sleep the way baby's do.

"Black and I have decided to try for a baby." Feather blushed into Johnny's sleeping face. "Black said it was ok with him, that's all I needed to know. I haven't swallowed a birth control pill since."

They laughed.

"The weird thing is the other day Champ and I were talking about y'all having a baby."

Johnny opened his eyes briefly and smiled at Feather.

"Hey man. It's Tee-Tee and her just love it, love it, love it." She pressed her nose gently against his with each 'love it'.

Looking serious Nikki sat on the bed next to them. "Feather I'm scared to go today."

"Why? It's just a Pap smear right?"

"Yes, but you're not supposed to have sex until after this appointment. And well uh…we sort of did."

"Girl?!!"

"Champ wouldn't wait. Soon as I stopped bleeding he was all over me." Nikki couldn't tell her that she hadn't stopped; she was too embarrassed.

Feather didn't say so, but she thought that was inconsiderate of Champ and stupid on Nikki's part. "Well what you gonna do?"

♣♣♣

It was twenty minutes before Dr. Sanders came in. Nikki was sitting up in the paper robe waiting and stressing.

"Good morning Ms. Collier, how are you?" He was especially glad to see Nikki she was such a beautiful girl. There was something about her that drew compassion from him.

"Fine."

"Lay back please." He sat on the seat below her and guided her feet into the stirrups.

"Do you have any questions?" He asked while conducting her internal exam.

Lying, uncomfortably on the table Nikki blurted out. "I need to take a pregnancy test."

"Today?" Dr. Sanders was slightly disappointed in her carelessness. She was not healed enough to engage in intercourse. He wondered why she would do that to herself.

"Yes. My boyfriend couldn't wait."

"I see." He removed his gloves then patted her legs for closure. "I'll have the nurse write up a lab slip for some blood work and send it to the lab with your cultures STAT."

"Thank you." Nikki purposely didn't look at him.

"I'll see you in two weeks. We'll talk about birth control at that time." Dr Sanders said it without veiling his disappointment.

Nikki was hurt by what she thought he thought of her. She dressed and went to the reception area for her paperwork.

Feather stood with Johnny, when she saw her approaching. "What'd he say?"

"I have to go to the lab and take a pregnancy test. He made me feel so stupid. Sometimes he can be so paternal."

"I like that in a doctor…I like to feel their concern." Feather comforted.

Nikki was in the lab for thirty minutes. After giving blood she relaxed some. She could call tomorrow for the results.

Dropping them off, Feather went home. Black was going to be leaving for work soon. She wanted to spend some time with him before he left for work.

"Call me later if you need to talk." Feather offered.

"Ok. Pray for me."

"I will." Feather was going to anyway.

♣♣♣

At 3 o'clock the phone rang.

"Hello Ms. Collier. This is Dr. Sanders."

"Yes." Nikki's heart was racing. *They said tomorrow…why is he calling today? It's only been a few hours*

"I'm calling about your lab work."

Nikki's tears formed. She just couldn't have another baby.

"Your pregnancy test was negative, however, there is another problem." She stopped crying then started right back. "You tested positive for an infection called Chlamydia. I've prescribed some Doxycyline. Take one tablet twice a day for seven consecutive days. Your prescription is for 28 doses there is enough for your partner as well. You must refrain from intercourse during this treatment. Excuse me a condom would be sufficient."

"Thank you." Nikki could barely bring herself to respond. She whispered those words not even sure that Dr.

Sanders had heard them or that she had actually spoken them.

She had been caught once picking her nose, she had fallen in the presence of a crowd, she even lost her manners in a public place, but never had she been this humiliated. Her hands trembled. As she clasped them together she noticed their cleanliness, then her jeans and her white tennis shoes. Her exterior was immaculate; her inside was putrid.

Nikki cried until tears would no longer form.

When Champ came home that evening he found her curled up on the bed with swollen eyes.

She knows.

"I got Chlamydia. A DISEASE! A sexually transmitted disease! You gave it to me you bastard!!"

"Shut up! It ain't no disease. It's an infection. You act like you got AIDS."

"I shouldn't have nothing. I fuck you and suck you until I'm comatose. You should be a happy man."

"If you were a better lay I wouldn't be out there." Champ was trying to hurt her.

His statement hurt Nikki, her breast milk began to leak. She couldn't understand why he was treating her like this.

"If you knew you had something why did you make love to me with it?" She cried.

"'Cause I wanted some! What you gon' do?!!" He started toward her. It was time to dominate her and sit her down. He was feeling cornered and didn't like it. He had taken care of it. Tina was beaten badly for infecting him.

Nikki rose off the bed. "Stay away from me, you and your dirty ass dick!"

The slap that slammed into her face was the first ever. All she could do was stand there looking stupid.

Seeing that she wasn't going to retaliate he walked over to his drawer grabbed a medicine bottle and threw it on the bed. It landed next to Johnny's head.

(Now she gon' think I was trying to hit the baby. Man, why she gotta trip like this. She could've told me she was infected. I could have apologized and it would've been over, but no...she had to do all this.) He grew angrier. "Nikki, take two of these until you get your own, then put them back. I got two days left so you need to hurry up and get your own."

He walked out of the room. A minute later Nikki heard the door close. She hated him.

Johnny started crying.

14

Black was working overtime again and Lillian was not available to pick up Feather from work. Charlotte, her co-worker, offered her a ride home.

The worst part of the trip was dealing with Charlotte's arrogance. Last month she became engaged and unbearable. As soon as Feather sat in the car Charlotte dropped a Modern Bride magazine in her lap. Of course, the ride home was filled with conversation pertaining to *her* wedding plans.

Oh well, I'll return it tomorrow. Feather thought dropping Charlotte's Bride magazine on the table. She hadn't meant to take it from the car.

Inside Feather busied her hands with her chores and her mind with her own wedding plans. She was loving Black and thanking the Lord for him.

When he arrived Feather prepared his plate, then continued with some pressing chores.

Setting his plate on the table, Black noticed the Modern Bride Magazine.

"Who's getting married?" He felt fear rushing him emotionally. What he expressed was outrage.

Feather was thoroughly offended by his attitude. She couldn't resist the opportunity to explore his feeling on marriage especially since he was in favor of starting a family.

"We are." She smiled playfully, but with a touch of seriousness.

"No we not." He stood with the book in his hand.

"And why not?" Indignation made its way to her tone.

"'Cause, I don't want to."

"Oh this is about what you want?"

"Yeah. You got that couch…the— "

"Furniture in exchange for wedding vows." She interrupted. "Sweetheart you got your values all mixed up."

"Girl gon' with that. I just ain't ready. I got enough sense to know that." Black was being honest. He'd seen it happen, people got married. Then changed. Then divorced. He didn't want to divorce Feather. He knew she was who he was meant to have, but for some reason he couldn't express himself that way.

"Black it's going on five years." There were tears spilling into her voice, but she was holding those in her eyes well. "We can start a F-A-M-I-L-Y—share the bills and the bed, but not the name. Let me tell you something. This what I have for you…(she pointed to her heart) is real. It don't get no better. You may luck up on a woman that can cook, run a house, and make love. And I'll go one better, you may find one prettier, but we all the same. So you keep looking and keep your lousy ass name. Lucky for me I was born with one." She turned without acknowledging his confusion and went back to her bedroom. In her heart she hoped he wouldn't follow like normal. Black had pissed her off beyond her control and he'd do right by staying out of her face. She was prepared to slap the breath from him.

Black dropped on the couch and rubbed his hands over his forehead in disbelief. *How could she think I'm looking for someone else?* Normally he would have followed her, but tonight he decided to give her her space. Besides, he needed some space himself.

Lying in bed Feather tried to dissolve the knot of pain in her throat without crying, until he came to bed.

The rest of the night was silent. Black slept on his side of the bed and Feather on hers. Both shocked at the others understanding of their relationship.

I assumed he was going to marry me. All this time I've loved him and he ain't been giving a damn about me. Not enough to spend a lifetime. What's happening to my life? First Daddy, now Black.

What is wrong with Feather? Another woman?? What is she talking about?? She should know me better than that.

♣♣♣

Driving home from work was awkward. Feather was distant.

At home she maintained her wifely duties. The house was clean, dinner was prepared and she had done something to make herself simply beautiful.

Black noticed it all. Loved it all, but couldn't show her. He could see through her beauty that she was hurting. She really thought that he didn't love her. And short of asking her to marry him, there was nothing he could say to erase the pain.

Black had every intention of marrying Feather. He loved Feather, but he was scared. The seriousness of marriage was terrifying. It meant that he had chosen one woman for the rest of his life. It felt so much like lockdown.

Tonight there was something else visible through Feather's beauty. It was determination. Black understood that if he didn't relay his feelings soon he was going to lose his woman. Feather had shared with him, in the beginning, that she would not stay in a relationship that was loveless or going nowhere.

Feather didn't want to leave Black, but she was forced to decide that way. If he had not explained his position on marriage or his plans for their future, by week's end, she was moving back to Lillian's.

Feather sat on the floor with her back against the sofa and her feet crossed at the ankles. She listened to Anita Baker pour her heart out to her lover as she poured hers out to Black. She hit each note and reached every range with ease. Like Anita she meant each lyric she sang. Black could stand no more. This message hit home. He walked into the room and turned the radio down.

"Feather, I love you. I want to marry you." He eased over to her on the floor. "I don't know how to say this I ...I ...I'm scared. I know a lot of people that get married and end up divorced. It's like after the vows the expectations change...suddenly what was all right before is annoying. I don't want to go through that. I don't want us to change."

"Black, we don't have to change. The only change we need to make is my last name. Do I nag you now? Do I deny you the things that bring you pleasure? Do I try to dominate you?"

"No baby."

"I am not good to you because I'm trying to get you to marry me. I am good to you because I want to be. This is who I am. I cannot change. What ever it is about me that you don't like now is all you will have to deal with; and that should be easy, you're dealing with it now."

"I know. I just, I'm—".

"You're not the only one choosing for life. I'm making a choice too. There are a lot of men out there. How do I know you're the right one?"

Black grew concerned. She did understand his confusion. "I am. I am the one."

"And so am I. I am the one for you."

"I love you baby." Black kissed Feather as he undressed her. The only thing that kept him from asking her to marry him then was Big Mama. Recently, he'd overheard her telling Tee 'Don't take to heart a proposal made while lying in bed, you don't always wake up married.' So Black would wait for a better time. Right now he needed to love his woman.

They made love right there. Every thing Black needed was given. Everything Feather wanted was provided.

Feather believed in his love again.

Black knew Feather was who he was meant to have.

15

The make up between Black and Feather lasted one week. It was "honey" this and "baby" that. They were making love every night. Just couldn't keep their hands off of one another.

Then Black messed up. He picked her up from work forty minutes late. She started panicking. Then he drove up.

"Babe, I'm sorry I'm late. I had to stop by the bank then by Jeff's for some weed."

"You mean to tell me you did that mess before picking me up."

"I miscalculated my time, well actually I would've been here, but seems like every car on the road was driven by folks with nothing but time."

"I can't believe you left me out here for forty minutes. It's dark and everything."

"It ain't like this place is deserted. It's always people at the airport, guards and everything. You need to chill."

"I need my own car." Feather tossed sarcastically. "How much did you get out of the bank?"

"Forty!" Black was getting pissed.

"Did you keep the ATM receipt? I need it to balance the checking account."

Feather was under his skin and she knew it, but picking her up late behind a joint had gotten under hers.

"Here," he handed her the slip.

They rode the rest of the way in silence. Black stopped at AM-PM Minimart before going home.

"I need to get some papers." He grumbled as he got out the car.

Feather wanted ice cream, but her pride wouldn't let her have it. She wouldn't dare ask him to bring her anything.

Not getting the ice cream rekindled her fighting fire.

"I ain't cooking, stop at Wendy's." She was purposely trying to urk him. He was too nonchalant about being late.

Black didn't say anything; he just drove to Wendy's before going home.

At home Black ate in the living room.

Feather went to the bedroom with her food.

At 8:00 pm Black called Feather into the living room.

"Babe that movie you wanted to see is on. The one about that man killing all them black boys and hiding them under his house."

She sat down. Touched that he was watching. He didn't care for the "women" movies she watched. Then he leaned over and kissed her cheek.

"Babe, I'm sorry about being late, but Jeff was down to one bag of purple. I had to go. We cool?" He smiled.

Feather smiled back accepting the Hagen Daaz container that he was easing from behind his back.

"Yeah we're cool." She loved him.

They watched the movie together. Every three spoonfuls Black got to taste her Butter Pecan ice cream.

16

Black and Champ hadn't really been talking. Black was working hard. He and Feather hadn't been anywhere or visited anyone in months. After work they went to bed and went to work on making a baby.

Nikki hadn't been out since Johnny was born. Her life had taken a different turn. She was not greeting the future she was sinking in the present. There had been tension in her home since Champ slapped her.

Champ knew that he had hurt Nikki. In his heart he was sorry. He couldn't bring himself to say it so he stayed away. He was spending time with Tina and a few other strays in the local clubs.

♣♣♣

Black dialed Champ.

"Hey man, y'all wanna go to the movies tonight?"

My way back in… "Yeah. Hold on." Champ was glad to hear from Black.

"Babe?" He called out to Nikki. "You feel like going to the movies with Black and Feather?"

"Yes, but what we gon' do with Johnny?"

Shit I forgot about him. "Man we're cool. We got this baby."

"Drop him off at Big Mama's. She said you could bring him anytime. Call her."

"Alright. I'll call."

Champ hung up the phone and called Big Mama.

"Hi Pat, how you doing?"

"Fine."

"Can I talk to Big Mama."

"Yeah hold on."

"Hello?"

"Hey Big Mama. This is Champ. I was wondering if you could watch Johnny while me and Nikki catch a movie with Black and Feather?"

"Sure baby. You know I can. Where's Nikki?"

"In the room you wanna talk to her?"

"Yeah."

Champ went to get Nikki. He placed his hand over the phone and whispered to her that it was Big Mama and she was keeping the baby.

"Hello."

"Hi baby. I just wanted to tell you to pack the baby some PJ's and plenty of diapers, in case you need to leave him until tomorrow."

"Ok, thank you."

"You're welcome. That's what Grandma's are for." Big Mama was sincere. She had wanted to get to Nikki for a long time, to make sure she was all right. Big Mama knew her troubles; she had loved a "Champ" when she was in the business of loving a man. She wanted to spare Nikki some of her grief.

Nikki hung up feeling better. She loved these people. They were good people. They always made her feel loved. She smiled.

Champ was pleased to see her smile again. He pulled her into him.

"Is my son sleep?"

"Yes."

"Do you wanna play?"

"Not really."

She knew she still loved Champ by her reaction to his touch. It was her not trusting him that made her say no.

Champ was not at all offended by her rejection. He was just glad the silence was broken.

The phone rang.

It was Black. "Did y'all call Big Mama?"

"Yes, we did. Where's my sister?" Nikki teased.

"Right here hold on." Black handed the phone to Feather.

♣♣♣

Black stepped into the bathroom as Feather stepped into the shower.

"Babe I'm about to blow it up!" He teased, unbuttoning his pants.

"Black! Why you always do that? You act like you eat flowers and sip on perfume. Boy, you stank!!"

"So, That's Life."

Truth is he enjoyed the music of the water and the dance of her silhouette against the shower curtain.

Feather was hotter than the water that thumped against her body.

"Babe, Nikki tell you?"

"Tell me what?"

"'Bout having V.D."

"No!" Feather stopped washing and stuck her head out of the shower. She was genuinely shocked. Nikki had not told her, but Feather understood because if it were her, she wouldn't have told either. Not that.

"Yep, Champ said he got it from a dopefein. He said she didn't have no money so she offered and he accepted. I don't understand him, he got a good woman at home and he running up in a dopefein. He'll run up in anything that'll stand still and got a crack."

"Black you need to talk to him. That's trifling and Nikki is good to him."

"He knows that he just doesn't care. Sometimes he talk about getting it together and doing right by Nikki and Johnathan, but he don't ever do it."

"I don't know how she put up with him. Once she tried explaining to me about his mother being dead and nobody wanting him and stuff, but how many years he gon' cry over that?" Feather snatched the curtain back.

Black was standing there with her towel, for drying, in his hands.

"How you gon' shit and wipe your hands on my towel?"

He sucked his teeth. "Girl dry off." He tossed her the towel.

She jumped out of its way.

"It ain't dirty. I washed my hands then dried them on the towel."

"Just get me another one."

"You do the laundry. It's on you." Black shook his head. "Just hurry up. The movie starts in two hours and it takes you that long to do your hair."

"I'm going to be ready. You need to be calling Champ and Nikki, she's much slower than me."

Nikki made Feather retract her statement. They dropped Johnny off at Big Mama's and were sitting in the living room waiting on her.

They arrived at the theater fifteen minutes early.

"Feather come with me to the bathroom please."

"Ok." Feather eased her hand from Black's and walked away with Nikki. As they approached the bathroom Feather noticed a tear slide down Nikki's face.

"What's wrong Nikki?"

"That girl out there in the jeans and red sweater approached me once and told me she could have my man if she wanted him. Girl, I'm so tired of doing battle with Champ and his women. You know we got our number changed and someone's still calling our house and hanging up." Another tear fell. She walked over to the sink and looked in the mirror. "I am so tired of his mess!!! I don't know what to do."

"Well, why do you put up with it?"

Nikki paused for a long time. (It was because she longed for family stability, the security of knowing she belonged to someone but she hadn't figured that out yet.) "I could say for my baby, but it was messed up before he got here. I guess I was hoping it would get better, after he did. Champ's been staying out all night for a while now, never have no money on the bills, he ain't right, Feather." Nikki was crying again.

"I know he don't have to do the things he do. He could be such a good man if he'd keep his promises."

"Promises?"

"Promises. He always promises it's going to get better. He swears he ain't gon' stay out no more. He says he's working on his temper. He slapped me once. I was so hurt. I still ain't over that and it's been a few months now. We don't even sleep together 'cause he gave me somethin' and I can't bring myself to let him touch me no more." She accepted the tissue that Feather had gotten for her. "Feather I ain't crazy. I know Champ ain't right. I just love him. When he holds me I feel like everything is going to be alright."

Feather was tempted to tell Nikki what she needed to hear, but she knew by her last statement that she wasn't ready to hear it. So she offered her the next best thing—a way to deal.

"Nikki, get it together. Don't ever let another woman see you cry. Don't give her the satisfaction. I'd go out there and take my place on his arm and…" Feather stopped herself, realizing she'd fight that way for Black because he was worth fighting for, but she wouldn't advise anyone to fight to keep Champ. "Well, you know. I wouldn't bow down."

Feather wasn't worried, she knew Nikki would never do any of that anyway. It wasn't in her.

After Nikki reapplied her makeup, and the Visine they found in the bottom of Feather's, huge, purse began to work; they went back to the lobby.

There was the girl boldly talking to Champ.

Nikki walked right over to him, slipped her hand into his, kissed his cheek and spoke to her.

Immediately Champ's attention turned to Nikki as he pulled her into him. He leaned over and kissed her back.

"I take it you didn't like my friend." He whispered.

"I think she didn't like me." She whispered back.

They walked into the blackness of the theater just before the first scene.

Nikki was proud of herself. It felt good to stand up for herself.

They sat down on a row about four feet from the door.

Black sat down next to Feather with one arm around her shoulder.

"What did you say to Nikki, had her acting like you?"

"Nothing." Feather smiled. She was proud of Nikki too.

Black leaned back into his seat and eased his hand into Feather's pants. She casually tossed her jacket over her lap and spread her feet apart.

Champ eased his hands into Nikki's bra, but bumped into a breast pad. His penis deflated. He hated breast pads.

She had purposely worn it to hinder him from rolling her nipple between his thumb and forefinger throughout the whole movie. She wasn't ready for him to touch her, even if it meant wearing breast pads on milkless breast. Although she still loved him she couldn't get past the things in the past—late nights, infections and hitting.

17

The family thing was not as Nikki imagined. She was hurt by the reality of her situation. Champ's luck had been down for months now. Nikki was paying all the bills. Mrs. Harris was reasonable, but with no help expensive. Things were so tight she had changed her brand of soap saving one whole dollar and depriving herself of the simplest of luxuries.

♣♣♣

Johnathan was warm to the touch. He was crying and his bowels were loose. His butt was beet red. At 2:38 am she was wondering how her baby's father could sleep through his screaming.

"Nikk, take him out of here."

Nikki was disgusted. She didn't want to argue, she got up, picked up her baby and walked into the living room.

Johnathan's wail intensified as if her touching him was the cause of his discomfort. He cried for thirty minutes or more before she dialed the advice nurse. The nurse said he was probably teething. Give him some children's Tylenol for the fever, keep him dry, and rub some baby Orajel on his gums. While speaking to the nurse, Nikki stuck her finger in his mouth and massaged his gums. He stopped crying.

Nikki went into the bathroom to look for some of the stuff the nurse recommended. She rocked Johnny in her arm, kissed a tube of (adult) Orajel in her free hand and bit down on its top. She twisted it off with her teeth, dabbed a little bit on her finger and put it on his gums. For the first time in what felt like forever his little eyes pressed shut. There was sweat on his face from the fever. The plumpness of his little body lay limp in Nikki's arm.

She put the medicine back then glanced around the bathroom. Champ's towel was on the floor. He'd smeared dirt on the decoration towels and the top to the toothpaste was missing.

Nikki looked into the mirror and started to cry. Walking back into her room and seeing the log of his body in the bed made her turn around. She slept on the couch that night and Johnny slept on her.

18

Lillian's first date with Bo to miniature golf had gotten her two more. They were getting along so well Lillian invited him for dinner.

He was bringing the wine and a movie.

She was preparing crab, and steak with a tossed salad. The steaks were marinating. The salad was in the fridge. The water for the crab was boiling. The butter for her famous garlic-butter sauce was sitting on the table. She pulled out her china and linen napkins, for the table. She had candles and incense. Najee was on the CD player. Just before he arrived all she would have to do was buzz around setting things into motion.

Suddenly Lillian was nervous. She had been comfortable all the other times, but reality had finally hit her. She liked this man. She'd been wearing all her best clothing, answering the phone on the first ring and glowing ever since she'd met him.

Lil walked past her room and glanced at the slacks on her bed. She was trying not to overdress; she needed her clothing to say this is a real date, but relaxed. She decided against tying her hair up before getting in the tub. Her curls were already tight. The steam would loosen them up to a nice bouncy curl that she preferred.

What am I doing? It's more than me enjoying Bo's company, I like him. Especially how alive I feel when he's around. Don't get excited and I won't get hurt.

Lillian slipped on her slacks and her sweater blouse and thought back to her relationship five years ago. How she let her guard down too soon and ended up hurt.

Ding. Dong.

Lillian looked at the clock. It was 5:55 pm. Dinner wasn't until 7:00 pm. She knew it wasn't Bo. He wouldn't dare come that much earlier. She slid into her slippers and went to get the door.

It was Black.......and Bo. He was standing to the side of Black out of her direct view.

"Hi baby, come on in. I almost forgot you were coming. Y'all bring my vacuum back here by Friday." Lil teased, walking away from the door.

"Alright." Bo answered over Black's shoulder.

Lillian jerked around. She hadn't seen him at first glance.

"Hey Shuggahh!" He greeted.

"Hi." Lillian looked like a little kid with her hand caught in the cookie jar. She still had that headband on, the one she was using to keep her curls out of her face while she bathed. She still had on slippers, no make up and now Black knew! She hadn't even told Feather yet. She wasn't sure where things were going with her and Bo and wanted to keep it discrete until she was sure.

Black could tell by Lillian's expression that he had seen too much.

"Alright Ms. Lil, Unc, see y'all later. Have a nice evening." He leaned into Lil as if to kiss her cheek, but whispered in her ear first. "I'll let you tell Feather how your date went. I know how y'all like to share everything."

Lil accepted the kiss and nodded ok. She knew Black was trying to tell her, her secret was safe with him and she appreciated it.

"You know why I'm early." Bo started. "'Cause I'm tired of seeing you all dolled up. I wanted to see you incognito. I like this natural thing. It makes you look younger." He kissed her cheek too as she tried to pass him to finish getting dressed.

"Thank you."

"Ooohh girl, it smells good in here. What we eating on?"

"Crab, steak and salad." She continued down the hall.

"Where you going?"

"To finish getting dressed."

"Baby, you're finished. I wanna look at you like this, ok?"

Lil paused for a long time. "At least let me put on my shoes." She was trying to ease to the bedroom for some earrings or something. She felt incomplete.

"For what. I ain't got on mine. You're at home. Relax. Girl I'm going to show you how to wind down." He walked over to her (she noticed that he had stepped out of his shoes. Must've been while she was at the door with Black.) He took her by the hand and led her back into the living room.

"That's Najee huh? I love him. That brother can blow a horn."

Lil went into the kitchen to finish their dinner. Bo was on her heels. He was helping. Lil was impressed. He handled himself well in the kitchen.

It took a few minutes for her to totally relax. All during dinner Bo stared at her. Offering silent praises.

"What movies did you get?"

"Superfly. The Mack and Body Chemistry. Which one you wanna look at first."

"Superfly." Lillian was slightly embarrassed as she responded.

"Girl, you alright with me." Bo slipped the tape in and plopped down on the couch.

By the time the movie was over Bo had fallen asleep with his head in Lil's lap, which was all right with her. She was able to enjoy the bathtub scene without embarrassment. Now she admired his features, hoping he was for real.

Bo woke and went home without even a slight advancement. He'd made love to Lillian all evening, with his eyes, mind and gesture. His holding back was not out of non-interest. It was out of respect.

Lil was glad too because she wasn't ready to get too serious. Honestly she was afraid.

19

Nikki relented two weeks after the movie outing and allowed Champ to make love to her. It was hard, but not as bad as she thought it was going to be. Her love came down midway and she was able to participate. His touch was healing. She loved being with him. Loved being in his arms.

Didn't matter, because the very next day he stayed out all night, came home broke, laid on her until he was satisfied then went to sleep.

For the second time in her life the results were positive. Johnathan was thirteen months and the baby she was carrying was two months. Dr. Sanders had given her the news this morning. She called in sick and stayed home.

Nikki thought of her mother and the many relationships she had been in, staying just to prove she was as strong as the next woman. Now Nikki understood, could even relate to the reasons her mother had for doing some of the things she had done in her life. Loneliness was a powerful, powerful force. Nikki knew it was abuse of lovers that turned her mother to drugs. Nikki also knew that she was here in this place in her life because she wasn't going to be alone again.

♣♣♣

"Are you pregnant?"

"Yes."

"Damn!!" Champ looked at her like she was the failure that she felt like she was.

"You need to do something about that!!"

"I am. I'm having a baby."

"Well, I ain't. Nikki you need to get rid of it before it's too late."

"It's already too late. I'm pregnant. I ain't having no abortion."

"And I ain't having no parts...No parts of the waking up and feeding. And I ain't buying no diapers. Your ass is on your own!" He walked out.

What else is new? She thought looking at the back of the front door.

Nikki sat in that spot all day, staring at the reflection of the brass plant holder against the hardwood floor. For the first time, she noticed the tiny hole in Grandma's antique sofa. There were dishes all over the kitchen. She thought about the clothes he probably left on the floor or all over the bed. Then she visualized the condition that he left the bathroom in. She began to cry.

Life had been so unkind to her. She was behind on all her bills. Mrs. Harris was pressuring her about catching up her daycare bill or finding Johnny somewhere else to go. Even after mentioning that to Champ he had not offered her a dime. Nikki cried more.

The phone rang.

"Hey Nikk."

"Hi."

"What are you doing?"

"Nothing."

"Black and I will be by there later. Is my brother home?"

"No. I can page him and tell him y'all coming"

"Ok, page him. We'll probably go out to dinner, our treat."

"Ok."

"Nikki, are you ok?"

Nikki kicked right into her mechanical mode. "Girl, I'm fine."

"Oh...ok. You sounded a little down."

"Nope."

"Alright, see you in a little while."

Nikki hung up and got herself together. It was time to pick Johnathan up from daycare.

Champ walked in.

"Champ, Feather called and asked that you be here later, they are coming by and have something they want to celebrate I'm sure. She was real excited."

"Did you tell her you were pregnant?"

"No."

"Good."

Nikki looked at him with unmasked hatred. "She said that we'd probably all go to dinner, their treat."

"I have money. I'll pay for us."

Nikki couldn't believe her ears. 'I have money'. She looked away from him.

Champ looked at her strange. Then he understood. He reached into his pocket and handed her eighty dollars. "Here, give this to Mrs. Harris for the baby's care."

Nikki didn't take it. "You give it to her. It's time to pick him up."

Champ stuck his money in his pocket. "Come on." They rode to Mrs. Harris' in silence.

Nikki got out. Champ sat there.

"Champ, you need to come in too. Aren't you going to pay her?"

Champ didn't respond. He just got out and went with Nikki to the door.

Mrs. Harris asked if she could speak to them in the kitchen. Nikki's heart was beating. She thought something was wrong with her baby.

"Mr. and Mrs. Andrews…I don't really know how to say this, but I can't continue to keep Johnathan."

Champ reached in his pocket and handed her the eighty dollars.

"Thank you, but still I cannot keep him anymore. He has been in my care for a year and some months now and you have only paid on time once. I just can't do it anymore."

"I understand." Nikki offered.

"Where is my son?" Champ was pissed.

"He's probably in the living room, my assistant is preparing him for pick up."

Champ turned and walked into the living room and snatched Johnathan out of the assistant's arms.

Mrs. Harris and Nikki stood awkwardly in the kitchen.

"Baby I'm sorry. I just can't…."

"Mrs. Harris, I understand. It's ok, really." They embraced.

"Nikki bring yo' ass on. Fuck that lady."

Mrs. Harris let her go. "Go on baby. Go." She patted Nikki on the shoulder and her heart became tender. She had no idea what Nikki was going through, had she known, she would have hung in there with her. She knew Champ's kind.

"Thank you." Nikki walked out. She was thoroughly embarrassed. Then she thought about the baby. She thought about abortion.

20

Black bought Feather a Toyota Camry. It was used but it was nice. He'd talked the owner down from $5,000 to $4,500, but only had $3,000 saved. Big Mama gave Black the $1,500 he needed to close the deal. He promised to pay her back.

She told him if he didn't mention it he didn't have to. She had too many grandkids to give each of them $1,500. And she preached about not making a difference so, it was important that it remained between the two of them.

Feather drove to Lillian's. She used her key.

Lillian jumped as they entered, so did Uncle Bo. They were watching TV, but their positions indicated they were lovers, watching TV. Lillian's hair was tossed back. Her feet were tucked under Uncle Bo's butt. His shirt and shoes were off.

"I guess I need to start knocking again." Feather teased. "Y'all need to see my new car!!" She turned to lead them outside. They followed her out the door.

Black felt like a man. He loved to see Feather happy, especially when it was because of something he did.

Everyone liked the car. Back inside they stood in Lillian's kitchen. Black had his arm dangling around Feather's shoulder as she leaned into him innocently.

"Mama, we're getting married…if that's ok with you?"

"It's ok. Are y'all pregnant?" Lillian tried not to show her joy/shock of Black's reference of 'Mama'.

"No. In love." Feather proudly stated.

"Well, you have my blessing. Congratulations" Bo offered.

Lillian hugged Feather.

"Well, hell go 'round up everybody. I'm gon' 'round up some groceries and we can celebrate." Bo announced.

Lillian was standing at his side again. She loved him, but ignored the feeling. He loved her too. He was holding on to his until the moment was right to present it.

Feather and Black headed to Champ's and then Big Mama's.

Lillian was relieved that her and Bo's relationship was out in the open.

♣♣♣

Nikki wasn't jealous; she was simply more aware of her own situation. She couldn't help but notice that Feather and Black were progressing. They were in love and they worked together. It hurt her to accept that as long as she was with Champ she would get no further in life, and she knew that was the case. So, she concealed her pain and went for a ride with Feather in her new car.

Nikki wanted to tell Feather about her pregnancy, but she felt so stupid and irresponsible for letting it happen. She was doing so well taking the pill until Champ complained that she was gaining too much weight and looked nasty. So, she stopped. He wouldn't wear a condom. He couldn't wait on the diaphragm to be inserted. And now he didn't want to deal with the result.

♣♣♣

While they were at a stoplight a guy flirted with Nikki. She flirted back. She needed that. Needed to be appreciated even if it was for her beauty and only for a minute. She didn't mean anything by it, but every once in a while she toyed around with the idea of someone loving her the way she wanted to be loved.

"Nikki, me and Black are getting married. We're celebrating tonight. Will you be my maid of honor?"

Tears rolled from Nikki's eyes. "Of course." She was crying for two reasons. She was happy for her friend that had become her sister. And she was angry at her own fate.

"Thanks. Don't cry. You're gonna start me crying."

"I'm sorry." Nikki sniffed.

They smiled.

♣♣♣

Black told Pat and Big Mama. They were ecstatic. Especially Big Mama, she kept looking at Feather sideways, then her stomach. Feather kept shaking her head "no" and smiling.

Black read their body language, but didn't say anything.

Tee came home shortly afterwards. She was ecstatic too. She really liked Feather. A few times Feather had given her good sound advice on men. Feather was the reason she was dating this guy now. Carl wasn't that cute, but he was good to her. He was very good to her. He had had a rough childhood and was looking for some joy. She provided him that or so he said.

♣♣♣

While everyone celebrated the engagement, Big Mama noticed Nikki's tears even though they weren't on her face. So, she eased alongside her and told her to come help her in the kitchen. In the kitchen she sat her down.

"Baby, I want you to *help* me understand why you so unhappy."

"I'm not unhappy Big Mama."

"Chile please, you'd do betta tellin' me you don't wanna talk about it. I can see your tears. I got Grandmother's vision."

"I got a lot on my mind. I need help with my son, he was put out of day care."

"I can help with that. I'll watch him while you work, but I thought you were having problems with his Daddy. I can help with that too."

Nikki thought it was nice of Big Mama to be concerned. Watching Johnny was going to be more than enough. She wouldn't dare burden her with her problems with Champ. "We're fine."

"Ok. Baby, Mama's here. I try to be here for all my babies, that includes you." Big Mama leaned over and kissed Nikki's forehead.

"Thank you." Nikki was so touched she had to swallow her tears before asking..."Big Mama, how much do you charge for babysitting?"

"I know you can't pay me right now; I ain't worried about that. You owe me a smile, some love, and the truth when I ask for it."

They hugged.

"Now, we betta get back to the party."

Nikki re-entered the living room smiling.

Big Mama was glad the time had come for them to begin a relationship. She intended to help Nikki remove her (love) blinders.

♣♣♣

Dinner was good. Bo ordered Chinese Food. Everyone was in a good/loving mood.

Black felt Lillian's genuine acceptance.

Feather thought she was dreaming. She knew she was blessed. She missed her Daddy, but still life was good.

Nikki's faith was restored. She was going to be all right.

The women decided to start the wedding planning next weekend.

21

Nikki accepted that she couldn't be in Feather's wedding. Now all she had to do was tell Feather.

"Hey. I was just about to call you. The wedding has been postponed until April. Time crept up on us so fast; I ain't nowhere near ready. The only decision we've made is to get married."

"Ok." Nikki was relieved; her situation had gotten the best of her. She couldn't swallow anymore tears. Couldn't hold anymore either.

"Nikk. What's wrong??" Feather was filling with tears too as her heart went soft. "Feather I'm pregnant. I'm scared... I'm tired...I'm unhappy."

"Oh Nikki." Feather felt so sorry for her. "It's going to be ok."

"I wish I could say the same. Girl, Big Mama is keeping Johnny because I couldn't afford to pay Mrs. Harris and she said she couldn't keep him anymore. Champ ain't helping none with the bills. And when I told him I was pregnant all he said was that I was on my own. He ain't buying a pamper. He ain't getting up with the new baby and he ain't gon' be bothered, period."

Feather grew angry. "Nikki, you decided to keep this baby. You will make away for this child. It's going to be ok. I will help as much as I can. I commend you for having a baby under these circumstances. You will receive your blessing."

"I wonder...maybe I should have at least considered abortion, but I just couldn't do it. Sometimes when it's just

Johnny and me we play and have the best time…just the two of us. I can't take that away from this baby. I know my life isn't what I hoped it to be, but I can't take someone else's because mine is the pits."

"Nikki, you're going to be fine. Abortion is not for everyone. I don't believe it's for me either. I don't blame you for having your baby; for doing what's best for you. I'm here for you. Whatever I can do to help, it's done."

"Thank you Feather so much. Now if you don't mind I'd still like to be your Maid of Honor."

"Girl, of course."

"Don't worry I'll be back down to size by then. The baby's due in early March."

"I wasn't worried."

"Feather although I feel better since talking to you, I still feel like a fool. Life's gotta get better than this."

"Girl this is life. Having a baby isn't your problem. It's the baby's father. Now I love Champ too, but I love you more. You need to be happy too Nikk. You don't even dress anymore. I'm <u>not</u> sayin' this to hurt you; I'm trying to help you. As a sister I need to tell you, it's my duty…Now, you have decided to have this child; you owe him a good life. You owe him a loving smile, a warm hug and tenderness. Get yourself together and have your baby. Love and raise your kids even if you have to do it by yourself."

"Thanks Feather…I needed that. I knew I was slipping, neglecting myself. I just lost interest in everything. I feel like people are talking about me. I hear them at work saying lil' stuff. It's going to be so hard carrying this baby and holding my head up."

"But it'll be done. You wanna go shopping?"

"Ok." Nikki put some effort into feeling better.

"Ok. I'm on my way." Feather hung up.

They shopped all afternoon. They even ate dinner out. Big Mama was keeping Johnathan overnight so there was a degree of freedom present for Nikki.

♣♣♣

Champ had the audacity to tell Black that Nikki was pregnant and he wasn't doing anything for the baby.

"Man what you mean you ain't buying no diapers?! You climbed yo' ass up there. It's time to reap the benefit." Black was floored by this news.

"I told her to get rid of it as soon as I found out." Champ was getting frustrated. Black had never shown concern about his dealings in the past.

"Champ how you part yo' lips to say something like that to her? Tell a woman, to kill y'all baby."

"Why you care?"

"What?!!! Boy, you need to grow up. Ya runnin' outta time."

"Man fuck you." Champ was pissed.

"Naw. You're a lousy father. I wouldn't wanna run the risk." Black snapped, sarcastically.

"You actin' like it's yo' baby!!"

Black's lips quivered with anger. Impulse told him to light into Champ. Maturity told him to walk away. He could not believe Champ sank to that level. He finally understood everyone's dislike for him.

"Dude, I'll hollah." Black had to struggle to get that out.

"What*evah*— "

Both men walked away slightly grieving. They knew it would never be the same. Too much had been said.

When Champ got home Nikki wasn't even there; no food had been cooked. He was pissed. So pissed he cursed Tina out.

He even called over to Big Mama's and she told him that she didn't know where Nikki was, but that she was keeping Johnny overnight.

♣♣♣

Feather dropped Nikki off at 11:00 pm she ignored Champ's 'where you been?' and went to bed. She was sound asleep before he left.

22

On the days that Feather could help Nikki she did. She picked her up from work, picked Johnny up from Big Mama's to keep Nikki off the bus for two hours. She had gone by a couple of times to help Nikki with her hair. Nikki had really let herself go.

The pregnancy was hard. The baby's schedule was opposite Nikki's so, when she slept it kicked. When she was awake she was chasing Johnny. He required a lot of attention. He was into the outlets, in the cabinets, in the toilet just into everything.

Champ was into just as much, Grandma's sofa was looking bad, beer cans were everywhere, the smell of smoke was throughout the house, the bathroom smelled like urine; he even peed on the seat, sometimes.

Nikki stopped caring. She cleaned whatever she had the energy to clean. She washed clothes, when everyone was one stitch from naked. Nothing was being cooked. (Nikki was clearly pregnant but thin nonetheless.)

She'd hit the bottom. The day she realized it she was standing over the face bowl rinsing a pair of panties for the next day and wondering what to pull out of the hamper to put on. The decorative towels no longer existed. She, herself, had used one the other day to bathe Johnny.

She had resolved to staying inside the apartment. Big Mama had been holding her every chance she got with those *'I'm here'* eyes that Nikki continued to ignore. She was so withdrawn that she missed Feather's famous birthday BBQ.

If suicide wouldn't damn her to hell she'd check out, but at this point, after all this, she was going to heaven.

♣♣♣

Wednesday Champ left to make some money. Nikki had thoroughly cleaned the house in his absence. She stood back when she was done and felt good about her accomplishment. Things were looking better just because she cleaned her house.

Saturday afternoon he came home while Nikki was at work took a shower, left his clothes on the floor, a dirty tub, and all his toiletries strewn across the countertop and his plate on the coffee table. After a hard day's work, a long bus ride and carrying Johnny for a block that is what she came home to.

"Hi."

"Hi." Champ returned without looking in her direction.

Nikki cringed. The baby kicked. "Come on Johnny. Let's eat." She walked into the kitchen and looked in the refrigerator. Yesterday Big Mama sent some baked chicken, rice and broccoli home with her. She was going to eat it today, but it was gone. She looked at the table. Champ had devoured the entire plate.

She went to the cabinet and grabbed a can of soup. There was no bread.

"Champ can you go to the store and get some bread. I'm making sandwiches for dinner."

"Naw. I ain't got no money. You?"

"No. That's ok."

Nikki knew he was lying. Her intuition told her so. He was too relaxed to be broke. If he were honestly broke he wouldn't be there. She learned that he came there to count his money and get a home-cooked meal. Once, she accused him of using her and he told her he didn't help her because he wasn't there enough to even be a problem. Every since that day, whenever he touched her, she moved.

Champ grew uncomfortable as he watched her make breakfast for dinner. Before she could finish cooking Johnathan stretched out on the living room, hardwood floor and fell asleep.

Champ watched him and the TV.

"Champ can you please lay my baby down. That floor is hard."

He picked up Johnny without argument.

"Thank you."

When the food was done Nikki put it away for tomorrow she wasn't hungry.

"Nikki, can we talk?"

"What?"

"What happened to us?"

"Why are you asking me that? You're the one that changed."

"I never changed. You kept getting pregnant."

"Champ I can't get pregnant by myself. You demanded that I stop taking the pill. You would never wait for me to insert the diaphragm, you would never do anything to help me."

"If you would have exercised some, you could have stayed on the pill."

"Champ I'm not even going to respond to that."

"Well, what do we do now?"

"We start talking more. You stop staying out all night. You stop treating my baby like he only has one parent. You stop destroying my house."

"Did you notice that you said '*my* baby', '*my* house'?"

Nikki had not noticed, now she did. "Champ I feel that way because I pay all the bills. I do all the parenting. I do all the cleaning. If you want recognition, help me."

"All right Nikki, I'll do better."

That night they showered together, and for the first time ever slept as a family. Champ on his side, Johnny in the middle and Nikki on her side, hopeful.

♣♣♣

Things were good for a week. Champ gave Nikki a little money; she stocked the cabinets and gave Big Mama sixty dollars for watching Johnny. The new baby was due anyday. Big Mama agreed to watch the new baby too. Nikki was eternally grateful for having her in her life.

They had gone to Big Mama's for the annual Superbowl party.

Lillian and Bo came together, but were still "just friends", literally.

Bo was loosing his mind with desire. So was Lillian, but she was investing in respect.

Black was reserved in his dealing with Champ.

The wedding plans were complete.

Johnny was walking well.

He made Feather's day by calling her name.

After the game everyone went their separate way. No sooner did Champ leave and Johnny lay down, for the night, did Nikki go into full labor.

"Hello?"

"Black? —"

"Ok. We're on our way."

Nikki got her bag and put it by the door. She could feel the pressure. The baby was coming or so it felt like it.

Black walked in, picked her up; carried her to the car. Feather had her huge purse on one shoulder and Johnny draped over the other. They slid into the back seat, closing the door as Black pulled away from the curb.

Feather went in with Nikki.

Black took Johnny and paged Champ, five times before he got there. He answered the first page, but didn't show up. So, Black kept paging him.

Finally he showed up, drunk. He was so drunk he fell into Black whining.

"Man, I can't do this baby stuff. My Mama died like this. I can't do it. I wasn't gon' come, but I had to keep things straight with you. I was wrong man, I know you ain't fucking Nikki."

"Champ don't even trip off of that. That's over. You need to get in there to see your son."

Feather walked out. She took one look at Champ and wanted to puke. He stumbled by her into Nikki's room. She was drifting off to sleep. She smelled alcohol before he opened his mouth.

"Babee, I can't do it. I can't watch you die. I can't." He dropped his head heavily into her shoulder, partially to stop the spinning, partially for sympathy.

Nikki heard him. Understood him, but didn't answer him. Joshua was 5lbs. 8ozs. and he was to blame. She couldn't accept that. While he whined she went to sleep.

23

Everything was set. Everyone that was going to Reno was loading up. Loyalty and habit kept Champ in the position of Bestman. "D" was a groomsmen and Tee a bridesmaid. Nikki was maid of honor. She had miraculously returned to even less than her normal weight.

Nikki used her income tax refund to sponsor her family's part of the trip. She went in on a Minivan with Feather and Black.

The ride down was a good time. The babies were sleeping. The girls sat in the back talking amongst themselves. Nikki told Feather about Joshua crying, saying that he was the most unhappy baby she had ever known. He cried all day and all night. Whether he was lying down, being held, sitting up, being rocked, he just cried unless he was with Big Mama. Like Nikki, Johnny and everyone else he loved him some Big Mama.

Big Mama told her that there was nothing wrong with that baby except he was feeling her pain and if she wanted him to stop crying she had to stop first. Big Mama told her that when Joshua was with her, he was the perfect baby.

Nikki agreed with Big Mama, she felt that he cried because when she was carrying him that's all she did, on the inside anyway.

Feather shared her disappointment of going from a Reno wedding, to a church wedding, back to a Reno wedding. As they talked the men listened to rap tapes so loud, that they could hardly hear each other.

"Black can you play something we can listen too?"

"Oh Babe, I didn't know you didn't like rap. I see yo' head back there bobbin.'"

Feather laughed. "Ok. Play something else. I'm tired of rap."

"You ready to cry too, huh Nikk?" Champ tossed in the back.

They laughed. Nikki was a sucker for R&B and everyone knew it.

♣♣♣

They arrived in Reno on schedule, checked into their rooms and parted ways.

Lillian and Bo rode down together, but registered in separate rooms. Lillian was still investing in respect; yet she bought a negligee, just in case temptation befriended her.

The wedding was the next day. So, aside from dinner, everyone was on his or her own for the evening there was six hours until dinner.

Big Mama was taking the kids to the one casino that honored their little needs. Everyone else was gambling.

♣♣♣

During dinner Bo leaned over and whispered in Lillian's ear.

"You know it really doesn't make any sense for us to keep avoiding the matter of sleeping together. I would love to feel you rub against me during the night." Bo was on his second drink.

Lillian turned to him and smiled. She was turned on, but didn't let on. Talking dirty to her in a public place was her weakness.

A few minutes later he leaned over again. "Lillian...I need to love you…please?"

Without disengaging from the conversation she was having with Pat, Lillian nodded "yes" to his question.

Bo sat down his third drink. He was not taking another sip, if Lillian was going to allow him to make love to her, he was going to do just that.

Bo never expected any of the things he received from *Ms* Lillian.

She wore the most gorgeous negligee. It was lace, embroidered with iridescent beads weaved throughout the bust and waist areas, coming to a point at the navel and lower back. The beads sparkled a crystal blue, with soft hints of lavender and of green, just a hint of yellow. Lillian's beauty coupled with this exquisite negligee was absolutely captivating…mind blowing. She attempted to pin her hair up, but instead it fell in all the right places; looking like the perfect wind had swept it into place.

Bo felt privileged to be within her presence.

As he lay in the king-sized bed she walked over to him, her heart racing with wonder of whether or not she should leave her security zone, and attempt to love this man.

Bo was so fine, he was almost unreal. He had the eyelashes of a woman; the complexion of well polished oak wood. His body was firm, yet surprisingly soft.

Lillian was afraid to touch him. She had leaned on him before, embraced him before, touched him before, but this time she would be touching his heart with hers.

He got out of bed to receive her.

She thought she noticed a sparkle in his eyes as she allowed her glance to fall upon him. He was blessed that way and she thanked the Lord for it. Until now, she had not concerned herself with this part of him. Laying that to rest she stepped into his open arms. She felt his readiness against her.

"You are so beautiful…Damn. You are beautiful."

"Thank you. You're something, yourself."

He smiled as she slid into bed with him, her bare leg brushed gently against his. To Bo Lillian felt like mink against his skin. He kissed her softly, once, twice, three…four times. He responded to her need to taste him. He entered her mouth with uninhibited passion. Passion burst from the both of them.

Lillian's beautiful gown was removed. Who removed it was a mystery.

Bo entered Lillian as graceful as a lover would a virgin. He was careful not to crush her delicate frame. She was a tiny woman under his huge torso and he was mindful of that.

She pulled him into her until he understood that he had been gentle long enough. "Baby, I appreciate the thought, but I'm not a schoolgirl and this isn't my first time."

"Ok. Baby…I just want you to enjoy me."

"Oh I am, but first you must give me of you."

He exploded at that moment.

Lillian smiled. She loved knowing that she took part in his experience of pleasure. She pushed back, tightened up and squeezed him inside of her; not wanting it to end. It didn't. He laid there with a good portion of his weight, not enough to bring about any discomfort, and he smiled from the inside out.

Lillian smiled too. It had been far too long since she felt this way.

"Your turn." Bo smiled. And began again.

Lillian was not prepared for her gift of love. She was better at giving than receiving. She shook her head "no" but it didn't stop anything. Bo massaged her body and soul with his own until Lillian cried tears of pleasure. He even stopped twice to prevent himself from sharing too much of her joy.

They lay exhausted for a short period of time. The physical lovemaking was off and on all night. Each time shorter than the last, but the true lovemaking began an infinite journey.

This time Bo was not going to play the "game" of love—the kind where he loves her reactions more than her actions.

Bo was the man Lillian had craved her whole life. He was whom she wanted during her marriage to Michael, in high school during her courtships, in her friends during her trials with dating. He made her stomach do somersaults, her pulse race; even her thoughts leave her. She melted at the sound of his voice.

He was whom she wanted to love, but now she was too afraid.

♣♣♣

There is no sight more beautiful than that of black people dressed in formal attire. The variety in the shades of their complexions seems to compliment any color. If they happen to accessorize with the glow of nostalgia and love it's an even more divine sight, so it was the morning of the wedding.

Feather stayed with Big Mama this night. Big Mama massaged her back, face, feet and even her hands. Touched up her nails and comforted her in ways only a mother could. She explained the myth of something old, something new, something borrowed, something blue. Then she offered her something old.

"Feather, Mama's gon' give ya something old tonight. The same thang my grandmother gave me on my wedding night. You ready?"

"Yes." Feather held out her hand.

"No matter what you do. Keep as much of yours and Black's business as you can hold to yo'self. I know sometime it gets rough and you need to talk, but talk to him. Keep yo' man satisfied yo' way. Don't worry ' bout what others are doing with their mates, you tend to yours. Don't ever make him feel less than a man. Men need to come to realizations on their own. Tellin' him what to do all the time is damaging to marriage. Take care of yourself…remind him always, of how you looked on this night. Remain thoughtful of his needs. Demand nonsexual romance from time to time. And, support him, sometimes even when he's wrong."

Feather smiled, she had just been given the "old" formula for a healthy marriage.

"Thank you, Big Mama."

"You're welcome sweetheart. Now I'm gon' give you something blue."

"Can I hold it?"

"Yes," Big Mama smiled. She handed Feather a box in the shape of a book.

Feather opened it. It was a Bible. Navy blue.

On the inside of the first page was the exact formula that Big Mama had just quoted her.

Feather was so touched.

"Yo' Mama and Mama-in-law have the sumthin' borrowed and sumthin new. They'll give it to ya' in the morning. Now let's get some sleep. You gotta big day ahead of you."

Feather lay awake half the night loving Black, Big Mama and her life in general. She counted her blessings, even the time she had with her Dad; some people didn't have that.

♣♣♣

For the longest time everyone had given Nicole praises for her beauty. She was a gorgeous woman, but not today. No one was prepared for the wealth of beauty that Feather graced them with at 2:45 pm. She walked down the aisle on the arm of her mother's play brother. She thought about her Dad with every step. Once she glanced upward so he could get a better view of her face if he were watching.

Black gasped with disbelief as she neared him. His stare at her during the exchange of vows lacked discretion, embarrassment or anything of a shy connotation. Some guests were embarrassed to watch his profession of love it was such a naked and private expression.

Feather was a smiling sunrise, a waterfall, a brook, a starlit sky... She was the essence of natural beauty.

Black was more than proud to know that he would lay next to her night after night for the rest of his life. He recited his vows with such passion that it caused Feather to stumble through hers.

"You may kiss the bride."

Black removed Feather's veil and offered her his cheek. She kissed it and everyone laughed aloud. Then he kissed her. Really kissed.

Dinner was immediately after the ceremony. Then everyone gathered in Feather and Black's suite. It was quite a celebration. Music, room service; it was a good time. People were in and out all night. At 1:00 am Feather was exhausted. She had been in her wedding gown the whole evening. Uncle Bo coerced everyone to clear the room, so the newlyweds could be newlyweds.

♣♣♣

Feather was exhausted. Black was exhausted. Neither wanted to go against the tradition of a sexfilled honeymoon, but both were too tired to honor it.

"Babe, don't take this the wrong way, but I'm tired." Black confessed.

"Me too." Feather slipped out of her wedding gown. She stood before Black in the daintiest underwear he had seen. "I was just thinking about the 'wifely' duties I've acquired and wondering where I was going to get the energy to make you a happy husband."

"Babe don't trip. This ain't a traditional marriage. We are gonna roll with the punches life throws us. I ain't even concerned with what everybody else is doing. You know Big Mama had a little talk with me before we left home. She told me to take care of my wife, and I plan to. It was the way she put it though. She said 'worry 'bout yo' own lil' red wagon. Yo' friends got theirs and don't you worry whether they push it or pull it. Jes' take care of yo' own. Hear?"

Black assumed Big Mama's posture as he quoted her, pushing his chest out in an exaggerated manner to illustrate her full bosom and leaning his head to the left as she did when speaking to him. He looked and sounded just like her.

Feather laughed. "Boy you crazy." Then she thought about her conversation with Big Mama last night. It was similar. Black had been given the formula too. She loved Big Mama. That loving brought forth a smile.

Black climbed into bed nude, so did Feather. Their bodies touched and she lay in his embrace. Neither became aroused. Their intimate life was such that it was never forced. And to do anything now would be forcing it. Black yawned.

"Don't do that." Feather demanded through a yawn also.

"I'm sorry…"

Feather wanted to talk. This was her favorite part of being in bed. "Babe, when did you realize that the moon was following you, whenever you were riding in a car at night?"

He laughed. "Man, I was little…I guess about eight years old. It tripped me out. I asked my mother why was it following us, and she said to make sure we got home safely."

"That must've been what their parents told them. My Daddy said Mama sent it so we could find our way, even if the lights went out."

He laughed again. "You know the funniest thing is you believe all that mess. Then you turn around and tell it to yo' kids." He paused. "I realized the clouds were moving on my own. I was mad about something and called myself pouting, so I fixed it on a cloud and it moved. I kept staring and it kept moving. Then I looked at another one and it was moving too. I thought I was the only one that knew they were moving, so I waited months before I told Big Mama. I remember her smile when I told her I had a secret. Then she said you think that's something wait until you realize you're alive. It took me along time to figure that one out and sometimes I'm not sure."

"She's right. I realized it when Daddy died. I knew I had to do that, so I must be alive."

The night grew quiet. Black held her while she slept. Shortly afterwards he fell asleep with his heart full of her. Just before sunrise he stroked her thigh lovingly and she opened her legs to receive him.

24

It must have been something in the air. Bo and Lillian had not left one another's side since the trip to Reno. Either she was at his house or her was at hers. She was losing weight—he was picking it up. People were starting to expect to see them together.

They lay on his living room, floor, drinking wine and listening to music. Lillian was in heaven. For years she had resigned to not having a relationship. She just didn't want to be bothered with the chore of love—the late nights, the mysterious hang-ups, the lying to cover up. Now here she was lying on the floor with a man whose mere voice had an unexplainable power over her.

Lillian was falling for Bo, but only in her heart. Her mind remembered the pains of love even if her heart was forgetting. Her mind wouldn't let her hurt like that anymore. It was made up. It would never do battle with rejection, with disappointment nor expectations.

Bo's heart was home. He was prepared to love this woman the way a man is supposed to love a woman. Not the doggish style he'd used in the past. Half the women in Oakland had cried behind him, some probably still. Love had been a sport for him. He was in it for the challenge; The challenge of women defending their hearts. He got the victory…they got the pain. Reflecting back, on that part of his life, he had some regrets. Some of the women he had mistreated were as dear as Lillian. They were kind, generous, good loving and passionate women.

They just wanted to be loved. Bo just wanted to see if he could possess them, once he did that the thrill was gone and so was he. Relationships had always been a game to him. Watching Lillian protect herself against him made him realize for the first time what he had done to other women… He was remorseful.

Now he was ready to try the love thing, the tell me your secrets, spot me while I fall back and that I'll catch you kind of love. He was ready to be honest at all cost. Bo was finally a one-woman man.

They lay on the floor for hours listening to music and talking. They liked the same kind of music.

They were in love.

Bo didn't tell because he knew she wasn't ready.

Lillian didn't tell because she didn't know how to.

25

Black was on the 11 pm 'til 7:30 am schedule. He wasn't tired right now, but about time to go to work, he knew sleep was going to get to him so he laid down anyway.

Feather called in sick and laid down too. She fondled him even though she didn't really want to make love. Not getting the response she was looking for she raised up his shirt and drew his nipple into her mouth.

Black was turned on. They made love and fell asleep.

He woke at 8:45 pm. He reached over, grabbed the phone, told his job a lie then woke Feather with his entrance.

It had been this way since the wedding.

Time rolled on fast after the wedding.

Things were getting back to normal. Hard times were creeping up. They received an increase in rent. Car insurance was up and Black's car was down, back to sharing, but still there was joy in their marriage.

♣♣♣

Depression was eating Nikki. She was 12lbs. underweight and it showed.

She was embarrassed and in pain all the time. And Joshua was still crying, all the time. She was tired. Sometimes she figured her body was shutting itself down so that she wouldn't have to look at Champ, should he decide to come home.

Nikki picked up the phone to call Feather. She had been meaning to for weeks but couldn't bring herself to steal any of her joy—hers was such a sad situation. She was considerate of the fact that she was honeymooning.

But oh how she had needed to talk to someone sometimes.

Before dialing Feather she called the Phone Company.

"Hello? Yes, I'd like to make arrangements on my bill... Fifty dollars next Friday and the balance on the fifteenth. Thank you."

She hung up. The phone rang immediately. "Hello?"

It was Feather. They talked briefly about nothing, just catching up.

Joshua was pulling up and Johnathan was repeating everything.

Feather was stressing so much over a baby for two straight months her period was late, but it always showed up as her hopes rose.

♣♣♣

Nikki learned that staying out of Champ's way, not depending on his income and keeping the babies quiet was one way to get some peace. He'd started staying out again about a week after they returned from Reno. The good/bad thing was that one night while he was out he totaled the car. The bad thing is it kept him home more.

Nikki picked up her paycheck and she was broke. She paid the rent, bought a bus pass, and gave Big Mama $85.00 for watching the boys. She had not paid her anything in two months. The money she had left was just enough to buy a roll of quarters to wash clothes.

When she arrived home Champ was there. He was sitting on the couch watching TV, sucking down a milkshake. Big Mama had fed the boys and as usual Nikki wasn't hungry.

"Hi."

"Hey."

She sat Joshua down on the floor. Johnathan ran over to play with him. He liked being a big brother. Joshua was as handsome as Johnathan. He too shared the beauty of his mother only.

Before she sat down Champ asked. "Did you pay the rent? The landlord left a message saying she couldn't wait any longer. She need the money by tomorrow."

"Yes."

Champ was relieved. He'd saved $1200 to get another car and didn't want to have to give it up on the rent.

"What about the phone bill?"

"You said you were going to pay it. I didn't have enough remember?"

Champ remembered, but hadn't realized it was this close to time to pay. He was going to get the car tomorrow he needed Nikki to pay that for him. He'd be ready next month. "What did you do with your check?" He thought, for sure, she made enough money to pay a $60 phone bill and the rent at the same time.

"I paid the rent, bought some quarters to wash, some diapers and a little food." She was yelling. She didn't tell him about giving Big Mama anything because she had already slipped and told him she wasn't charging her. "Oh and I bought my bus pass for work." She yelled sarcastically.

Champ had never seen this side of her. She was livid.

He got mad. "Then you need to make arrangements on the phone bill. I'm broke." Champ was trying to see if she'd miraculously come up with some money. The bill wasn't, but $56.83.

"I can't call them. Those were the arrangements!" Nikki didn't mean to yell, but she was frustrated.

"Then they'll just turn the Mothafucka off." Champ yelled back. "Matter-of-fact they can have all this shit. I'm out. Fuck this damn struggle."

Nikki thought he was abandoning them. Soon as he walked towards the room it registered that way in her mind. She followed him.

"Babe, I'll call the phone company, don't leave us." Fear of being alone was creeping up her back, up her front, slapping her all upside the head. She started crying. "Champ we can work it out."

The boys were in the doorway. Joshua had crawled there behind Johnathan. Johnathan was starting to cry. He wasn't crying for Champ to stay. He was crying because his mother was crying.

Champ ended up staying. Nikki didn't wash clothes as she'd planned. She catered to him all night. She was off the next day, so she decided to skip her chores and love her man.

She bathed everyone that night including Champ. She gave the boys a drop of cold medicine to put and keep them asleep.

During the night she made love to Champ like her life depended on it. She spent the entire evening on top. And when he suggested she "go down" she went.

At about four something she got up to use the bathroom. She knocked his pants onto the floor. Out of his pocket fell a wad of money (The money for the car.) Nikki felt like someone had poured a bucket of refuse on her. That was it Champ was a dog and she wasn't ever fucking him again. This time she meant it. It didn't matter, though, she had conceived again on this last time.

♣♣♣

The next morning Nikki washed clothes. During the sorting she checked the pockets and in Champ's jean pocket she found a fifty-dollar bill. She pushed it into her bra without missing a beat.

26

Big Mama crocheted on a blanket every evening, while waiting on Nikki to pick up the boys. She thought that might make it a little easier for Nikki to tell her.

Nikki's weakness was starting to strain Big Mama. She wanted her to get it together, to understand that Champ was running her in the ground. She wanted her to see that she was letting herself go. Nikki's hair had been in a ponytail all year long. Her nails were all different lengths, she was frail, dark circles had formed under her eyes. She was in a bad way. Big Mama was getting angry because she wasn't even fighting anymore. She was just letting Champ wipe his feet on her.

Nikki walked in the door. Her clothes were hanging off of her. Her ponytail was ragged. Big Mama could tell she hadn't brushed it this morning. That was all she could take.

"Nicole, when are you going to tell me?"

"Tell you what Big Mama?"

"'Bout the new baby you carryin'?" Big Mama put the crochet down, walked over to her and laid her palm on her stomach. It was already hardening.

Nikki grew paler. She had let pregnancy cross her mind twice. She knew her period was late, she blamed the inconsistency on stress. Nicole had drawn on her own Grandma's wisdom. Surely He knew she couldn't have another baby. She had prayed a sincere yet, bargaining prayer. She had even fasted and prayed for two days not eating or drinking anything. She had been a good girl; she repented and confessed all of her sins.

"I've known for 'bout three weeks." Big Mama took Nikki's index finger and placed it on the soft spot of her neck, just below her Adams apple. Thu-dunt, Thu-dunt, thu-dunt.

Nikki felt the rhythm of her pulse there.

"That's your baby's heartbeat. That's how I got caught too, so don't feel bad."

Nikki fell into Big Mama. That was the final blow. Fasting made her weak, the baby made her tired and the truth knocked her down.

Big Mama held her for along time.

Pat came in and left them there. She took the boys in her room and turned on cartoons. Joshua looked sleepy, so she rocked him, then laid him down.

"Hush baby. It's ok. I ain't putting you down and I ain't mad at you. I'm making that blanket for this baby. I'm keepin' 'dis one too, but I ain't keepin' nan 'nother one. It just don't make no sense, y'all having babies like y'all doing. Ain't that much love betweenst y'all."

Nikki was vibrating with sobs. (Her need for change was revealing itself.) She was scared to go forward, but knew she couldn't go back or stay there, not at this point in her life. This was a sinkhole.

Big Mama sat her down, and got her a cold towel. It was going to be awhile before she let her go home. Nikki was not leaving until she understood love—and that she was not in its realms.

"Baby you need to get yourself together. You're letting Champ bury you alive. How y'all say it, he ain't *'all that'* that you gotta be hurting like this for him. The first time I met you, I wanted to tell you this…but I know that life has to run its course and I can't interfere with that. Nikki let me tell you something…Champ is not the man for you. Yes, I know you're afraid to be alone. Yes, I know you need love, baby if you can take what Champ's puttin' down, you ain't gon' have a problem sleeping alone for a while. It won't be forever. You're young, beautiful and loving. That's just what men are looking for." Big Mama was holding Nikki close to her; speaking mainly into the top of her head. Nikki was still crying. "Champ is not a man. He's a boy with heavy burdens and a lost soul. I used to be in a relationship with a man like that. I was battered for six years. I kept trying to tell myself if I loved him hard enough and long enough he would be ok. I felt like nobody had ever loved him, so that's why he was the way he was. The truth is he wasn't worthy of love that's why nobody loved him. See, I wasn't the first one to try. Sometimes we buy into that strong Black woman mess. Well, strength is in your head. You betta wise up and save your life. Understand your worth and beauty. You're beautiful enough to just be looked at. Any man in his right mind would want to love you. Nicole you know what you gotta do. Find your courage baby…it's there."

Nikki was warming from the cold fear she had been living with. She understood Big Mama. She was right. Nicole knew it was time to leave Champ. Empowerment rose up in her.

Big Mama could see the light of understanding go on in Nikki's head. She knew this was the beginning of a long journey for Nikki.

"Baby, here's what I want you to do. You have a Bible?"

Nikki nodded yes.

"Read the twenty-third Psalms every night before you go to bed. Ask the Lord to stay with you every morning when you get up. Start eating right, comb your hair and get your clothes together. If you gon' brang this baby into the world you owe him a chance." Big Mama kissed Nikki's forehead.

Joshua started crying in the other room; Big Mama went to get him as Nikki sat on the couch in deep thought. She was going to get herself together. She was going to do it.

She stayed over to Big Mama's that night until 9:30 pm. Big Mama made her eat and brush her ponytail before Pat dropped her and her babies off at home.

Champ wasn't home and didn't come home that night.

27

"Nikk, why you got him in the bed?" Champ was about to sit on Joshua.

"Ssh. Don't wake him up." Nikki whispered. "'Cause he's a baby and I want him here. Ain't nobody else ever on that side of the bed."

Nikki had been acting strange for months now. She was tripping with him last month at Black and Feather's for no reason. Now she was getting smart for no reason. Champ ignored her.

"Champ, I saw your friend pick you up. Please don't have your women come to my house."

"I checked her about that, but look don't think 'cause you everybody's Mama you can tell me what to do! I ain't one of yo' kids."

"Oh, I know you don't have a Mama." (Nikki was trying to hurt him with her statement. She'd been stabbing at him every chance she got.) "All I'm saying is don't have your women come here, remember you moved in with me."

"You're right and I can move my ass out!!" Nikki had reached his limit for her.

Pregnant with her third child, going into her final trimester and miserable, she wanted to piss him off. She wanted to hurt him back. "So, you 'd just leave me and your kids here. You don't love us!!"

The baby kicked. Joshua began to cry; Nikki picked him up. Johnny came from his room and stood in the doorway tears already in his eyes. He was learning to cry for himself as well as for his mother. He had learned about being tired. And he was tired of his parents.

"You the one don't care nothing about me. You don't give a shit about what I'm going through. My Mama died giving birth to me how do you think that make me feel!! I ain't got nobody!" He walked closer to the bed… "And every time I turn around you pregnant."

Johnathan walked his little self all the way into the room. He was going on three years old, and prepared to kick his Daddy's butt.

"Shut yo' damn mouth!!" Champ yelled at Joshua.

Nikki felt a throbbing sensation in the pit of her stomach. Her fetus flinched. Her nose flared. "Don't talk to my baby like that. You're the reason he's crying. You're the reason we all crying!!"

"What?! Y'all just sorry. They just like you. Gonna be some lil' fags crying over everythang. You crying 'bout a girl coming to pick me up, you ain't givin' it up. You ain't slept with me since you been pregnant. Ain't nobody waiting no seven months on you. You might not be fucking, but that ain't stopping me."

Nikki thought back to the night she gave him sincere pleasure, and that money fell out of his pockets, she had vowed to never lay with him again and she meant it. If a woman picked him up everyday, she would help him get ready if it meant she didn't have to lay with him. She didn't respond.

He continued. "And if I wanted it I would take it. You better be glad I don't want you."

At this point tears steadily flowed from her eyes. It wasn't the things he was saying it was the way he was talking. It was the realization that he was just there for a place to stay. His presence had nothing to do with her or their children.

In her heart Nikki was letting go of Champ. She wasn't as empowered as she had been at Big Mama's, just more aware of her situation.

Johnathan eased his way over to the bed and beside Nikki. She had placed Joshua on her other side because of her protruding stomach.

Champ stood, silent, in front of them. The entire picture turned his stomach—Nikki, a baby in her and one on each side. He walked out of the room. A minute later the front door closed.

Nikki sat there with her boys for nearly an hour. She was confused. She wanted Champ to leave. She wanted him to stay. She wanted to start over. She wanted him to love her. She wanted what she had always dreamed of. Nikki was at her lowest point.

After feeding the boys, she bathed them, put them in bed and read them a story. They lay in her bed until they fell asleep, then she took them to their room. She felt like an organized, struggling, yet contented mother.

She needed and appreciated this break. Champ would eventually be back.

Nikki cried for all the bad and wrong and painful occurrences in her life. She cried because she feared that she would never find love.

There was no logic in allowing Champ to sleep with other women and there was no way she would allow him to sleep with her again. She cried because she knew getting Champ out of her life was going to be harder than getting him out of her heart.

Lying in her bed, all cried out she dialed Big Mama, but hung up before she could answer. Then she dialed Feather and hung up as Black answered. Nikki slid out of bed onto her knees and she prayed a prayer for serenity, love, strength and deliverance that she didn't even know she was capable of.

That night sleep came easy.

The next morning there was a peace with her that had never been with her before. She had an understanding of life that she had never known. Champ was not going to hurt her anymore because she wasn't going to let him. Again Nicole was empowered with a strength that helped her believe she would be all right.

28

Lillian realized she was in love when Bo went out of town on business. She had become sick, literally unable to function. It wasn't that she couldn't do anything; she didn't want to do anything. She knew it was love, but she wouldn't acknowledge it. Lillian didn't know what to do with love...except run from it. In her opinion love was another name for pain. Bearing pain was not one of her strong features.

"Hey Babe."

When she heard his voice she felt alive again.

Bo continued. "Hell, I should've brought you with me. I didn't know I was going to miss you like this."

"I miss you too."

"When I get back we gotta talk. I wanna have you girl. I want to wake up with you, go to bed with you."

"Are you suggesting that we move in together?...'Cause I'm too old for shacking."

"Naw. I'm suggesting that you find a lot somewhere and we build a little nest for us to grow old in. One of my buddies is an architect, he'll draw up the plans...that's no problem."

On this business trip, Bo had reunited with a few old friends that were still happily married or just plain married, but they weren't alone. He realized that he didn't want to be either.

"You must be marrying me Mr. Loverman." Lillian teased.

"Whatever it takes." Bo chuckled, assuming they were on the same accord. "I'm gonna have to talk to you later Babe. We're about to get ready to head back to this meeting. It's almost over. Two more days and I'll be home."

"Ok, I'll talk to you later."

"I love you Lil."

"I love you too baby."

Lillian lost about thirty years off her life. She was feeling giddy like a teenager experiencing love for the first time.

She had given up on ever being in a relationship, let alone married. She smiled.

♣♣♣

Lillian picked Bo up at the airport. It seemed like an eternity since they last touched. They talked everyday that he was away, but she wanted to kiss him, touch him, enjoy him.

Bo got in the car.

Lillian was wearing a cream pantsuit and she was beautiful. The pearls in her ears highlighted a natural glow of her skin.

Bo was taken aback. "Hey Shugah!"

"Hi honey."

"Lil are you really going to marry me?"

"Yeah."

"Then I think we need to rethink that living together thing. Hell, I like to went crazy without you. Everyday I was so hard I could break concrete."

"Bo!" Lillian blushed.

"Let's go home and fix that."

"Which home?"

"The closest one."

The animal came out in both of them as they sought passion from one another. They were up half the night exploring one another as though, the six days apart had changed something.

Lillian went to work from Bo's, wondering where she wanted to build her new house. Wondering, who to tell first. She had never been so happy.

At work Lillian told no one. Somewhere between Bo's house and parking the car Lillian became terrified of being married. She walked around in a daze all day, wondering what she had gotten herself into. She loved Bo. Without a doubt, but ready to go through the fire with him? Well, that was something all together different. She had been through the fire of love before. She had been burned by it more than once.

Her marriage to Michael was so rigid and structured. It lacked passion and spontaneity. Lillian had tried a few times to be loose and free with him, but Michael seemed to not like that side of her so she buried that. Now Bo wanted her to dig it up and show it to him. What if it's not what he wanted? Lillian had practiced being sophisticated. She had mastered *'sedity'* now she had to find the root of down to earth and replant herself. How?

That night she returned to Bo's. Foreplay for them was just as good as the real thing. They made love like two people that had the rest of their lives to reach their peak.

Bo slept like a baby.

Lillian was awake all night. Her agreement to marry Bo had been impulsive and in some ways immature. Marriage is so hard. The punishment for failure is divorce. The one thing she did know was that she couldn't handle that.

The next morning she was moving about the kitchen rather slow.

"What's wrong Lil?"

"Nothing."

"You look like a woman with a lot on her mind. Since, the only thing we've discussed is marriage, I'm going to assume it's that."

"Bo what are you talking about?"

"I'm talking about your pre-occupation. I'm too old to be a fool Lil, and I know this marriage thing is too much for you."

Lil couldn't lie anymore. She needed to tell him that she loved him dearly, but she couldn't marry him. It wouldn't come out. "I love you too. Please believe that. You're right. I am not exactly ready."

"Ok. I understand. Are you ready for this relationship?"

"Yes." Lillian was pleased to know that she could maintain the relationship without the stress of marriage.

"Well, let's proceed." He pulled Lillian into his arms and kissed the top of her head. Love had taken hold of him. Bo wanted Lillian bad enough to wait for her.

He knew that she was afraid of his love. Just like he knew that sipping wine from the wide rimmed wine glass, sculptured nails, neatly pressed slacks and weekly professional styled hair was something she enjoyed, but she'd be just as comfortable grabbing a beer from the fridge and drinking it from the bottle.

"Put these dishes away. Let's go get something to eat. I know you get tired of cooking."

"Ok." Lillian was grateful for this man and his love. She cursed herself for not being able to love him to the fullest of her ability. At breakfast Lillian was happy and it showed. The tension of negativity wore off Bo as Lillian ordered steak, eggs, and a beer. (She was finding her way back down to earth.) Bo smiled to himself…He loved this little woman.

29

On the other side of town a completely different occurrence was taking place. Champ had decided, again, to stay out all night actually, three nights. His girlfriend had come by and picked him up three days ago. At which time Nikki had explained to him that she needed some money for food, she had used all of hers for rent and other utilities.

Champ noticed that he was not needed at home as he had been. He knew his clout was dwindling too. He had not been questioned about his whereabouts; not been catered too, not been spoken to, not even missed. Nikki seemed glad to see him go. She ironed his pants and put his condoms back in his rear pocket.

On one occasion she told him she would meet him at Black's for the get together—if he planned on going, because she and the boys were certain to be there.

Champ took all that into consideration when she asked him for some money for food.

"Here." He tossed two dollars and some change on the table before her.

"What am I supposed to do with that?"

"Get something to eat."

"What?"

"Buy some food."

"I can't buy nothing for me and two babies with two dollars." Nikki was livid, but didn't show it. Champ had gotten the best of her on too many occasions. She was finally hurting him. Yes, the nights that he was home and she slept on the couch or with one of the boys was getting to him, this childish move was proof.

"Buy some Top Ramen, a pack of Kool-Aid and some of them 2 for a $1 cookies. Don't tell me you can't shop anymore."

"I'm just tired. Thank you. I'll pay you back when I get my check." Nikki's tears pressed against her throat, her baby kicked, but she didn't falter. She picked up the money and started talking to the boys.

It amazed her that with tears and hatred balled up in her throat, she was still able to squeeze out the loving tone a mother uses to talk to her children. "Go get your coats... we're walking to the store." Nikki walked past Champ, as he stood defeated.

Returning from the store she saw Champ and his girlfriend pull away from the curb. She thought about the crease she'd put in his jeans and started to cry.

All the power that Nikki had over the last couple of months leaked from her as she fed her children the 25cent meal their father sprang for. It was strange how empowerment came and went. One minute she could care less, the next, her very life depended on the same thing that used to not matter.

♣♣♣

Champ came home three days later. The door slammed shut.

"Nikk, I'm home."

"We're back here."

He stomped in there.

She could tell by his stomp that he was mad about something.

He entered the bathroom, stood over Nikki as she bathed the boys.

She looked up to see the threat of departure in his eyes. She remembered the 24-hour Notice on the electric bill and the refrigerator that was still near empty. The boys had been eating over Big Mama's mostly and she hadn't been eating at all.

"Hi Champ."

"Hi Champ? I thought for sure you'd have some food in this house by now! Ain't no food in here Nikki! I ain't crazy! Hell, it's dinner time if it was some food in here you would be done cooked."

"I made some tuna. I am tired. I didn't feel like cooking today. I started my maternity leave and I was going to try and rest before the baby comes."

"All you think about is babies. I don't want no damn tuna!" He stepped up on her, touching her belly with his.

"Do you want me to fry some party wings and some potatoes? It ain't too much else here."

"Nothing here! Yeah you right. No man either. I'm out!" He stomped out of the bathroom with a little more haste than his entrance. He had intended to come home and piss Nikki off; she had truly pissed him off before he left and that's why he stayed gone so long, to show her he didn't need her either.

Champ was going back where he came from until Nikki was ready to act like his woman. His woman usually had dinner cooked and greeted him like he meant something to her. Lately, Nikki had been acting like he didn't really matter.

He knew she needed him there. That's why he left to teach her a lesson. He knew his absence was hurting her. That's what he was trying to do until she straightened up. In the beginning it was so good. She was perfect.

A new panic swallowed Nikki. There was something different about his anger, this time he wasn't bluffing; he had a plan to leave them. Maybe he was really leaving her…them…for good...Nikki remembered her dream. The man/husband, the home, the kids, the love, the picket fence…So, she couldn't have it all, but at least she could have the man and the kids.

"Wait Champ I'll find something else to cook." She wiped her hands on her dress and started after him. Cracks already forming in her heart. The children's eyes were filling with tears.

Joshua sat in the tub looking confused and crying because Johnathan and his mother were crying. Johnathan was crying for himself too. He could feel the troubles of his parents. He couldn't explain it, but he knew.

"Champ I'm sorry."

"That's why I'm leaving. Leaving yo' sorry ass and all these damn kids right here. I don't need this shit. You the reason I'm sinking. And every time (his voice rose two octaves) I turn around, you pregnant. (His eyes were filled with a mixture of disgust and something that resembled hatred) I can't take care of all of these damn kids!" He walked in the bedroom and over to the closet. He grabbed his duffel bag and started snatching his belongings from around the room, throwing them into the bag.

"Champ talk to me. It's more than I didn't cook. Look the house is clean; I'm bathing our sons. I'll cook in a minute. Just don't leave. Please don't leave me." She leaned on the wall. The labor of begging, fear and the fetus were taking their toll on her.

Champ was unable to conceal his smile. There were days when he simply needed to feel like he was needed at any cost. He had the kind of pain that fed off of other people's pain.

"I'm out. I'm tired of the threatening bills, the empty ass 'fridge and yo' crying ass kids. Get outta my face." His eyes were full of disgust as he tried to pass between the doorway and Nikki.

She grabbed him, involuntarily, but grabbed him none-the-less. He shoved her, she held on.

The commotion of loud voices and falling items caused both boys to ease from the bathroom into the bedroom, naked, wet and confused.

Johnathan cried out when he saw Champ's hand draw back. As his hand slammed into Nikki's face, Johnathan leaped right onto his Daddy's leg. He wrapped his limbs around Champ's leg, sinking every one of his teeth into his Dad's thigh. He pinched his flesh until he broke its skin, and was still holding on with the grip of a Pitbull terrier.

Champ danced around the room trying to shake him off. When he realized what was going on, he reached down with a good portion of his force and snatched Johnathan off of him. Then threw him against the wall, knocking the wind from him.

Nikki rose off the floor, and at that exact moment, there was a rising in her. It was in her spirit. It was in her eyes. Her fist too, as they slammed against Champ's face. His left eye, then his cheek, then his mouth. She was firing punches onto his face, with all her pain.

Finally, he grabbed her wrist, both of them and flung her to the floor. Again she rose, taking him by surprise. She leaped at him with the grace of a gazelle. She clawed all of his face filling her fingernails with his skin. She slapped, spit, kicked, kneed and bit him with all her might, and for once she didn't cry. Her fear of being alone was gone.

Exhaustion was creeping on him—when she also relented, but to his surprise she wasn't through. He grabbed his bag, called her a sack of crazy bitches, promised her death and was on his way out the door when she charged at him with a butcher's knife in one hand and a cast iron skillet in the other. She threw the skillet grazing his shoulder, he would have retaliated but the knife was coming forth. He barely escaped. She stabbed at him again, just as Johnny caught his breath.

"Mama!!" She stopped, realized what she was doing and froze. Tears were running down her face uncontrollably.

Champ took this opportunity to teach her a lesson. He punched her in the face fast and furiously so many times, that she could not defend herself. He punched her until she slid down the wall and sat there. He then picked up his things and departed. Dazed at what had just happened, he leaned against the other side of the door for a minute before walking away. He had come home to get his ego stroked and nearly lost his life.

Johnathan and Joshua eased over to Nikki. Blood, moisture, pain and confusion dripping from each of them, together they cried briefly. Nikki had faced and fought her fear, and she knew she had won. She thought *To hell with that 24hour notice on the electric bill, I'm going to buy some candles, food and some new locks with my last money.*

30

"Feather!" Nikki sobbed into the phone. The pounding of pain was pressing outward against her entire face.

Feather sat straight up.

"What's wrong? What's wrong Nikki?" Tears stung her eyes as the feeling of helplessness crawled all over her. This wasn't about the baby; she'd heard Nikki's cry of baby distress before this was something serious.

"Champ. He-we...." Nikki didn't know where to begin. "Can you come?"

"I'm on my way." Feather hung up before Nikki did. She grabbed her huge purse and headed out the door. Black was coming in the door as she was rushing out.

"What's wrong?" Black was following Feather down the steps.

"Nikki called crying…Black something is wrong. Really wrong! She sounded horrible."

"Probably Champ." Black's intuition told him this was it for Champ. Nikki had probably reached her limit. He had noticed the last couple of times when Champ and Nikki were together, they weren't. Feather had noticed too, but neither of them said anything. Actually, they were silently glad that Nikki was wising up.

♣♣♣

"Who is it?"

"It's Feather."

Nikki opened the door and fell into Feather's arms. It was difficult for Feather to support her. First, Nikki was awkward with the protruding stomach and she was quite taller than Feather who was already weighed down with her purse.

Black cringed at the sight of her battered face. He pulled her away from Feather.

"What happened to you?!" He yelled at Nikki. He didn't intend to. He was shocked. He knew Champ had done this and he was hurt.

Feather gasped at the sight of her too. "Oh Nikki." She began to cry.

Black stepped through the entry way and into the house. Both women followed him inside.

"Where are the boys?" Feather cried looking at the blood-splattered wall, the skillet and the knife.

Nikki was crying too hard to respond.

Feather rushed to their room. They weren't there. She rushed into Nikki's room there they were; both of them sound asleep. She crept back into the living room.

Black embraced Nikki as she continued crying.

From where Feather stood she could see specks of blood on the wall and an indentation in the doorframe, with a skillet lying on the floor a short distance away. Then she noticed a butcher's knife on the opposite side of the room. She pointed these things out to Black with her eyes.

He took in the setting of the room.

"Nikki where's Champ? Did you hurt him?"

She shook her head no.

"Nikki are you ok?"

"Yes,"

"What happened?" Black had to know.

"Champ came home after three days of being in the street and was mad because I hadn't cooked. It ain't nothing here to cook. He left me two dollars for food three days ago!" Nikki's swollen face contorted even more. She was really beaten. Black wanted to fight Champ more than ever. He wanted to whip him like he had beaten Nikki. Nikki's eyes filled with tears again. "I ain't staying with Champ. I can't. It's over. I will raise my kids myself. He hit my baby."

"What?!"

"He slammed Johnny into the wall so hard, my baby couldn't breathe and before I knew it I was going crazy on him…When my baby was lying there I wanted to kill Champ. I really wanted to do it…I never knew how much I hated him and I do. I hate that man."

Black was livid. Johnny was almost 3 years old. It made no sense for Champ to be hitting on him like that.

Feather cried silently. She hated Champ too.

"I don't care how lonely I get…I gotta let this go. I just can't take this no more. Somebody's gonna get hurt, and it don't have to be him or me, it could be one of my babies. I can't live with that."

Feather looked at Nikki's face and let the tears fall from her cheeks. She had not wanted to get involved. She was careful to stay out of it, maybe if she had told her to leave this wouldn't have happened.

Black's pacing broke her concentration. Looking at him Feather was concerned. He was truly mad.

"Feather, I didn't even realize how frightened my babies were. Johnathan cried until I told him that his Daddy wasn't coming back."

Black paced around the room.

Nikki's tears flowed. Her face was swelling, turning shades of blue, purple, red and black. Her hair was ragged, yet Feather could see peace in the shadows of her pain.

"Get the kids up, we're going to my house." Black walked out the door.

Feather and Nikki moved without hesitation. They packed in silence. Feather got Johnny and Joshua some clothes, while Nikki got stuff together.

In her room Nikki passed the mirror. For the first time in a long time she looked like herself. Beyond the bruises and puffiness she could see herself as she was before Champ. The only thing missing was the fear. Despite the lifting of the burden, Nikki continued to cry.

♣♣♣

Black sat behind the wheel of the car wondering if he would ever be able to understand Champ.

He had two beautiful sons and a damn good woman. She was intelligent. She kept the house clean. She could cook. She had a job. Some men are just plain stupid.

At the apartment, Feather prepared the sofa bed, and the boys lay in her bed until she finished.

Black and Nikki sat in the kitchen talking about what lead up to the fight. Nikki told him everything. She went back to the stuff during her pregnancy with Johnny.

He didn't' know Champ was over there acting a fool like that. He knew Champ had some hang-ups, but he just didn't know he was doing all that. Nikki was grateful for them, but the embarrassment that she felt showed even through her scars.

"Hey Sis, we're gonna get through this. You and the boys are going to be fine. As their Godfather I'm going to see to it that they never suffer again. So, don't feel like it's all on you."

"Yeah, we're here Nikki, It's ok." Feather agreed with Black.

All Nikki could do was nod. She was truly touched by their love. It meant a lot to know that regardless how much they loved Champ their humanities allowed them to do what was right. Life had finally shone her a kind light.

♣♣♣

Instead of disturbing the children, Nikki slept in their room and Black and Feather slept on the sofabed.

"I am so mad. I could rip his ass apart. Babe, did you see her face?! That don't make no sense. I'm done. I can't deal with Champ no more. Tomorrow, I'm going to change the locks at her apartment; you go to the bank. Y'all go buy some more food…you know, stuff for the kids. And pay her electric bill, or on it, or something to keep it on. I think she should stay until after the baby. We can't send her home like that."

"Ok. You know what Black...I love you. I was thinking the same thing about her being over there by herself. That baby is due in a couple of months. We can manage that long."

"Yeah, we can. I kept thinking back to when we first met her and we were playing that game and she said her biggest fear was being alone. If we don't let her stay she will probably grow weak for Champ when he gets back in her face."

"Do you really think he's going to try to get back in her face?"

"Babe, he's a man. Any man that has a good thing always tries to go back once he learns that it was good. He'd be a fool not to."

♣♣♣

Neither Nikki nor the kids were a problem.

She was on maternity leave so she kept them at home with her, instead of worrying Big Mama.

Everyday when Black and Feather came home she had prepared dinner, set a gorgeous table and the disinfectants could be smelled upon opening the front door.

The boys were well behaved. So much so that it made Black nervous. He noticed the signs of abused children. These kids were afraid to play. Not just in the house, period. Joshua literally did not talk unless he had to. Black made up his mind to start spending quality time with them.

Feather had found a new appreciation for Black. She loved her husband. As long as she was with him she knew she wouldn't be going through the mess Nikki had gone through. It was killing her not to touch him, but she didn't want to make Nikki uncomfortable. The last thing she needed was to sit under two lovebirds.

It had been three weeks since Champ and Nikki separated. He had not called Black's looking for his family. No one had called him regarding his family.

He had crossed Nikki's mind a few times some days more than others. She replaced those thoughts with the memory of her battered face. As always, she was ok.

Big Mama had come to Black's to see Nikki and the boys. Before leaving she gave Nikki a new maternity dress. It was really pretty. She had even bought a hair bow to match, since Nikki was still wearing that ponytail.

"I know you only have a short while to go, but Mama know sometime you need something to make you feel good. Ain't nothing like some new clothes to soothe heartache".

"Thank you Big Mama. This is so nice of you."

Big Mama also slipped her twenty dollars before she left, for her pocket.

Nikki loved her.

That night Nikki explained to Black and Feather that she needed to return home. She needed to prepare for the baby and start dealing with her situation.

"Thank you for helping me get on my feet again." She smiled. Her face was almost back to normal. "I think I need to go home tonight. I have imposed on you two enough."

"Nikki you're ok." They sang in unison.

"I need to do this. I need to do some thinking before the baby comes. I need to take some inventory of my life."

They understood. "Ok. I'll drop you off after dinner."

"Thank you." Nikki almost cried then.

It was a tender moment for everyone.

♣♣♣

Arriving home Nikki felt a little uncomfortable. She really didn't want to step back into her life, but it was hers and she had to deal with it, in order to fix it.

Approaching the door she saw a note stuck in it. She pulled it out and opened it. At first glance she recognized Champ's handwriting. She didn't even read it, just opened the door and went on in. The house was exactly as she left it the skillet was still near the door and the knife on the floor. The house was dark and full of sadness. It was depressing.

Black, Feather and the boys entered moments later.

Nikki was holding her tears convincingly. Black and Feather stayed only a moment then they were off, leaving Nikki and her family alone to start repairing their lives.

♣♣♣

"Hello?"

"Hey Nicole. I came home a couple of days after we got into it and uh…you changed the locks?"

Nicole's heart was beating faster and faster. Her anger was forming. Her face still showed traces of how he'd beaten her.

"Yes. I did."

"Well, what's up?"

"What do you mean what's up?"

"What's up? Did you get my note?"

"I got it, but I didn't read it."

"So, we can't talk?"

"No. I don't have nothing to say."

"Well, I do."

"Well, I don't want to hear it."

"What??!"

"I don't want to hear it."

"I'm on my way."

"Ok, but I ain't backing down this time, so come on."

He hung up. Nicole didn't even bother getting worried. She sat a pot of water on to boil and went back to her thoughts. She was making a list of things to do when the phone rang again.

"Hello?"

"Nikk. We need to talk. I've been buying clothes and shit. I need my stuff. Just let me come get my stuff."

"You can pick it up tomorrow. It's 2:30 am. You've been without your stuff for three weeks now…one more day ain't gon' hurt you. And please don't call here anymore. My kids are sleep and I don't appreciate my phone ringing at this time of night." She hung up before he could respond. Tears were coming. She had to hang up because she wanted to say ok. She wanted him to say what she needed to hear and mean it.

The phone rang. She unplugged it without answering it. Her tears flowed into the morning.

♣♣♣

Champs knock scared Nikki. It was 10:15 am. The kids were still sleep. Nikki got up.

"Who is it?"

"Me."

Nikki cracked the door. "What?"

"I want to talk to you."

"About what?"

"Us, the kids, our situation."

Nikki felt the tug on her heartstring. "Champ, you can have 5 minutes. I don't want my boys to wake up and see you here. I promised them you wouldn't be back."

"Ok."

Nikki could see the hurt in his face. She stepped aside.

He walked in.

They stepped into the kitchen.

Nikki refilled the pot of water and turned the fire up as high as it would go.

Champ looked at her then the pot.

She looked away.

"What's the water for?"

"You if you decide to get out of hand with me. You have 5 minutes…what?"

"I want to come home. I know I was wrong. I'll help you more financially; I'll stay home more. I don't know what else to say."

"And that's just why I can't let you stay. You didn't say any of the stuff I needed you to say."

"What?"

"What about I'm sorry, I love you, I love my kids…I'll get a job…I'll do whatever it takes." She was crying. "For the entire time that I was with you I loved you…I wonder why, you never loved me?"

"I loved you Nikk. I still do. I will do whatever you want."

"Don't do what I want. Do what your heart tells you to do. Never mind Champ…Go!! That's what you do. GO."

"I ain't going nowhere."

Nikki picked up the pot of boiling water, "oh yeah sweetheart, you're going."

Champ looked at her. Her eyes were full of hatred and begging him to act a fool. She wanted to throw that water on him.

He sensed it. "I want my things."

"Come back at 1:00 pm and I'll have them ready. Bring something big enough for your television and your stereo too."

"Don't be trying to keep none of my shit Nikk." He didn't want to appear weak, yet there was nothing he could do except wait until 1:00 o'clock in afternoon like she said or give her a reason to give him a hot bath in the kitchen.

"I ain't."

Champ walked out of the house again, defeated.

The rest of the morning Nikki fed the boys. Washed their hair, played with them for a little while then finally began packing Champ's things.

He called at just before one o'clock.

"I'm on my way."

"Ok."

Nikki and Johnathan sat all the bags on the front porch then she dragged the stereo and TV out there too. When

Champ pulled up he was pissed. He snatched his belongings up.

Nikki stood in the window, watching him.

"Fuck you. Fuck all of y'all."

Nikki knew she had done the right thing, He had not changed at all.

31

Living without Champ wasn't as hard as Nikki thought. Knowing he wasn't coming home really helped her get to sleep. Knowing exactly how much money she had and what she had to do with it helped her sleep through the night.

The fact that her boys seemed happy made it all worthwhile.

Joshua still wasn't talking—he wasn't crying either.

Big Mama had come to get them regardless of Nikki being on maternity leave.

Champ was calling and yelling profane words over the phone, occasionally. He went so far as to say if he saw Nikki on the street what all he was going to do to her. Each call he sounded more and more angry. Nikki grew concerned.

♣♣♣

Today Nikki was going shopping with Feather. She was going to replace her bathroom décor; it was the last thing she could do before the baby arrived. The day before she changed the boys room around. Black unstacked the bunkbeds and she washed their curtains. Everything in the house was in a different place. She even cleaned the sofa bringing it back to its original whiteness.

After the baby she planned to redecorate the entire apartment, start saving money, buy a car and pay Big Mama something on a regular basis, for all her help. She prayed for Godspeed and promised Him that she'd do what was right if He helped her out of this mess.

After shopping Feather visited for a while. They put the crib together and placed it in Nikki's room.

Champ called twice. Nikki was surprised that he wasn't unpleasant at all.

He called a third time when Nicole went to walk Feather to the door. This time he left a message.

Things were good for Nikki. Life wasn't what she had planned it to be; however, she was glad to be out of the war.

After dressing the boys for bed Nicole sat on the sofa, propped her feet up and stared at her favorite corner of the house. The sun was down, so the brass pot didn't shine against the hardwood floor, but it was still a serene picture.

The phone rang.

"Hello?"

"Hey girl, I forgot to call you when I got here. What are you doing?"

"Nothing. Just put the boys to bed."

"Are you ok?"

"Yes. You don't have to worry when it's time I'll call. I got a week left. I hope it's on time. I mean she's on time. It better be a girl this time."

"I hope so too. I know you all right. I just feel for you. I don't know what I'd do if I was in your situation."

"You don't have to worry because you would've left long before I did. I stayed in it because I was afraid to be by myself. Ain't that something? I did all that so that I didn't have to be by myself. Hmph...and where am I? BY MYSELF."

"You want me to come back?"

"Girl, no. In a minute my brother's gonna start tripping about you being over here so much. I appreciate what you're trying to do, but I gotta be alone at some point. And how are you going to make a baby from over here?"

"I know. I just feel for you. I feel for the boys too."

"I was just talking to Johnny. He's deep. I would never have guessed he is as enlightened as to what's going on as he is. I know now for sure Champ can't ever come back here. Girl, my baby told me if he does he doesn't want to stay here. He wants to go live with Uncle Black. I was crushed. That's why I'm getting it together. I don't want my baby to feel like that." Nikki decided to stop all that crying, so she swallowed the tears that were forming.

"You gonna be alright. Determination beats failure all the time."

"I know. I needed this break from Champ. I really did."

"Ok. Call me if you need anything. I'm going to go in here and try to make you a niece or nephew, your brother just walked in."

"Ok. Thanks. And tell Black I said hi."

"Nikki, I love you."

"I love you too."

32

Big Mama was keeping the boys again. The baby's due date had come and gone, and she was 6 days past that. Dr. Sanders suggested that she walk to encourage her body to begin labor. So, everyday just before Big Mama or Feather dropped the boys off, Nikki strolled to the store for junk food.

Champ called everyday now that Nikki was home. It didn't matter she didn't buy the lies anymore. Oh, they were sweet. Especially the last message she pulled off of the answering machine.

"Nikki....This is the last time I'm going to call. I know my calling like this is hard on you and my boys. I just wanted to know if I could take you out sometime? Maybe we could start over? I am trying to make some changes in my life. I'm seeing a counselor. I've gone to visit my mother and my grandmother's graves. I realize that I didn't have anything to do with my mother dying. Nikki, I love you please page me when you get this message. I want to come home. I want to be with my family. Y'all all I really have."

The machine cut him off before he could say anything else. Nikki stood listening with tears in her eyes. Once again her heart went soft for him. She was glad he was in counseling. Pleased to know that, maybe, no other woman would have to go through with him what she'd been through.

She slipped on her shoes and began her walk. In the store she browsed around. After purchasing her items she left.

The man in line behind her asked the cashier if he knew her.

"Yes. She's really a nice lady."

"And…Gorgeous."

"Yeah, that too."

Nikki strolled home never knowing she had been admired.

"Nikki. Why haven't you called me back?"

"I've been busy." Nikki put the key in the lock. (The look finally registered. Champ looked like he had been doing some hard drugs or something. He was twitching around his mouth, his eyes were open as wide as they could open, and he seemed off balance.)

She entered the house quickly. As she closed the door he pushed against it. She secured the lock and walked to the window.

"You betta call me girl…You betta…Don't make me hurt you." He slurred as he staggered off.

A few minutes later Feather arrived with the boys. Nikki tried to act normal, but Feather saw right through her.

"What's wrong with you?"

"Girl, Champ came by here today and he looked like my mother. My mother is an addict and she looks bad. Champ didn't look as bad as her because she's been doing it for years." Nikki began to cry a little.

"Nikki, it's going to be all right. He's going to leave you alone eventually. Right now he's probably just shocked that you've been holding your own this long. I am certainly proud of you. I really am. You are really doing well by yourself and your family."

"I know. That's not it. I'm sad because yesterday I thought about loving him again. Not because I need to, but because I wanted to be loved. I listened to one of his messages and I let it get to me a little."

"But you didn't let it get you to the point that you faltered. See Nikki it's time for you to start trusting in the Lord. He's going to protect you. Why do you think Champ showed up here today? That wasn't nobody, but the Lord protecting you—revealing to you the truth. Helping you to see that nothing has changed with him. Things will only get worse if you go back. Listen to Him."

"Girl I feel foolish to have even thought for one second of going back to him."

"Nikki. You are human. You are in a vulnerable state in your life. It's gotta be scary standing in your shoes, but you're doing beautifully. You're going to be ok. There are going to be times when you feel like you need a man. You've had someone in your life for a long time. Whether he was good or bad is irrelevant…he was there and now that he's gone you're going to feel that emptiness—that void in your life. It's going to be hard at times and sometimes it will be a breeze. Don't matter you will weather the storm because you have to. It's all a part of life."

"You been hanging out with Big Mama too long." Nikki laughed.

"I am getting just like her." Feather smiled back.

♣♣♣

Later that night after Feather left and the boys were asleep, Nikki lay in her bed alone. She reached over for no apparent reason and listened to Champ's message again. Again she was glad to be out of that relationship. Suddenly a pain ripped through her left side. Sitting up straight she noticed the shadow outside her door.

"Come her Johnny."

He walked into the bedroom. Too young to know to wipe his tears, he tried to hide them.

"What's wrong?" Nikki picked him up in spite of her condition.

"I'm scared."

"Of what?"

"Daddy."

"Why? Daddy's not here."

"'Cause he's coming home and fight some more." Johnathan started to cry even though he tried not to.

"No he's not. I'm not going to let him." Nikki rarely had this type of one on one with her son because Champ had forbidden it. Calling him a little candy ass girl. So, both mother and child tried to act tougher than they really were. Not today. Today and from now on they could cry if they wanted to. He was a baby. He was her baby and he was scared.

"I know you want to." He fussed.

"Why do you think that?"

"'Cause you keep listening to his messages. I wish you would just hang up." He expressed his hatred of his situation.

"Johnny sometimes Mama needs to hear Daddy's messages so she can remember not to let him come home. I don't expect you to understand, but I expect you to trust me. He won't be back." She promised.

Nikki's pain was worse than that Champ had inflicted. All this time she thought her baby was too young to be effected by what was going on between her and Champ.

The phone rang.

"Hello?"

"Hey, Nikk. Can I talk to you? I'm sorry 'bout scaring you earlier."

"No Champ I'm sorry. Sorry that I have no more chances to give you. Please stop calling here." She gently placed the phone on the hook.

Johnny smiled into her smile with brightness she'd never seen before.

33

When Feather suggested that she keep the boy's overnight Nikki was against it. Letting them go would mean staying in the house alone. As it stands caring for them prevented her from totally focusing on her pain.

Nikki wanted to cry. She needed to cry. The bottled up emotions of loving Champ and now, living without him was killing her. It wasn't so much that she needed him. She just couldn't understand why he had mistreated her. In searching herself, she didn't find enough wrong with her to make a man abuse her the way Champ had. She knew his sexual appetite was fed on aggression and she tried to accommodate him, but certain times it was too much. She was more of a romantic, partial to gentleness and loving/soothing touches.

For every reason and no reason at all, Nikki burst into tears. She cried like never before. Her cries contained no tears they were deep grunted moans and sighs, pleading noises. She cried for herself, her children, their father, her mother and her grandmother. Nikki cried all day. She didn't change her clothes, didn't eat, didn't brush her teeth…just cried and fell in and out of sleep.

The next morning she did the same thing. Only this day she thought to feed her baby so she ate.

Despite all she had been through, Nikki was healthier and much better without him.

Feather called to see if the boys could stay another night.

This time Nikki happily agreed. Her healing had begun. When Champ called that day, Nikki hung up on him and dialed the Telephone Company. In minutes she had a new phone number. After calling Feather and informing her of the new number she cleaned the house again.

Suddenly she had a burst of energy. So, she decided to groom herself. Half way through curling her hair her arms gave out. She brushed her hair back, into its famous ponytail. Looking in the mirror, Nikki laughed aloud. The laughter kept coming. It was flowing from her as uncontrollably as the tears that preceded it.

She jumped up and went in the room to get the new dress that Big Mama had bought her. In it she looked divine. It was the way she looked during her pregnancy with Johnathan.

Nikki reflected back to her changed locks, new telephone number, clean house and the fact that although her bills were delinquent, she could see them current once she returned to work. Feeling good, Nikki reached into her makeup bag and applied enhancements to her beautiful face. She was pleased with the outcome. All this time Nikki thought she had lost herself, but today she realized she had simply been misplaced. She felt good.

More and more she realized just how unhealthy her relationship with Champ had been. She would never love like that again. Matter of fact never would she compromise so much of herself for a man.

Nikki walked to the store. In her mind she composed a small list of goodies. Suddenly she missed her boys.

The lines were moving really slow.

The man behind Nikki was staring at her; she could feel the weight of his eyes. Twice she turned and smiled and twice he nodded politely. With each glance a pleasant warmth filled her just a little bit more. She knew she was flirting with him and he was flirting back. She was enjoying it. She almost forgot she was pregnant and for a moment her situation. As Nikki began to realize she should not entertain thoughts pertaining to this man, he spoke.

"Excuse me, you look awfully nice pregnant. It's very becoming. Not all women carry that well. First one?" He raised his left eyebrow slightly while lowering the right one a very sexy sort of look. He was gorgeous.

"No. Last one. Thank you." Nikki smiled and wanted to turn away but couldn't.

"What's your name?" He was harmlessly probing.

"Nikki." She hated herself for that stupid reply. She was acting like a complete idiot. *'Nikki'*, like she was a kid. She thought about her comment.

"Nicole. Please say it's Nicole. I love that name. Always have." He pleaded with fate, aloud.

"Yes. It is really Nicole. And yours?"

"Phillip." He gestured for her to move forward.

"Oh." That was all she could say. Nikki was totally out of character, but he was gorgeous and he was flirting too.

"You live around here Nicole?" Phil was gentle.

"Yeah." Suddenly Nikki remembered Champ. This was the same way she met Champ. The same relaxed behavior that got her in the predicament she was in right now. She decided to end the conversation.

"Me too."

They were leaving the store together. He was walking right next to her. To look at them was to assume they were together.

"Here let me carry that for you." Phil was taking Nikki's bags out of her hand before she could object.

"Looks like I'm going your way." They were standing at the corner at a traffic light waiting for their signal to walk.

"You walking too?"

"Yes. I'm walking too." Phil mocked her.

"I didn't mean it like that. I guess I just thought your car was in the lot."

"Oh, I have a car, I just walked to the store."

"I wish that were my case."

"Why don't you have a car?"

"I don't really know… Babies, bills, stress."

"You still need a car. Are you married?" Phil had meant to ask that along time ago, but didn't want to find a reason to leave her alone.

"No. Single. You?"

"Single. Lonely…etc..."

Something stirred in both of them. Each being relieved to know the other was available and wondering how if at all this pregnancy would complicate that. Also, both knowing they would probably never see each other again. Life has its way of teasing.

"You don't look lonely."

"Oh yeah? How am I supposed to look?" He drooped his eyes and dropped his lip into a pout.

"You so silly." Her grin faded from her face and her playful tap stopped mid air. Champ was parked in front of her house.

"Nicole are you ok?"

"No. That's my ex-boyfriend. You better go." She was frantically trying to get her bags from him.

"Ex-boyfriend right?"

Nikki nodded her head yes and pulled at the bags that Phil refused to let go of.

"Does he know he's ex?"

"Yeah, but he won't go. It's complicated. It's only been a few months."

"That's long enough. Come on." Phil firmly removed her grip from the bag and started walking in the direction of the car.

"No. He-he—he's gonna act a fool. Please just go." She pleaded.

Despite his anger at her fear and because he didn't really know her, Phil was on the verge of relenting when Champ got out the car and started towards them.

More intense fear claimed Nikki's face. She didn't want to get this nice man involved in her domestic affairs.

"What's up Nikk? Who the fuck is this?" Champ was hurt more than he was angry. She was supposed to take him back at least one more time.

"Phillip Bordeaux and you?"

"That's my ex-boyfriend Leslie. Let's go."

"Ex-boyfriend? Bitch I own you?"

Phillip's nostrils flared and again he raised his left brow. At this point Nicole could not do or say anything to make him leave. She was much too beautiful to be going through this mess with anyone. Most importantly, she was a woman.

"Dude, it's over. Why don't you just gon'?" Phil gave Nicole all the bags and grabbed her wrist. "Come on Nicole."

To her surprise her feet moved at the request of this stranger.

"Bitch you bett' not move." Champ was livid. He was not taking any more of this liberation from Nikki. When he tried to call her and the number was changed he rushed over to put a stop to all this nonsense.

By now Nikki was pissed too. She kept walking with Phillip; he no longer had to coerce her. She was tired of being called bitch.

"Go on Nicole." Phillip assured her although he wasn't moving anymore.

"What did I say!!" Champ flared up, taking a step in her direction.

Phillip grabbed Champ's arm, stopping him dead in his tracks.

Nicole kept on walking. When she got to the porch she turned to find Champ against a neighbors car and Phil in front of him, sharing what looked like threatening words. Soon he raised up off of him and started in her direction.

Champ caught his breath then charged Phil as he started up the steps. Hit him from behind just like a football player. Phil went down, but sprang right back up. He hit Champ in the jaw, then stomach, and then jaw again. Champ remained standing, but not well enough to retaliate. When Phil closed the door behind him, Champ was vomiting at the curb.

"Are you ok?" Nikki asked through her tears. Somehow this was her fault. Maybe she should've stayed in the house. She was shaking.

"I'm fine." Phil pulled her into him and let her cry.

"I'm sorry." She regained her composure. "I've been through a lot with him. I'm tired of all this. That man has ruined my life. I know there's got to be more to my life than this! I can't take it any more. Sometimes I wonder if he wasn't born to purposely make sure I was unhappy."

"There is more to life than this." Phil brushed her hair back and wiped her cheek. There is joy and laughter and love and babies (he touched her stomach) and hope and of course situations like the one you're in. Sweetheart it's your life, make it what you want it to be. Dude was a mistake. Correct him. You'll be alright after that." He smiled warmly.

It was a contagious smile. Nikki found herself smiling too.

"Can I use your bathroom?"

"Sure." She started down the hall. He grabbed their bags and started after her.

"First door on the right."

"Where's the kitchen?" He raised the bags in explanation.

"Right there." She pointed straight ahead.

He sat the bags down and proceeded to the bathroom.

Walking into a room that burst into burgundy, black, and gray with hints of white, the odor of disinfectants lurking. Everything was spotless. Lined neatly. Folded decoratively. Straightened to perfection. He almost didn't' use it.

"You have a lovely bathroom. It's too pretty to use."

"Did you?" She teased.

"Yes I had to, but I didn't dry my hands on your towels. I used my pants."

Nikki smiled, forcing the memory of Champ wiping on everything from her head. "You could have used the two small ones on the rack nearest the sink. They are for drying."

He sat down on the couch next to her. "Was that the baby's father?"

"Yes." Nikki was really embarrassed now. Suddenly she too wondered how she'd ever let him touch her, in the name of love and make a baby. Three babies.

"Was he always like that or just jealous?"

"Always like that. That's why we're not together."

"You poor thing." Phil touched her cheek softly. If he had known her better he would've kissed her. She had and angelic look about her that he found hard to resist.

They talked like that the whole evening—about everything and nothing. Off and on Nikki's stomach tightened.

At 11:00 pm he decided he should go. He certainly didn't want to wear out his welcome. By night's end he was comfortable enough to kiss her cheek and as he did she tensed with pain.

"Don't go yet Phil…Let me get your stuff from the kitchen." She whispered through her pain.

"Woman I thought you were in labor." He relaxed.

Nikki smiled and walked carefully into the kitchen.

"Phillip!!" She yelled. She never made it to his bags on the countertop.

"What? What's wrong?" He ran into the kitchen. Nikki looked at the floor. She stood in a puddle of water.

"My water just broke." She was calm, but scared and unprepared, emotionally for delivery.

"Is this it?" Phil was obviously scared.

"Yes. I think so. Yes, I'm sure. Call an ambulance."

Nikki was gripping the table through another contraction.

"How much time we got? I got time to run back to the store and get my car?"

He was already headed out the door as Nikki nodded positively.

"I'll be right back."

Pain was ripping through Nikki the entire time. She stood exactly where he'd left her only now she seemed more dampened and tired. Her stomach looked like it had dropped even to him, someone who didn't know a thing about childbirth.

"Where's your bag or something?"

"In my room." A few seconds passed before she could finish her sentence. "I wan...wanna…change first."

Phil raised his one eyebrow, "Now?"

Nikki was going to get indignant when another contraction stabbed her and she felt her first jolt of vaginal pressure.

"That's ok…Let's go." She started towards the door.

Phil ran down the hall opening doors until he found one that lead to her room and her bag. He beat Nikki to the car, put the bag in and went back, scooped her moist body up sat her in the car, went back a third time and got her purse and locked the door.

Nikki started to moan on the way to the hospital. She was breathing hard and sweating, but still she was beautiful.

For a brief moment Phil wished this was his baby and Nikki through all her pain was wishing the same thing. She knew Phil was a decent man, the kind that would make a good father.

They arrived at the hospital as tears began to roll down her cheeks. "This is killing me Phil. I've been trying to hold it since we got in the car."

"We're here now Nicole. You can let go." Phil's demeanor/tone of voice willed calmness to her even though he was terrified.

A nurse came over with a wheel chair.

"How many minutes apart?"

"About one or two." They sang in unison, both impressed with the others accuracy.

"I wanna push. I gotta push." Nikki whined.

"Just hold on. Ms., hold on."

The nurse stopped at the nurse's stations for the admitting paperwork.

Phillip innocently offered Nikki his hand in comfort. She nearly crushed every bone in his hand. He felt the tingle up to his elbow. She glanced up at him appreciative and apologetic at the same time.

Finally, the nurse rolled her into a birthing room. She was prepared for delivery quickly. Phillip turned the corner at the door and went into another door marked waiting room and sat.

Nikki wanted to call him, but was too preoccupied with pain to know how.

Four good pushes and Nikki's third son entered the world. Eight pounds and six ounces. She'd name him Justin Phillip Andrews.

"Mr. Bordeaux she wants you now."

Phillip raised his head out of his hands.

He followed the nurse to the room. There she was. His angel, lying in bed groggy and exhausted.

"It's a boy." She whispered.

"Where is he?" He whispered too. They way people who are whispered to do.

"Being cleaned and dressed." She mumbled.

"I thought it took longer."

"This is my third time." Even through her exhaustion Nikki managed to pry her eyes open wide enough to see his expression. She assumed he would leave now. Three kids was a lot of responsibility to accept.

Phil didn't flinch at all. He showed no signs of departure.

"Do you have a daughter already?"

"No. All boys."

"Looks like they need a father." He seriously/jokingly tossed the question.

"You applying for the job?" She seriously/jokingly replied, but before he could answer she stopped him. "Don't answer that. I am out of line. Please forget I said that." She was drifting to sleep as she apologized.

"It's ok, it's ok. Can I call anyone or do anything else for you?"

"Yes. Call my sister. She has my boys." She rattled off the number. "Her name is Feather."

♣♣♣

"Hello, may I speak to Feather?" Phillip raised one brow as the unfamiliar name rolled off of his tongue.

"Yes. Just a minute." Black woke Feather. "Feather. Babe…Telephone." He didn't go back to sleep. He stayed up and eavesdropped on the 2:30 am phone call from a man that he didn't know especially one calling for Feather instead of Maya.

"Thank you for calling. Tell her we'll be there first thing in the morning. Thanks again for calling."

She turned to Black. "Babe, Nikki had the baby, another boy. That was her friend Phillip Bordeaux. He's there with her. I don't know him do you?"

"No."

Feather rolled back under Black, silently praying for her own childbearing moment. Keeping the boys the last two nights had the hands of her maternal clock whirling.

Phillip hung up the phone. He was feeling giddy for no reason at all. That baby didn't belong to him, but he was proud to be a part of his birth. There was a connection to him, the turn of today's events and that baby. He stared across the room at a sleeping Nicole. She'd fallen asleep before he even finished dialing. He watched her chest as it rose and fell. Finally, satisfied with the engraving of her image into his mind he approached the bed and kissed her forehead. Then whispered lighter than a blown kiss, "Goodnight Nicole."

Phillip knew that he wanted this woman. As he stood before her he knew that he wanted to be a part of her life. Somehow he would.

Nikki lay sleep in the one thing she'd always wanted—adoration, not even knowing it.

Champ was not notified of the baby's birth.

34

The next morning Nikki lay in the hospital bed looking at little Justin, wondering how much pain and sadness life was going to throw his way. If he could stay as he was right this moment she'd be the happiest mother breathing.

Looking out the window she noticed the sky was dark…blue/gray…kind of sad looking. Looked like rain. Then from nowhere a tear…then two...then a river until she was weeping.

"Mother's blues." The nurse said as she came in. "Yeah, Mother's blues. I got that way with each of mine and I have five."

She took Nikki's hand gently in hers, while sitting on the side of her bed. "Go on and cry baby…don't mind me. Just cry. I know all about it. You look at your beautiful, perfect baby then you see the ugly cruel world waiting on him."

Nikki was crying. That's exactly what she was feeling.

The nurse's hands were aged hands so Nikki assumed they were rough. "I used to think the same thing. These hands been older than me since I got 'em." She responded as if she'd read Nikki's mind. "My grandmother said they were working hands and I'd carry love through them. I guess she was right. They just look bad Sweetie, but they feel just fine."

Her presence made Nikki cry more. Her own mother entered her mind. She wanted her. She wanted her to want her back. She wanted Justin to have a grandmother. Oh! There were so many things wrong with her life. If only she could have cleaned the world up some before her baby entered it. In her agony she lost a little moan.

"Go on baby, let it out." The nurse sat there holding her. Holding her like Big Mama would have. She starred out the window with Nikki…she was in search of peace herself.

That's exactly how Phillip found them.

"Hmph." He cleared his throat.

Both women were startled. The nurse stood.

"I'll check your pressure later." She patted Nikki's hand before leaving.

"Mother's blues. She'll be fine, once you get her home." She whispered to Phillip as she passed him.

He nodded without understanding what she meant. He did like the part about…once you get her home.

"Nicole are you ok?"

"Yes." Nikki tried to regain her composure.

"What's Mother's Blues?" He raised his one eyebrow.

"I guess another name for depression."

"Look." He picked up a gift bag. Inside Nikki found a bunch of sports embroidered clothing and a picture frame with sports paraphernalia outlining it.

Nikki was out done. Who was this man? Phillip was everything she used to look for. He was the man she had wanted Champ to be.

"And these are for you." He bent down again and came up with a dozen roses.

"Thank you, Phillip. You really shouldn't have. You don't even know me. This is so sweet." Nikki started to cry again.

"Come on Nicole. I'm a man. You just gave birth that's a beautiful thing…the roses were to compliment your beauty…that's all. Is this him?" Phillip asked turning to the baby resting in the little hospital bed next to Nikki's."

"Yes. That's my son. Justin Phillip Andrews." Nikki smiled.

"Phillip?" Phillip turned his head with a jerk. "Were you going to name him that before you met me?" He asked.

"I hadn't really given it much thought with all that was going on. All I could come up with was Lamont and I didn't really like the sound of that with Justin. Are you offended?" Nikki had not even considered his feelings. She'd decided on the name as a way to hold on to one of life's pleasant moments as she didn't know if or when she would encounter any more.

"Of course not. I'm honored. I'm surprised that's all." He wanted to kiss her, but he knew that was inappropriate. On his drive home last night, early that morning, he's wished for this baby and in a twisted sort of way he'd gotten him. He also wished for his mother, maybe he'd end up with her too. Maybe?

There was a silent passing of admiration between the two when Black walked in.

He too had a bouquet of flowers and a present for the new family member. His expression read "Who is this man?"

Black walked in introducing himself. "I'm Black, Nikki's brother how you doing?" He extended his hand. Phil shook it.

"Phillip. Fine. And you?"

"Alright."

"What's up sis? Congratulations. Where he at? Can't you have anything, but boys?" Black kissed Nikki's cheek. She felt awkward and knew he did too. After all, he was her brother because of Champ. Nikki wondered if she did find it somewhere in her heart to love again would she lose her family?

Phillip was taken by surprise at the scene, he sensed some tension, but saw the love.

"Mama!!" Johnathan rushed past Phil into Black and to his mother. "Where my brother?"

"Hold up. Say excuse me." Johnathan spoke to Phil, but looked at Black.

"Ok. That's a big boy." Black praised.

"This is your new brother." Black picked up the baby and held him down to Johnny's level.

Feather walked in with Joshua on her hip and that huge purse on her shoulder. Immediately she assumed the handsome man standing near Black was the same man that called her last night.

"Hello." She said to Phil as she sat her purse on the foot of the bed and stood Joshua on the floor.

"Thanks for calling last night." She smiled approvingly.

"No problem." Phil said mostly to Black as he accepted Justin like a pro, when Black handed him the baby.

"You did that real good. How many kids you have?"

"None. I just love kids, it comes natural, I guess...Don't even have siblings."

"Me either. Just these knuckle heads of Nikki's."

The men were getting acquainted when Feather sat on the bed.

"Girl, congratulations two times." Feather pointed discreetly at Phil and smiled.

"He's just a friend."

"A friend from where?"

"I met him yesterday and went into labor and he ended up bringing me here. I didn't really expect him to come back." Nikki was trying to act as though it meant nothing to her but she was touched by Phillip's presentation of himself. Despite her strain to not fantasize she was.

"Well, you better thank the Lord he did. Maybe he'll stay? And he's cute." Feather joked.

"What's his name Nikk?" Black interrupted.

"Justin Phillip Andrews." Nikki and Phillip answered in unison.

Feather wished she were nearer to Black. She knew he was going through some changes with Phillip's presence. She was wise enough to know that even when you are sincerely through with someone you still hurt for him or her when you know of their loss, even if they don't. Champ was like a brother to Black. Man or not it was going to take some getting used to not kicking it with him, not talking to him etc. She knew that.

"Nice. I knew it was going to start with 'J'." Black joked.

Phillip wondered after he'd spoken if he should have. His intent was to add nonchalance to '*Phillip*' so Nikki would be able to say it. There was something about her brother that made him, think he was having a hard time with him being there. If Nikki's pull on his heart wasn't so strong he would have left, but the more he looked at her the more he had to. To him she possessed the kind of face you could look at forever and never get bored.

Nikki was glad Phil had spoken, she'd almost lost her voice on his name, but hearing Phil's voice gave her the courage she lacked. She didn't want to hurt Black.

Black understood. He saw the chemistry, the attraction between the two. He knew that this man wanted more than friendship from Nikki. And she obviously wanted something from him too. Naming her baby after him, that was rather serious. Black was hopeful that he meant her some good. She so deserved it. The best thing about Phillip was that he didn't seem to mind dealing with the kids. That was commendable.

Black wasn't sure he could do that, especially if he had none.

35

It was a perfect morning, a photographer's dream. Nature's serene images were vivid. The sky was perfect blue. The grass was green and the scent of a neighbor's bacon filled the air. It was morning.

It was also one of the rare mornings when Feather woke first. She eased out of the bed careful not to wake Black. She went to the bathroom. She stepped into a hot shower, washed her hair and her body and stepped out. Looking at her nude self in the mirror, she wondered what she would look like if she were pregnant.

Then she reached under the cabinet and retrieved the last of her pregnancy testing kits. She'd been picking them up regularly as her period had been playing tricks on her, but always it showed up after the negative results of the test.

Feather was starting to wonder why she wasn't getting pregnant. Nikki had had a baby since she'd stopped taking birth control pills. She peed in the cup. Siphoned it. Dropped five drops on the pallet and continued grooming herself.

When she finished she walked out of the bathroom and back into the room, forgetting to check the results.

She entered the room as Black woke. He peeked from under his sleep and smiled. "Hey gorgeous."

"Hey." She answered. Plopping down next to him, opening her robe unveiling her nudity.

"I was talking to her." He pointed to the teddy bear, for Justin, sitting on the chest of drawers behind Feather.

"Yeah right. Well, you can sleep with her tonight."

"Then how you gon' pay for yo' keep?" He rushed her, pulling her back into his arms and the bed. He knew her well enough to know she was going to pop him when his remark registered.

Feather wrestled lightly. She was still appreciating the morning's beauty. This was the kind of day made especially for loving moments. A good day for making pleasant memories.

Black released her. "What are your plans for today?" I think I'm gon' hang around here. Probably stop by Big Mama's and see what she cooking."

"I'm going over to Nikki's. I'm supposed to be doing her hair. I'm so tired of that ponytail. Plus I think she's trying to impress Phillip."

"I think she likes him too."

"I know he likes her. Every time I go over there he's there. I mean every time. It's been three months since Justin was born and Phillip hasn't left her side yet."

"I hope he's sincere."

"He is. The boys like him too. You know I was thinking about having them over for dinner or something soon. What do you think?"

"That's cool." Black tried to sound like he was ok with it, but he really wasn't sure. Sometimes he missed the times when they used to get together. Then he flashed back to the month before seeing Champ on the street. He was looking like an addict—even tried to talk crazy to him. Black knew it was the drugs talking so he didn't even respond.

Black got up. Reached into the drawer, threw some socks and some underwear on the bed and was picking out the rest of his clothes. "Babe, can you iron these shorts for me." He glanced at her and walked out the room.

Feather felt his discomfort.

She wanted him to spend some time with Phillip. She knew that they would get along well if he just gave it a chance. Nikki was happy too. Maybe if he saw them together he would understand.

Thinking about what was developing between Nikki and Phillip made Feather crave newness.

Her marriage was becoming routine. She missed going to breakfast, dinner, movies, and stuff.

Black passed her going to the closet for towels. Feather fixed her mouth to say something along those lines to him when she heard the shower.

Black crept back into the hall before getting in the shower. He felt her desire. "Hey Babe you wanna go to breakfast before you go to Nikki's?"

Feather smiled to herself, swallowed those exact words and yelled back "yes".

She got up plugged in the iron and started spreading up the bed while she decided what she was going to wear. Something loose so she could eat good. Suddenly she was very hungry.

Black entered the bathroom glanced at the test pallet, then stepped into the shower. A minute later it registered. He got out, walked into the room mad and naked. He couldn't believe that Feather would do him like that, but when he saw her expression he realized she didn't know. So, he maintained his angry face and tossed the pallet to her. She reached on the bed, grabbed the pallet; looked at it.

It was positive. She never expected it to be. "I'm pregnant?!" She whispered through her tears.

"Yep." He pulled her into him.

"Wanna make sure?" Black whispered, as they both eased to the floor and made the most careful and delicate love they'd ever made.

36

"Babe who we gon' tell first?"

"Let's tell Big Mama."

"Ok."

♣♣♣

"Hello?"

"Big Mama. This is Black and Feather." Feather was on the other phone. "We have something to tell you".

"What is it baby?"

"Feather's pregnant." Black could feel Feather's smile from the bedroom. He was in the living room on the phone.

"Oh that's good. Congratulations baby. Ooh Mama so happy."

"Thank you." Feather eased in.

"Is Mama there?" Black asked.

"No baby. She went somewhere with a friend. It ain't gone work though. That fella that she left with stood right here in this living room and ain't spoke to me yet. I was sitting here on the couch and I didn't speak to him either. Every once in a while I gets hellish like that. You want me to tell her, or have her call you?"

"Have her call us." Black requested.

"Bye Big Mama." Feather said.

"Bye baby, I'll talk with y'all later."

♣♣♣

Lillian and Bo had just started making love.

"Go ahead and get it. Then unplug it." Bo rose up enough to let Lillian get the phone. She cursed fate.

"Hello?"

"Hi Mama. It's me and Black. We have something to tell you."

"Aahh!! Bo, Feather's pregnant!!" Lillian screamed.

Black and Feather pulled the phone away from their ears with huge smiles.

Lil got back on the phone.

"Ms. Lil, we're not pregnant." Black spoke seriously into the phone.

Lillian dropped her mouth. She was embarrassed. She had been dreaming of death and usually that meant someone is born.

"I'm just kidding!! We're pregnant." Black laughed.

"Boy!! I'm a beat your butt, I hope this baby don't have your sense of humor. One of you is enough. Congratulations. I am so happy."

"Thank you Mama. Tell Bo to get on the phone." Feather said, "I know he's there."

Feather was happy for her mother. Lillian seemed alive—real. Feather had begun to really enjoy her.

"Hi, Uncle Bo are you gonna make my mother into an honest woman before my baby get here?"

"I'm trying to Feather. Congratulations baby girl. Now we gone see can we do what you just did." Bo teased.

Lillian hit him. "Bo, don't talk to my baby like that."

Black and Feather could hear the slap.

"Your baby is having a baby…she knows what time it is." Bo laughed.

Feather blushed. She was happy for her mother. She wondered if her and Black would still be that loving when they were their ages.

"We just called about the baby. Didn't mean to interrupt anything." Black teased.

"We're supposed to be going by Mama's later, why don't y'all round everybody up and meet us over there? we'll celebrate." Bo invited.

"Ok."

"Alright."

"Bye."

Lillian and Bo went back to their lovemaking.

♣♣♣

Before Black could hang up good the phone rang.

It was Pat. After telling her they called Nikki.

Phillip answered.

"Hello?"

"Hey man this is Black. What's up?"

Phil acknowledged Black's effort. He had not tried to befriend him because he sensed that something was making Black keep his distance and he wasn't going to crowd him. Once he learned of his true relationship to Nicole he understood. He also figured he'd come around, but until then Phillip stayed out of his way. Today he knew that Black was reaching towards friendship. Phil accepted. He liked Black from day one. His sincerity had him thinking he was Nicole's biological brother. He liked how he and his woman were there for Nicole. He liked how he handled the boys.

"Nuthin, chillin'."

"Where's Nikk? Tell her to pick up the other phone, but don't you hang up."

"Hello?" Nikki picked up.

"Hi Auntie Nikki."

"Hi." Nikki wondered what was wrong with Feather. Then it registered. "Are you pregnant?"

"Yes."

"Ah shit!" Nikki screamed.

Phil yelled congratulations too. He was trying to talk to Black. Nikki was trying to talk to Feather. Finally, they all calmed down.

"Yeah man...Meet us at Big Mama's tonight for a little celebration."

"All right see you there."

"Feather I'll see you tonight." Nikki slid in as the phones were being hung up.

"Ok."

"Ok. Bye."

Feather sat on the bed wondering if anyone had told Big Mama that they were having a party.

Black accepted Phillip as a friend. His baby's arrival was evident that life was moving on. So was he.

Phillip was sincerely happy for them. He only wished it were him. He loved Nikki's kids. Loved them, but still he wanted his own. Then he smiled as he heard Justin cry. He and Nikki had never kissed, never even talked about it. There was nothing more than an attraction, protected by a good friendship, between them. Phillip hung out at her house most of the time because he hated being alone. He loved family. Especially hers.

Nikki was glad for Feather. She had seen her sadness in watching her care for Justin. She had allowed the boys more time over to her house as a way of comforting her. She knew when she asked for them it was because she needed to nurse her maternal clock. Nikki loved her enough to share her children; after all she was their Godmother.

♣♣♣

After leaving the celebration at Big Mama's Phil took Nikki and the boys home, as usual, he stayed a while.

Nikki had noticed that everyone at Big Mama's liked him. She felt good to have him as her guest at the get-together.

It felt so natural. He was at home the minute he walked in. Saying 'Yes Mam' to Big Mama when she called upon him had won him a place in the family and everyone knew it. Black went so far as to say 'Welcome…you in now.'

Phillip mingled well. He talked to the women and the kids too. Seemed like he knew just what to say to each person. He won Pat and Lillian's hearts when he changed Justin's diaper and tended to him while Nikki helped in the kitchen. Black and Bo simply liked the way he juggled his attention from child to child, even remembering to give Joshua some attention; though he was easily forgotten because of his quietness.

♣♣♣

"I've had a lot of girlfriends. They just never worked out. I'm just a bad judge of character."

"I find that hard to believe. You are a good man. I mean an ideal man. You have a job, a car, and your own place. That sounds like a good catch to me."

"Then why aren't you trying to catch me?" (He paused long enough to let her answer, but she didn't). "'Cause you're the first person to consider those traits as qualities not opportunities. The women I've dealt with had me getting layaways out for Christmas. Being mentors to their fatherless children while they ran the street with other men. I even had one girl tell me I was too nice to her." Phil raised his eyebrow and shook his head in disbelief.

"You lying."

"Fo' real! I don't fault them though. Some of them brothers out there do the same thing to them, but before they know the game and it scars them for life. I just hate that it's gotta be like that."

"I know the feeling. Just the other day I sat back and took a good look at my life. I felt like there's gotta be something wrong with my loving 'cause no matter how I give it, I don't get it back. My own mother trips." Nikki had never spoke of her pain from her mother's negligence to anyone. Not Feather. Not even Champ. There was a calmness about Phillip that let her explore herself in his presence. It was like a mirror. Almost like he wasn't really there, but he was and he was listening. He soaked everything in like a sponge. He just loved her quietly. He understood he could not be her man cause her wounds were raw and deep. So, he'd just be her friend. He had to be something to be able to look at her to be able to touch her even if it was an accident in passing. Once he even found himself wishing he were her brother just to guarantee himself a place in her life.

"What about your parents? Do you all get along?" Nikki broke his trance.

"Yeah. We do. They just asked about you. Wondering who you were and what happened to their weekly visits. Pops—Pops is cool. I just love him. Brew, sports, and fishing and he loves Mom. I almost envy them. They got each other and they're happy. Hell, I'm younger with better opportunities and less settled. They've been together since college." He paused, raised his one eyebrow and said, "How do you know? I mean when you make your vows how do you know the other person isn't lying?"

"I don't know. I've always been afraid of that. Because I'm a faller and I fall hard. Head first—just bloop." Nikki pressed her palms together then imitated the motion of a diver.

Phillip smiled. "Me too. I'm a faller too." He could no longer ignore the similarities of their hearts.

He wondered how he could get her to see that he could love her like the man in her dreams. He was the man in her dreams. Only he was real, sitting before her, wanting her, knowing she wasn't ready to have him. So, he had to let her keep dreaming. As his love for her came down on him his expression changed to sadness and he lost a sigh.

"What's wrong?" Nikki sensed his pain.

"Nothing. I hate to leave, but it's getting late." Again he raised his brow in regret.

"I know." Nikki was referring to her own regret. He didn't catch her plea for him to stay.

"I'll call you tomorrow." He stood.

"All right. Be careful."

They walked to the door. Phil bent to kiss her cheek, but stopped and grabbed her. He pulled her into him and held her as though that was the last time he'd ever see her. Then he kissed her cheek and slowly released her.

"Lock this door." He pinched her nose and walked out.

Nikki locked the door after he stepped on the other side of it, but she couldn't walk away. She leaned into it and peeked out the peephole. There he was sitting in his car, starring straight ahead. She stood, watching him until he drove away.

Ten minutes later Nikki realized that Phillip had fallen in love with her.

Love was not something she was ready to deal with. Not now, probably not ever.

In separate beds, Phillip and Nikki loved each other all night. Her while scared to let go and allow it to happen and him while tired of holding it and preventing it from happening.

37

Feather was five months pregnant when the Superbowl rolled around again. As usual the party was at their house.

Nikki's personal business had circulated through the family. Everyone knew that she and Phillip were in love despite their 'just friends' label.

Nikki made it a point to look her best. Phillip had a lot to do with that. She knew he was attracted to her and she liked the attention. This was her way of keeping him interested should she ever find the courage to love him. Something in her gut kept her from letting go and loving this man. This man that was so good to her and her sons. Her boys were getting from him what they would never have gotten from their father.

Pretty was too little a word to describe her. The girl was head-turning gorgeous. Even women appreciated her beauty. The ones that were jealous got over it quick, because she was down to earth. Her experiences had her well grounded. Of course, she knew she was pretty, she was also aware that Life abused her just as it did the less attractive.

It pleased her that she had someone to accompany her to family functions and help her out, versus struggling and stressing alone. Phillip was a very pleasant part of her life. When things did get rough, whether she asked for his help or not, he helped. Since Johnathan started school and she couldn't always get him from school to Big Mama Phillip did. He took him and picked him up on the days she couldn't.

They were the perfect little family, only they were 'just friends'.

Big Mama had prepared vegetable trays and Buffalo wings for the game. Feather cooked her famous spaghetti and fried chicken. Nikki tossed a salad. Lillian brought the beverages.

The game was about to begin. People were taking their places. Women were sitting on the floor between their mate's legs or on their laps. Kids were buzzing around. The whole gang, excluding Champ, was there.

Tee brought Carl. Carl wasn't fine, but something about him made him attractive. He was the man Feather had advised her to keep, because he was good to her. She thanked her again tonight for the advice.

Big Mama knew he was the one for Tee the minute he greeted her. He was sincere and decent and it was visible. He was respectful. Very gentlemanly. He was a perfect fit into the family.

Everyone settled in. Even the kids were quiet as the teams filled the field.

A knock bounced off the door. Black scanned the room quickly. Everyone that was expected was already there. Black wondered.

Feather hunched in answer to his questioning glance.

It was Champ.

He dropped in unannounced/uninvited to see Nikki. He knew she would be with Feather and Black today. They were a family of tradition and Superbowl was a tradition. He had been going by her house and seen her and that M-F he'd fought with several times. He wanted to catch her alone. He knew she wouldn't have the balls to bring him to HIS brother's house. And if she did, Black would set her straight.

Champ still had plans on returning home. He had stayed in many places since leaving and was tired of that. He'd even grown tired of Tina. Now he was staying with some girl he met at a night club. Lately all he could think about was Nikki and his sons. Champ had no idea of the new baby's sex. He'd seen Nikki and *that man* with a carrier seat, when he'd gone by, but couldn't see if the baby were a girl or not.

Black stood there awkwardly. Champ had tried to clean himself up, but anyone with eyes could see that he had been in the streets living an addict's life. Black couldn't turn him away, yet he didn't want to be bothered. He had outgrown Champ. He was about to be a father and didn't need to deal with the mess Champ was putting down.

"What's up Brahh? Long time no hear from" Champ offered.

"Nuthin' man."

Champ eased around Black into the house.

Black was embarrassed for him. Although he looked good compared to the last time he saw him on the street, he looked terrible compared to his normal self. Black hoped that he'd grown up some and could walk away from this situation like a man.

Nikki was sitting in a chair watching the game. Phillip was standing over her with a beer in his hand. Big Mama was cleaning Joshua's nose. Lillian was talking baby talk to Justin.

Champ started towards Nikki.

Black grabbed his arm.

He wiggled free.

"Hold up man. We need to talk." Black explained.

"'Bout what? I came to talk to Nikki."

"About that. Man I don't think she wants to talk to you. Plus she's here with a friend. You know I ain't telling you to leave, but chill."

Everyone's attention turned to them.

"A friend?" He spoke louder. He recognized Phillip.

Johnathan eased over to Phillip; fear in his eyes. Phillip sat his beer down and picked him up.

"It's ok little man. I got ya. Ain't' nothing going to happen." He whispered in Johnny's ear.

Champ took in the whole scene. His pain turned to anger. When he looked back into Black's face he was hurt even more. Feeling like he had nothing else to lose he exploded.

"Man fuck you and that stanky ass bitch Nikki!" Champ yelled at Black.

Phil eased Johnny down into Nikki's lap. Bo eased up on Phil's side. Big Mama stood up; passing Joshua to Feather, she was closest to Black and Champ.

"Champ go. Man get out. I ain't got time for no shit."

"So, that's where your loyalty is? You choosing Nikki over me?! I was right you must be fucking her! I bet you Feather didn't know that."

"Man you ain't shit. You worthless ass bastard. Naw-naw I have her over here 'cause she's a friend of MINE. But you wouldn't know nothing about that."

"I knew your ass was fake from the beginning. You and yo' BITCH!"

Black hit Champ so fast the people watching didn't see it. Big Mama was watching for it and she didn't see it.

Champ hit him back. Black hit Champ in the jaw. Big Mama was on them by then. She grabbed Champ.

"Bllaacckk!! Black! Stop it!

Black froze.

Bo came forward when his Mama got involved.

Champ was squirming in Big Mama's arms, talking loud and profane. She ushered him outside with Bo and Phil's help.

Black stood there pissed. Carl was standing with him at this point. Big Mama got Champ outside and turned him loose. Phil and Bo were at the door watching.

Outside Big Mama talked to Champ.

Champ started to cry. Actual tears fell from his eyes.

For a brief moment Big Mama felt compassion for him. She offered. "It's gonna be ok baby. You gotta change your ways. People don't care 'bout the way you carrying on. Now you done mistreated that girl and them kids long enough. She's tired. If ya care anything about them…Let 'em go."

"I don't care nothing 'bout her. Man she ain't shit. Nikki's fucked up. That niggah don't want her. Don't nobody want her with all MY kids."

"Looka here boy. You watch your mouth when you talk ta me. I ain't no friend of yours. You gon' respect me. Or I'll tear an extra hole in yo' ass." Big Mama's nostrils opened and her voice was low and heavy as the words pushed from between her closed teeth. Her eyes were dripping with serious sternness like syrup onto pancakes.

Champ chilled.

Big Mama stepped down one of the steps closer into his view.

"I was asking you to go. Now I'm telling you. Get yo' ass on 'way from here and leave my kids alone. Everyone of 'em even the ones you thank is yours. Don't ever darken 'dis doorstep again. You hear me?"

Champ took one step down. One more and he was on the pavement. From there he responded. "Fuck you Bitch!! Fuck all y'all." He grabbed his thang and cupped it. Phil and Bo rushed out the door to see him trotting away. Big Mama was walking towards them… Phil passed her. She grabbed his arm.

"Let him go baby. He ain't coming back. You come on in here with Mama. 'Cause you gon; owe me some change before this night end. You betted on the wrong team, kid."

38

Phillip and Black were getting along well. They had started running together. Phil was the kind of friend Black had wanted in Champ. Their last outing, Phil invited Black fishing with him, his cousin, his Dad and Johnny.

It was a nice time. They didn't catch any fish but Black figured out that they hadn't really planned to. They sat around talking mess and laughing and drinking beer. Occasionally someone picked on Johnny and the little silly things he did.

While they were gone Feather tried to get Nikki to tell her how she really felt about Phil.

"He's ok. I could love him, but I can't. That mess I went through with Champ has changed me Feather. I don't think I'll ever be the same. I mean I can not go back to that."

"Girl, Phil ain't nothing like that. He ain't hardly gonna be acting like Champ."

"I know but…I'm burnt out on the whole love thing. I think I need to spend some time by myself so, that I can get a grip on what I want and don't want. That's how Champ kept me…he knew my weakness was being alone. I still don't want to be alone, but I don't want to be dependent on no man anymore either."

"You can love Phil without becoming totally dependent on him. I love me some Black, but I think if I had to live without him, for whatever reason I could. Yes, it would be hard, but I could do it. I don't let my every little thing include him. I do some things that only I can do and I allow him to have things just for him. Sometimes I get selfish, but hell I'm human. It's easier to let him go and keep him than to squeeze him and lose him."

"I know. Champ was away more than he was at home. I was in love with the "idea" of love not the real thing."

"You mean you could see that and you don't recognize the real thing? Phillip is in love with you. Ain't no man hanging around and doing all that he's doing 'cause they like you. He wasn't appointed your personal attendant. He loves you. Most important he loves your children. Sometimes I forget Justin is not his."

"Me too. They love him too. The other day Johnathan told me that he wanted to call him Daddy. He said when Phil pick him up and the teacher refer to him as Johnny's Dad they don't tell her no different. I smiled. I thought it was cute. Then he asked me if he could call him Dad. For a minute I was stuck. Then I told him to ask him. I guess I wanted to know if the vibes I'm getting are real or if I'm so horny I'm seeing things."

They laughed.

"Both." Feather teased.

"Girl, I'm bought ready to drop this baby. I'm tired. Why didn't you tell me it was this hard? You made it look so easy."

Feather made it look easy too. Her nails were beautiful. Her hair had grown its full length. Her skin was flawless, and she glowed with joy.

♣♣♣

Now that Champ had severed himself from Black, Black and Phil began a true friendship.

"Man you know I got this problem. I thought maybe you could help me with, I can't seem to figure out Nikki. I like her man. I wanna kick it with her, but I don't think she want to be with me."

"Phil, man you gonna have to be patient and more aggressive. Nikki is not going to come around by herself. She's probably afraid. Champ had her going through it. I don't know exactly why she stayed so long, but she did. Nikki's a good woman. A good woman. And because of that she's easy to use. She knows it."

"I know she's a good woman." Phil accepted the joint and hit it. "I have dated a lot and she's the best woman I've ever met. She's warm and sensitive. She's what I've been looking for. A real woman."

"Man I'm glad Johnny rode with your Pops. I was dying to hit this." Black changed the subject.

"You? Pops took him 'cause I asked him to. I told him we needed to talk. Jus' so we could hit this joint."

"Let me ask you something Phil. If Nikki meets somebody else what you gonna do about the relationship you're building with her kids?" Black had to know that. Johnny had had a good time and he really liked Phil's father. Black didn't want him to get hurt in all this.

"Man I don't know. I've grown to love them lil' dudes. I guess just hope Nicole let me stay in their lives. I think about that sometimes. I can't wait forever. I mean hell I'm trying but…"

Black was pleased with his answer.

"Stop at the store, so we can get some fish." Black smiled. "You know the girls gonna wanna fry some."

Phillip rolled with laughter.

After picking Johnny up from his Dad they proceeded to Nikki's.

Nikki and Feather were in the house waiting. Feather laughed when she saw the grocery bag with the fish in it. Nikki volunteered to cook it while everyone relaxed.

Phillip walked in the kitchen twice and twice she ignored the warm feeling that melted over her when he was near her. Nikki was afraid to admit it, but she loved this man. In the last ten months she had seen him everyday except last night, while he was fishing, and he was sorely missed.

Phil was last to leave. As usual, he didn't want to. He wanted to stay. Not make love and all that, just be around her. He wanted to know if she snored. If she got up to use the bathroom during the night. What position she slept in.

"Good night Nicole." He left.

In his car every song on the radio reminded him of her. Including the ones that were older than their friendship. He wanted her.

Nikki lay in bed alone. The boys were finally back in their room and beds. Since her separation from Champ she had been allowing them to sleep in her bed. She needed their security as much as they needed hers. Justin was in his crib in her room but her actual bed was empty of children.

Nikki missed the warmth of a man. For the first time she wondered if the little men, though there were three, were going to be enough to last her a lifetime.

The sound of the house settling frightened her. Phil eased into her mind. She wondered if he were there would he check the house or simply pull her closer into his comfort. Nikki knew if she were bold enough to be totally honest with herself she would have to say that she wanted her relationship with this man to be more than friends.

♣♣♣

On Colleen Bordeaux's birthday she would be graced with the presence of Nicole Collier, the woman responsible for her son's smile.

Phil was on his way to pick up Nikki and the boys. He'd already called, letting them know he was on his way.

Nicole primped in the mirror trying her best to represent him well as the doorbell rang.

She walked to the door careful not to snag her stockings. She opened the door without even asking who it was—she knew it was Phil.

He walked in without wiping his feet. Phil always wiped his feet. She recognized the mannerism. She turned to look at him.

"Champ what are you doing here?"

Her hair had grown since the baby and she had not cut it; Phil liked it this way. Once he complimented her and that determined it. The hair was for keeps. She had arched her eyebrows for the first time and she looked marvelous.

The beauty he'd cheated himself out of pained Champ; there was something in her eyes that assured him it was over. It was happiness. She had found it.

"You look good."

Nikki didn't comment.

"Where my kids? I heard the last one was a boy too." He knew that sounded stupid, but it was out of his mouth.

Nikki was disgusted the baby was ten months old and here he comes.

"What's his name?" Champ stepped further into the house.

"Hold on Champ. You're not welcome here. My sons are asleep and we're on our way out. I already have a restraining order against you. So, I think you better go." Nikki walked over to the phone, forgetting all about nursing her stockings.

"Wait Nikki… I just came to see the boys. I gotta right to see them."

"So, sue me Champ. Take me to court. Let the judge set a time and a place, but in the meantime, GET OUT OF MY HOUSE and don't ever come here again."

Nikki prayed he would go. She had promised Johnny he wouldn't be back. Everyone in her life was finally settled and now here he comes to upset her household. Not to mention Phil. What if this scared him off? Truth is Nikki was searching her heart for the courage to love him. She didn't want to ruin the opportunity by having him think she couldn't get rid of her past.

"So, that's how it is? Well, fuck you then. I can't see'em I ain't doing shit for 'em."

Nikki laughed a hearty laugh.

Champ walked away.

Nikki was about to close the front door when she saw Phil's car pull up. He smiled and got out.

He saw Champ, but was not threatened at all.

"Nicole are you ready to go?"

She was tipping down the hall. Careful again not to run her stockings.

Phil saw a mass of hair and a fuschia skirt.

"I'll be right there. Justin's crying."

He followed her. She was in her room with one knee on the bed and one foot on the floor.

"Nicole?" Phil could hardly believe his eyes. She was beautiful. If he didn't' know any better he'd say a goddess.

"Ssh. I don't want him to wake up 'til we are ready to walk out the door." She stood completely up to find the most striking man she'd ever seen standing before her. The kind of man that remained in dreams, yes him and his pulse were standing in her bedroom. Her inhale was far from discreet. She had to catch her breath. Phillip was taking it away.

"Well, Mr. Bordeaux you look very…I mean very handsome."

"You look rather tasty yourself." He licked his lips to further emphasize his expression.

"You like?" She posed quickly.

"I love." Phil was honest. This was the first time he'd seen Nikki put an effort into being beautiful. He didn't know she could look any better.

Johnathan came to the door.

"Hi Phil."

"Hey man. You ready to go."

John nodded yes.

"Go get your brother then."

"Let's go."

Johnny ran out.

At first Nikki wanted to tell Phil about Champ's visit, but decided not to. It was his day.

Mr. Bordeaux opened the door.

"Hi son. Hello Ms." He kissed Nikki's cheek.

"Hello Mr. Bordeaux." She exchanged.

"And who are these little soldiers?" Mr. B asked.

"That's Joshua and that's Justin. You know me. I went on your boat." Johnathan pointed to his brothers.

"Come on in Joshua and Justin." Mr. B stepped back.

Nikki was impressed. This was a gorgeous house. An entire wall of the living room was mirrored. The furniture was antique and ivory in color. The kitchen was humongous and filled with people.

Johnathan was right on Phil's heels as he entered the kitchen.

Everyone greeted Phil and because he was there Johnathan too.

Questions filled the room in all types of tones from slang to proper southern drawls in every dialect known to Nikki.

"Hey Phil." "Boy look how you growed." "Come here let me see that baby."

"Who's baby is 'dis?" "This the young lady you's sweet on?"

They seemed to all be talking at the same time. The questions sounded like run together sentences. Phillip laughed at them. His family was quite a bunch. He hoped Nikki understood, they sucked their teeth at the table, licked their fingers, said exactly what they were thinking, before thinking it through sometimes. Some of them acted stuck up and like the more grounded ones were embarrassing them. Phil loved them all. Being an only child he appreciated all types of people; enjoyed the exchange.

"This is Nicole…Nicole this is my family." It was too many to go one by one. He'd do that later.

"Hello Nicole." They sang in the unharmonized tradition of "Happy Birthday" at a child's birthday party.

"Hello Family." Nikki smiled genuinely. She liked them already. Their love warmed her family oriented spirit.

"Where's the birthday girl?" Phil asked.

"Out back. You know, at the grill."

Phil, Nikki and her children proceeded to the grill.

As soon as they walked out the patio door all hell broke lose in the kitchen. Those that knew Colleen knew she was going to give that poor girl grief.

Colleen noticed Nikki right away. She was very pleased. She understood why Phillip was smiling so, lately. Nicole was adorable with baby face innocence and the most beautiful smile. Colleen almost smiled her approval but she didn't like that little one on her son's hip. The closer they came to reaching her she was further struck by Nikki's beauty. So much so that she was willing to pardon the baby. That's when she noticed Johnathan and Joshua in their shadows.

She immediately made direct eye contact with Nicole. They spoke with their eyes the way women do. Phillip missed the whole line of communication between them.

It was understood by the time they stood face to face that Nicole's and Phillip's friendship was about to experience some difficulties. The smooth sailing was over. Here comes the storm. Nicole was finally, glad that she had suppressed her feelings for Phillip. She had weathered one major, hideous storm in her life and she wasn't tackling another one, even if it meant giving up his friendship.

Nicole, being a woman, understood this lady's concern. Collen thought her worth far less than her son deserved. Therefore, Nikki resolved to being polite, eating and leaving never to return. Mrs. Bordeaux had nothing to worry about. Nikki was through fighting for and with men.

"Mama this is Nicole Collier. My…"

"Friend. It's a pleasure to meet you Mrs. Bordeaux. These are *my* boys Johnathan, Joshua and Justin. Thanks for having us." Nikki interrupted. She withheld the hug that usually swelled within her when she meets new people. Especially people that belonged to people that she cared about.

The confirmation that she wasn't after Phil was accepted and appreciated. Colleen smiled. "Welcome, Nicole and her sons." She knelt down to make acquaintance of John and Joshua. Joshua grabbed her cheek, pinched it then stopped behind Phil.

"Hi. He's shy. That's Joshua. He don't talk to nobody 'cause our Daddy is mean."

Nicole was embarrassed. Phil was embarrassed for her, but he fixed it.

"He's just a quiet kind of guy. And you are a talker."

Colleen ignored the remark, but she heard it. She knew Phillip well enough to know he was trying to make up for Champ's meanness. She would be making sure that she needed him around there more to keep him from Nikki's boys.

They returned to the house. The evening moved pleasantly forward. Phil's family was a great bunch of people. Very entertaining too. Nikki was comfortable enough to take her shoes off, but she stayed on top of things by tending to her boys herself. Unlike around her family where she allowed them to take they're little troubles to Phillip too.

She stopped Johnny several times as he sought out Phillip to either tell on someone, complain or request something. Phillip noticed, but didn't say anything. He was too excited that his mother was behaving normal. He expected less hospitality from her.

She had even fixed Justin's bottle for Nikki and laid him down when he fell asleep. Phil had no idea that Nicole had assured her that she would never be apart of his life; which allowed Colleen to relax more than usual.

"Good night everyone." They were leaving. They had had a good time. Johnny more than anyone. He kissed and hugged everyone before they left.

At the door Colleen and Jimmy Bordeaux said their good-byes.

"Bye Grandpa B and Cozy." Johnathan laughed. He'd heard Mr. Bordeaux refer to Colleen that way all day long. (It was his pet name for her). He came up with Grandpa B on his own.

"See ya next time baby." Colleen smiled. She genuinely liked him. Her heartstring hadn't been pulled in a long time.

"Bye…Lil' man." Jimmy smiled too.

♣♣♣

The boys fell asleep on the way home.

"Nicole do you like'em?"

"Yes. They're sweet." Nikki had thought Black's family was the most loving group of people she'd met. Now she realized that real black, functional, families did exist. She was feeling real good.

"What about Mama? She liked you. Do you know she has never welcomed anyone I've brought home the way she welcomed you?"

Nikki wanted to tell him why, but didn't have the heart to hurt him.

"I like your mother too. Everyone was really nice."

Phillip sensed something different about Nicole, but couldn't put his finger on it. After helping her in he left. She indicated that she was going straight to bed. He caught the hint. Didn't want to leave, but knew he had to.

At home he realized that he was tired of going home every night. Colleen's acceptance of Nicole had given him courage to present himself to Nicole in a romantic way. It was time for him to wake her from her dream of a man and give her one. If Colleen liked her it was time to move…if that wasn't a sign there would never be one. For Phillip that was a green light and he was going for it.

39

Black's supervisor tapped him on the shoulder. "Andre there's a phone call for you in my office, it's urgent."

Black became unsettled as he rushed to take the call. His supervisor stood by his side not to be nosy, but to be of support if necessary. Black didn't get too many personal calls.

"My wife is in labor…it's too soon." Black explained over his shoulder as he trotted out of the door. He cursed himself for not stopping for gas this morning. He'd drive as far as he could then run the rest if it came to that. Black didn't know if baby's born at seven months survived or not, but his had to. Suddenly this fetus became a person in his mind.

Black ended his prayer without Amen. He focused back on the road. A minute later he was at the hospital.

He walked into the hospital frantically.

"I'm looking for Maya Singleton. I'm her husband Andre Singleton."

"When was she admitted?"

"I don't know. She's having a baby and she was brought here from work."

"Ok." The nurse punched some keys on the computer and was about to respond when Black spotted Uncle Bo. He walked away from the nurse's station without a thank you.

"Uncle Bo?!"

Bo turned towards him. "Man I told Lil you'd probably be over here. They just brought Feather in from work. Her water broke and she started full-fledged labor. She's in delivery now. Lil's with her, this way...hurry."

Black was already running away.

Uncle Bo was waiting on Pat, Big Mama and Tee. He had called Phillip and Nikki too. Phil said they were coming if they could get a sitter if not at least Nikki would be there.

Pat and family walked in. Carl was there too. Phil and Nikki both walked in right after them. The Bordeaux's kept the boys. Nikki wasn't even hesitant about Colleen keeping her children she knew she didn't like her, but trusted she wouldn't hurt her kids. Plus Mr. Bordeaux was there and he was very loving. Nikki needed to be there for her sister. After Uncle Bo explained what he knew so far every female in the room started to cry. Big Mama was trying to hold it together, but her pain was felt too. All they could do was wait. And pray.

The tears in Black's eyes matched those in Lillian's. Feather was crying too—she was afraid, if Black was crying something must be wrong.

Feather sat up one more time. This was the final push. There was silence in the room. Everyone was looking down at her bottom area, waiting on the baby's wail. It never came. The baby plopped out silent. The doctor handed the baby to another doctor who weighed and measured, then placed it in an incubator.

♣♣♣

"It's a girl." The first doctor announced. She's too early so we can't allow you to handle her. As soon as we get you cleaned and settled we'll let you see her. She's fine."

It seemed like forever before the Pediatrician rolled the little incubator over to them. Feather cried some more, out of fresh fear. Mikal was so tiny she didn't look healthy like other baby's. Yet, she was perfect. She looked just like Black. Every little feature looked like it would develop into the same ones he possessed.

Feather and Black looked at each other and were as proud as proud could be. Everything perfect about them had united and lay before them in their beautiful daughter.

Lillian looked at her and thought *Thank you God*. She walked out after kissing Black and Feather, she wanted to kiss the baby but the nurse was taking her away.

"Black she's so little."

"I know baby. She's early and you're no giant."

"I know, but 3lbs 7ozs. They're not going to let her go home."

"Babe…just think how little she would've been if you hadn't been a pig." He smiled. "Let's just be thankful she's alive. I was so scared. I was praying all the way here."

"Ok." Feather calmed down. She knew he was right. She started falling asleep while they were still talking. "Black please don't ask me to name my baby Maxine. I know you like girls with masculine names, but I don't like Maxine or Max…I don't like Samantha either. I know I agreed that you could name the girl, but that's because I thought it was a boy." She smiled weakly.

Black smiled too. "What do you want to name her?"

"How about Michael. We can spell it M-I-K-A-L so it will look cute, like for a girl...you can even call her Mikey...I think we'll both be happy with that."

"Whatever you want." Black was just glad his family was ok. It no longer mattered what they called her just so long as they had her.

Black could tell by Feather's mumble that she was going to sleep. He walked down to the nursery. On his way he felt good about his daughter. She had given him something that no one else could give him—security within his own skin. He had never admitted to having a complex about being dark. Sometimes, he was irritated when people said he was good-looking "to be dark". Looking at his child he knew she was going to be as dark as him. Mikal had shown him that black truly was beautiful.

♣♣♣

It's a girl. She's ok. She got some complications, but she looks like a fighter to me.

Relief brushed over everyone, but they knew not to relent with the praying.

Lillian was leaning into Bo as she shared the news of the new baby.

Together they walked to the nursery. Black was at the nursery window looking at the baby that looked just like him. Wondering what life had in store for her and hoping it would be kind to her. Everyone saw him as he turned his eyes up towards the ceiling and said "Thanks Man."

No one let it carry any weight. They were silently thanking him too.

40

"Phil can you come over her after you get off from work?" Nikki was crying into the phone. She had had all she could take.

The notice was on the door when she came home from work. She didn't think it was anything more than a rent increase, which she wasn't prepared to handle either.

Her check cleared on the 23rd of the month. It had already gone through once but it wasn't like she hadn't paid. When she called the property Management Company they explained that she had been consistently late with the rent and that they were not going to renew her lease. It would expire in thirty days and she had exactly that to vacate the premises. She offered to sign a new contract with a much stiffer stipulation about paying late, but they refused to even consider the idea. Nikki humbled herself. She made an attempt to explain to the person that she was a single parent with three children and she was doing the best that she could, but if given the opportunity she would manage to do better. The response remained the same.

"Nicole what's wrong?" He was on the other side of town, but still Nicole knew he had raised his left eyebrow when he asked the question.

"I need to talk to you."

"Ok. I'm on my way now." Phillip hung up the phone and left his job.

Nicole answered the door with tears in her eyes.

"What's wrong Nicole?" He picked her chin up and wiped her tears.

She handed him the eviction notice.

He smiled. "Babe, this is not so bad. You can just stay with me."

"I can't come stay with you. You only have two bedrooms and one you said is full of weights."

"I can put the weights in my parent's garage or storage or something, but that's not a problem. We'll turn that room into the boy's room. We can even get a bed in there for Justin. He's too big for that crib now."

Nikki was touched by his gesture, in her heart she knew she could never do that. (Putting the weights in Colleen's garage brought her back to reality.)

"Thank you for making me realize that it's not that bad. I feel a little better. I need to start looking for a place it's as simple as that."

Phillip was saddened by the slight rejection, but proud of the fact that she considered him enough of a friend to turn to in need.

"Relax. It's going to be ok. Plus you're moving from this place and Champ's memory. Good things come from change." He smiled. "Pizza, on me."

Nikki was grateful to have Phillip in her life.

"Did I do that?"

"What?"

"Put that smile on your face?" Phillip raised his brow.

"Yes." Nikki blushed. She was painfully aware at that moment that she was in love with Phillip. No matter how she tried to deny it.

Nikki wanted to love him. She wanted to love him the way she had loved Champ. With hot meals and backrubs. She wanted to bathe him.

"Are you going to call in the pizza or do you want me to?" She asked, breaking her own concentration, hoping to ground herself in the security of their friendship.

"You call it in. I'll pick it up." He walked into the kitchen. Looking at her had given him an erection and he was embarrassed.

Nikki really felt better about her situation. Tomorrow she would get a newspaper and start looking for an apartment.

♣♣♣

The evening was long. The boys fell asleep about eleven, Nikki and Phillip stayed up talking until about three o'clock in the morning.

"Ok Mr. Philosopher why are you alone?"

"For the reasons I just told you. I am waiting for the right person."

"You're not assisting in any way?"

"Nope. Just waiting." Phillip wanted to say "on you" but didn't want to tamper with fate.

"What is your idea of a good woman?" Nikki was toying around with fate… knowing she was scared to death of being hurt. Waiting on Phillip to answer she began entertaining sinful thoughts featuring Mr. Phillip Bordeaux.

"A woman that knows how to treat a man. I'm the kind of man that likes to come home from a hard day's work and watch the kids fight over who gets to pull off my boots. I want home-cooked meals and an annual Fourth of July BBQ. Robbing Peter to pay Paul. Using income tax returns to take local vacations. Saving all my life for a boat cruise that I don't get to take until all the kids are grown and gone. I'm a simple man. You know anyone like that?" Phil knew he had described Nikki down to her core. He was hoping she knew it too. In his opinion they were made for each other.

"And if I tell you I did know someone like that would you like to meet her?"

Nikki's expression couldn't be read. Phillip didn't know if she were flirting or serious or joking or what. He was hesitant, but he answered honestly. "...Yes."

Nikki extended her hand. "I am Nicole Collier and you are?"

"Phillip Bordeaux" Phil didn't know what to make of what had just happened. He was hoping she was saying what he was saying but he wasn't sure. In his mind he wanted to kiss her and so he leaned over and looked deep into her eyes and asked, "Are you the girl of my dreams?"

Instead of answering she placed her lips on his and allowed him to quench her thirst for hands on loving.

Her breasts were as soft as cotton candy. Phillip could feel her melting within his touch. He knew from the bottom of his heart that she had been loving him as long as he had been loving her. She confirmed by unzipping his pants.

Phillip obliged Nikki's request to wear a condom.

His expression of love for her was delicate and sincere. He truly had a way with her body. He traveled along its paths as though he'd traveled them before. (In his mind he had) He hit all the right spots. Stroked all the secret places, found the hidden treasure and handled it like it was the priceless possession of a royal man.

That morning Nikki woke feeling like a woman. Champ had never made her feel like this. She reached over to Phil and pinched him.

He turned over. "What's up?"

"I wanted to make sure I wasn't dreaming?"

"So you pinched me?"

"Yeah…I hate to be pinched. So I figured if you woke up it wouldn't be a dream."

"So are you still going to look for an apartment? Or are you gonna come with me?"

"I don't know?" Nikki looked so adorable to him he had to smile.

"You can decide later. Just promise me you will at least consider it."

Nikki wanted to pack right then, but she didn't feel it was appropriate. Maybe she should play a little hard to get. Then she remembered her dream. With her dream lover she played no games and neither did he.

"Babe, I know how you got the boys…you're a hell of a woman."

"Oh yeah? Well, you ain't seen nothing yet." Nikki's expression informed him that she too was shocked at her response. They laughed.

"Nikki you can ask me?"

"I don't want to know anything."

"You don't want to know how I knew exactly what to do to please you?"

Nikki blushed. That had run across her mind during lovemaking.

"I have been making love to you for a long time. In my mind." He raised his one eyebrow.

Nikki felt herself get moist. She got up. She decided to move in with Phillip, but she wasn't going to move until her thirty days were up; mainly because of the way the lady at the property management had spoken to her.

She thought briefly of Colleen's reaction, then shook it off.

41

Phil rose. "Babe I'm going to run by my place to get some clothes. You need anything while I'm out?"

"Like what?"

"Like something for breakfast…Never mind. I should have known you were still floating."

Nikki tossed a pillow at him. "Ok Romeo it wasn't that good."

"Yeah right." Phillip stopped at the crib and got Justin. He was awake and standing there like he wanted out. He laid him in the bed with Nicole. "Ok. Babe. I'll be right back."

Nikki watched him walk away in his drawers. It was the first time she noticed how nice his body was. She lay there in love and playing with her son.

Phillip came back with a list of things he knew she needed for breakfast. "Do you need anything else?"

"No." Nikki smiled.

He bent over to kiss her.

"No…I haven't brushed."

"Me neither." He kissed her anyway. "And him either…" He touched Justin's nose as he smiled into his face.

After he left. Nikki grabbed the phone and called Feather.

"Hey girl, what you doing?"

Feather was in a joyous mood herself. This was the first night that she slept the whole night through. Today Mikal came home. Leaving her baby for the past fifteen weeks was much harder than delivering her. Feather's heart had been heavy everyday that she went to see her. No matter how long she stayed it was never enough time. There were days that she cried the whole while she was there. She longed to touch her skin. She longed to pull her through the incubator. She was ready to start being a Mommy. The time was finally here.

"I'm getting ready to go pick up my baby. You know she comes home today." Feather beamed.

"Yes, we'll be over later after y'all get settled, but guess what I did?"

"You didn't??" Feather sat up in a more comfortable position. Black shifted his position too.

"Yes, I did it with Phillip."

"How did you get there??!!...*'I don't....'I can't'*" Feather teased.

"Well, first of all I got evicted."

"What?"

"They said I was consistently late so I had to go. Anyway, I was upset so I called Phillip, he came over, we talked about it and then he opened his home to me and my children. After we put the kids to bed we started talking like we normally do and the conversation became about love. At some point during the conversation I realized I loved him... and well, he shared his love for me too...Next thing I know he was laying next to me and it was morning."

"So how do you feel? I ain't gone ask you how it was, but you know I wanna know."

They laughed.

"I feel great. And it was great." Nikki laughed some more.

"I am so happy for you. Well, are you moving in with him?"

"Hell yeah. I haven't told him yet. I need to get it right in my mind. His mother is a trip. I told you how she acted when I met her. I know she don't like me. I'm trying to get it in my mind that I deserve this love. I deserve some happiness and I can't let Mrs. Bordeaux or anyone else cheat me out of this."

"That's right. You need to do what's best for you and your children. You're not going to find another man like him. Phillip is like Black. Someone raised them to be men. Girl you betta go for it. It's a lot of males out there, but not a lot of men."

"I know. I just get so tired of fighting. Now I gotta fight his Mama for him."

"Nikki you are crazy." Feather smiled. "Just think about all that you went through with Champ…and kicking Mrs. Bordeaux's butt will be easy."

"I know…you know the best part about leaving him alone? Girl when I got my check up after Justin and didn't have to worry about pregnancy or infections. I hadn't got a normal Pap smear result since I'd met him." Nikki laughed. (Big Mama ran across her mind. She was right. It wouldn't always hurt.).

Feather laughed too. She was so happy she didn't know what to do. She was looking forward to seeing them tonight as a family finally.

Nikki was hopeful that she had finally reached the top of Life's circle; surely she had already been on the bottom.

Black turned over. Feather told him about Nikki and Phillip. "Babe guess who done hooked up?"

"Nikki and Phil." He rolled over again. "It's about time."

"He already knew?" Nikki asked overhearing Black's comment.

"Uh-huh..."

"Well, let me get up and get dressed. When he get back I don't wanna be lying in the same spot, he already think he done something."

"Ok. I'll see y'all tonight."

Phillip returned with the groceries. Nikki cooked breakfast in her pajamas and Phil straightened up the house.

He had the boys attempt to make their beds. And when it was time to eat he held only one of Justin's fingers as Justin walked into the kitchen. He was Justin's father. He was the only man he'd known. Nikki had never felt more at home in her home before.

♣♣♣

Mikal came home to a room full of helium balloons and a family she didn't even know she had.

Everyone noticed the love between Nikki and Phillip. They were a couple without making the announcement. The toast to Mikey's homecoming warranted a kiss, and Phillip kissed Nikki naturally, like he had been doing it all his life. Johnathan noticed and was pleased too. He had decided to call Phillip "Daddy" the next time he addressed him, he had come to trust and love him.

Big Mama smiled when she saw his little eyes fill with hope. He was the one tugging on her heartstring now. She planned to do for him what she had done for Black.

Watching Feather and Black standing dead center of their joy, watching Nikki reach for hers made Lillian painfully aware that she could have the same light shining from her. She too could blind people with her light of happiness if only she'd let go and let it happen. Bo loved her the way these young men loved their women. The young women loved them in return. Why couldn't she? What made Lillian think that if she reached for his love he was going to snatch it back?

Throughout the room growth was occurring. Revelations were being made. People were giving in to life and all that it has to offer.

As the guest left Black and Feather began living life as a family. Neither knew how truly good the other was feeling. There were no words to describe it.

Life was busy for the next couple of weeks.

Nikki and Phillip were preparing for the move, struggling to keep their hands off each other in front of the children and getting to know each other. Phillip shared with her his desire to have a child.

"Just one baby... I know you're through. I know..., but I just want one."

"Maybe when Justin's in school. I want to do it right if I must do it again." Nikki was being honest, but the absolute truth is she didn't want to do it again at all.

The thirty days were up.

Black was helping Phillip move. Big Mama was keeping all the babies while they moved, including Mikey.

Feather and Nikki went over and decided where to put things. Nikki sold most of Grandma's stuff and used the money to buy a new bedroom set for her sons. She bought two bunk beds and all the boyish decorations.

Phillip's place was scarcely furnished so she bought things to enhance it. A new entertainment center, a second VCR, sets of curtains and throw rugs, bathroom decorations for the main bathroom. She bought towels and stuff. By the time the night ended it looked like they had been living together for years.

Black and Feather went home and made love after putting Mikey to sleep.

Phillip and Nikki did the same thing only they had Justin. When Phillip went to get the boys Big Mama offered to keep them, but Justin wouldn't stay. Naturally Phillip took him home with him.

"I should call you sunshine." Phillip smiled.

"Why?"

"Look how you came in here and added color and radiance to this drabby old place."

"It was easy. You have nice things to work with." Nikki looked into his face. He was sitting on the couch with Justin sleeping on him. "Phil, is this real? Am I really who you want?"

"Yes. You're who I've been looking for. I love you, Nicole."

"I love you too."

They put Justin in his new room and made love briefly. They were tired when they started so after relieving each other they fell straight to sleep. When Justin woke during the night in the strange room, in the strange bed, Phil went and got him and laid him next to his Mama; who never even heard him crying. As they slept Phil watched his family and felt complete.

The next morning he got up and loaded his trunk with the weights. Everything looked so nice yet they cluttered the kitchen.

"Hey Mama. I need to put my weights in your garage for a while."

"Alright baby. You ain't working out no more?"

"Yes…I'll be doing it from here now. I need the room—Nikki's staying with me now."

"With you now?" Colleen was pissed. "With me. She's my woman."

"Your what?" Colleen couldn't take anymore, *next he'll be saying she pregnant.* "Woman my ass. She got all them damn babies and she's using you to take care of them. She's your pimp!! Next she'll be pregnant."

Phillip was confused. Colleen had acted like she liked Nikki, now she was showing her true colors. This time he didn't care. Too many times he'd concerned himself with his mother's opinion. He was a man; it was time for her to respect that. "And if she were pregnant I'd be glad."

Colleen's mouth flew open.

Phillip had never defended himself against her. "Mama Nikki is not like that. She loves me."

"You got it all wrong!! You the one loving, if there's any loving going on."

"Can I store my weights in your garage or not?"

"I don't care." Colleen walked away.

Before leaving Phil stopped by the kitchen and kissed her cheek anyway. It was hard, but she was his mother and he respected her.

Upon returning home Phil's joy was restored. Nikki cooked neckbones, cabbage, hotwater cornbread and corn on the cob. She fixed his plate and made sure the kids were quiet. It was like she knew he had been through something despite the fact that he didn't mention it.

Living together was a fairytale that came true.

Phil helped with the chores, the kids and the finances. They discussed finances a week after settling down.

Big Mama was figured into the budget as #1. Nikki was responsible for daycare—Big Mama was to receive $650 a month. Nikki took care of utilities and insurances. Phillip took care of the rent and the groceries. Each was responsible for depositing at least $100 a month into the joint savings. The other money was theirs to do whatever. It was a plan.

In two months Nikki had $400 saved and everyone had new clothes.

"Nikki, we need two cars."

"I know I'm saving for my own now."

"Ok. I was thinking we'd get a utility vehicle. The kids are getting big."

"I don't want to drive a SUV everyday."

"Then you drive the Jetta and I'll drive the SUV."

Nikki could not say 'no' to him. Sitting there his eyebrow raised and so damn fine. "Ok baby." She smiled.

There was easiness about their love for one another that both of them appreciated.

Nikki cleaned the kitchen loving her man. The house was full of noises that a family make and she was pleased to hear its' music.

♣♣♣

Colleen had been mad since Phillip left her house. She had to let Nikki know. Just had to.

"Hello?" Nikki answered.

"You think you slick. Enjoy your visit 'cause you ain't staying." Colleen angrily pushed the words through the phone.

"Mrs. Bordeaux. I know I assured you that we were just friends, I didn't lie to you…we were then, but I love Phillip."

"Girl please." Colleen hung up.

Nikki stood there with the receiver in her hand wondering how she was going to deal with this.

42

"Shugah you know I really like that Phil. Have you ever checked out how he handles Nikki's kids?"

"Yeah I think it's sweet."

"I was looking at her and I saw you."

"You saw me?"

"Yeah. When we first met her she was in a bad way. She got out of that then stepped into something good. All year long she was hollering "Just my friend" and you could look at either of them and see the love."

"Uh-huh." Lillian knew where he was going.

"I wonder how much longer before you step into something good. I'm a good man Lillian. I ain't gonna hurt you. I realize you're the kind of woman that needs a man to herself. I am that man. I wasn't always, but I am now."

"I'll step soon. You wanna watch a movie or something?"

"I want an answer."

"I said soon."

"I want an answer I'm tired of waiting. I am this man whether I'm with you or not. I can go be true to someone else. There are a lot of women looking for a good man. I chose you, but Shugah you making me feel like I'm not what you want. I keep telling you I want you. I need to know if you want me?"

Lillian wanted him. She loved him.

"Yes I want you."

"Then marry me and let's go on with the loving."

"I can't. I need more time."

"You got it." Bo stood.

Pride, pain, embarrassment and fear kept Lillian from crying out. She watched him walk out the door.

Bo was hurt. He was also determined to move on with his life. He had been fooling around with Lillian for close to five years. Hell, Joshua was starting school this fall and when he met Lillian, he wasn't even born.

43

Big Mama knew something was wrong when neither Bo nor Lillian came to Christmas dinner. Lillian sent her gifts by Feather and Black, and Bo dropped his the week before. Everyone noticed their absence, but since they were both absent assumed they were together. Big Mama knew different.

Mikey was the cutest thing. She was frilled down in her little dress, looking just like her Daddy. They all wore the same color coordination. The evening was uneventful and laid back unusually quite for their family.

Underneath the silence all kinds of things were going on.

Johnathan had finally asked Phillip if he could call him Daddy. Phil answered "of course" with sincerity.

Black and Feather were buying a SUV also, a present for one another.

Big Mama was thinking about opening a daycare.

Tee was thinking about moving in with Carl.

Carl wanted to get married.

Joshua was talking up a storm.

Colleen was at home pissed because Phillip wasn't home for the holidays. The same crowd was there so the house was full, but she missed her baby. For that she disliked Nikki more.

Bo was home alone chilling and watching TV.

Lillian was home alone crying and wanting him.

♣♣♣

He opened the door.

"Merry Christmas."

"Merry Christmas."

She stepped in. "I brought some mistletoe. May I have a kiss?"

Bo kissed her. They made love right there on the floor in front of the front door.

Nothing had changed. She loved him and he her. She was still scared and he was still tired of waiting.

"Bo, I love you. I really do. I just don't have the courage to love you right."

"So, are you ending it?"

"No. I'm scared."

"Lillian were you beaten?"

"No."

"Cheated on?"

"Not that I know of."

"Then just what type of scarring do you have?"

"I was deceived. I thought Michael loved me. I changed myself to suit his needs. I became the woman he wanted me to be and he still was unhappy. I did everything that he asked of me. Everything and still he was unhappy."

"You were not deceived. You were foolish. You shouldn't have done all that. If Michael married you one person, then that's whom he wanted. Not who you became."

"I know now..., but I am a changing person. We all are and if I change on you then what?"

"Then you changed. I am not leaving. I'm loving you now and you're changing. I love you Lil."

"Bo, I'm scared. It seems like nothing is ever going to be right. Just when I think it is, something happens."

"You know what. I used to think life could be perfect too. If I was with a woman and she gained a little weight I was outta there. If her kids suddenly became unruly I was outta there. If things were not perfect I was outta there. Then one day Mama pulled me aside and told me that I was living in a world full of shit and it don't make no sense for me to try to stay clean 'cause if shits all around you, it's gon' get on you. This world ain't perfect. The only thing perfect in it is us."

Lillian cried some more then she offered herself to Bo. As he accepted her loving he granted her the time she needed. Lillian was the woman he had grown up to love.

44

Bills filled the mailboxes, kids had homework, days were too short to meet all of its' demands, loving was scheduled and work was hard.

Phillip sat on the bed. He swallowed hard. This thing with Nikki had rocked him harder than he cared to be rocked. He was proud she was standing up for herself. What he didn't like was the inconvenient timing. Nor how it was affecting him. When she should have been standing up to Champ she was sitting there letting him walk all over her. Now she wanted to stand up to him. He wanted to support her decision but he couldn't. It hurt too much to keep dealing with it so he decided to let it go.

"Babe you hungry?" Nikki asked from the kitchen. She was fixing plates.

Phillip stood in the doorway. She was beautiful. He could see his gift of happiness all over her face. He knew he made her happy. His love was good for her as hers was for him.

"Naw." He walked away. Phil was weak for her and it was killing him. He was willing to give up his desire to accommodate hers.

The house was silent. The kids were aware of the tension and were on their best behavior. Johnathan wondered if things were going to end up like when they lived with Champ.

That night Nikki lay on her side, Phillip on his, careful not to touch one another.

"Phil, I'm sorry…Maybe we can try again later. It's just too soon for me." She was letting her tears flow. Her leg brushed his. She really did want to make him happy, but she couldn't keep going through the same thing over and over again.

"Nikki, you full of shit!!" Phillip was low and forceful in his response. He didn't want to wake the kids. "Everything is about you, I had to wait a year to touch you…You weren't ready. Now I have to sit back and let you abort my baby. You messed off your beginning, now you wanna deny me mine. I shouldn't have ever loved you." He didn't mean that last part. He couldn't have *not loved* her if he tried. He said it to hurt her. She needed to feel his pain.

Nikki listened to his heart for she knew that's who was speaking to her. She was crying now. Phillip was a natural father. The kind of man she wanted her children to be born of. "How can you say I don't love you?"

"If you cared Nicole you'd have my baby. I could see you being scared, feeling like you drowning, but I'm not that man. I'm not the one that dogged you. Love me like I love you. You loving me like you should've loved Champ. How you have three babies for a man who don't give a shit about you or them and then deny the man that would die for either of you his child? How?" Tears rattled in his throat. The pain in his voice was no comparison to what showed on his face.

Nikki couldn't take it. She walked out of their room and into the bathroom. She threw up. She wasn't ready to spit shine her heart and give it away. She had given enough. He was asking for all of her. She loved him, made him aware of it, now he wanted her to prove that love.

Phil sat up while she was in the bathroom. He was emotionally exhausted. Then there was Justin easing from his room to theirs. Phil picked him up without hesitation. Justin's urine wet his arm as he did so. Phil didn't get angry. He held him away from himself and started towards the main bathroom.

"You know what son, you need to tell me when you have to go to the bathroom. You're too big to be going on yourself. Ok?"

"Ok Daddy." Justin tilted his head apologetically.

Nikki walked out of their bathroom to intake the whole scene. Silently she watched Phil prepare to clean him up. Justin slept with them that night. The conversation ended due to his presence. Nikki lay on her side with her eyes shut, but awake. Phil lay on his side the same way.

Some days Nikki would forget she was even pregnant until she looked at Phil. He was still hurting. Her appointment couldn't come fast enough. The doctor said she must be eight weeks before they could perform the surgery. (Two weeks to go).

"Mama where's Daddy?"

"In the back why?"

"Can we have company?"

Nikki was about to say she didn't care when Phil responded.

"If it's Brian tell him to go home and get your game cartridge first. I told you about trading and not getting your stuff back. After that yes."

Nikki walked away feeling bad. She loved the father he was. She loved the way he did just about everything, except desire this baby.

45

Lillian wanted to let go of her fears and love Bo, especially since he was no longer pressuring her to marry him.

She agreed to find a lot and begin building their lover's nest because she didn't want to lose him.

Almost daily an acceptable piece of land for sale came across her desk. Never did she mention them to Bo and if he asked she lied. 'I haven't seen anything I like yet."

He smiled excited that she was looking.

Although, Lil was preoccupied with her dilemma no one saw the strain on the love they had for each other. The teasing of them getting married was still being done, but less. Big Mama knew they would find their way to the altar. Her concentrating and prayers were on Pat and Tee.

Tee and Carl's relationship had developed over night. They were as loving as an old married couple. Big Mama didn't see Tee staying around the house much longer. She was twenty-two now and obviously a woman. She fixed Carl's plate, called him Baby, and stroked him lovingly as the rest of the women.

Pat was dating someone new also. He was the most promising date she had, but Big Mama didn't like him. There was something about him that made her uncomfortable. She hadn't yet put her finger on it.

Mikey must have known it was her birthday. She whined all day. No one other than Black could touch her. Not even Big Mama who kept her little butt everyday. Now that

Johnny and Joshua were both in school and Justin was potty trained, at least during the day; he wet the bed at night. Big Mama only had him and Mikey so they were usually fighting for her attention. Today Mikey wanted her daddy and that's it.

Mikey was the physical size of a six-month-old infant at one-year-old. She was trying to walk a little and it was the strangest sight, her being so tiny. Black and Feather were proud. Their lives were good. Black had just bought a Chevy Denali. They were moving to Hayward in a month or so and saving to buy a home. Nothing had changed between them since the wedding.

Nikki watched Phillip watch Mikey all night and wondered what was going through his mind. She knew him well enough to know that the sight of that baby was probably making him hopeful that she'd change her mind, and it was killing her to know she wasn't. It was days like this that made her hate Champ more. If he had not mistreated her, she would not be too scared to love the man that loves her. Phillip was her dream lover, yet she couldn't love him with the strength he deserved. He deserved uninhibited love. He deserved her best. Champ had stolen that from her. The little bit of unconditional love remaining she was protecting. Her heart began to break for him so she looked away.

Phillip knew she was watching. He tried to remain composed. It was not his intention to persuade her to change her mind about keeping the baby; he was trying to understand how she could give up something as adorable as Mikey.

No one knew they were going through something. With the boys now calling Phillip 'Daddy' the illusion of happy family was more vivid than ever.

After the party Feather whispered into Black's ear "Y'all look so cute."

Mikey lay on his chest falling asleep.

Feather smiled, the cute part was that Mikey wasn't the only one asleep. Black was falling himself and when he realized he was sleep he woke up and looked around to see if Feather was watching. Each time she smiled.

"Forget you Feather, I'm tired. This girl done wore me out."

"Do you think Mikey's ever going to catch up to her age?"

"Yes. What if she grow up to be big like Big Mama?"

"That would look crazy especially with me being her mother."

Feather picked her up off of him. "I'm going to put her to bed. You go to."

Black smiled as she walked away. She had kept enough weight from Mikey's pregnancy to get him aroused as she walked. She was much curvier and thicker. Black liked it. It was just enough.

This night like plenty others Black and Feather went to bed and straight to sleep. Lovemaking was still there, but Mikal was their everything.

46

Three days later the tension in Nikki and Phillip's home began to thaw. Nikki was not going to change her mind. Phillip accepted the decision. He had no choice. The one thing he made perfectly clear was that he *accepted* the decision, not supported it so he would not be going with her or picking her up.

"Ok." Nikki left the room just in case he wanted to talk about it. She didn't want to talk about it. It was time for things to get back to normal.

"Mama can I go outside?"

"For an hour."

"Mama, I'm just out front."

"Johnny I said an hour, don't waste it in here."

Phil came into the living room.

Nikki had just sat down. She was going to watch TV with Joshua. He was lying on the floor watching cartoons.

"Nicole, I'm going by my Dad's I'll be home for dinner. I'll take Justin with me."

"Ok." Nikki nodded. It was hard making eye contact now. Hard to look into each other's face and see the other's pain.

Joshua looked up into Phil's face.

"You wanna go too?" Phil recognized that look.

Joshua jumped up in answer to the question.

"Well, I'm taking Johnny too, might as well take'em all. We'll be back."

"Be careful."

Soon as they walked out Nikki called Feather.

"Hey girl, what you doing?"

"Nothing. 'Bout to cook. I get so tired of cooking everyday, but I hate for my baby to eat junk."

"Me too and I gotta cook for an army."

Feather sensed that something was wrong.

"What's wrong Nikk?"

"What's always wrong?"

"Are you sure?"

"Yes. I'm not keeping it though. I already told Phillip. He's having a hard time with my decision. I was calling to see if you would go with me. He won't."

"Yes. Let me know when."

"On the 22nd at 8:45 am."

"Ok. Are you ok?"

"Yeah...I'm ok." Her voice started to fail.

Part of Feather was disappointed. The other part was sad for Phil. The part that was left understood that they probably didn't need a baby first dash out the box.

"Oh Nikki you're going to be ok."

"He wants this baby. Girl we had an argument about it. He said I shouldn't even be tripping. If I had three babies for Champ having one for him should be easy."

Feather agreed.

"I can't make him understand that I'm scared. What if he don't really love me? What if we don't make it? When do I get my turn? I just wanna be loved." Nikki's tears were falling, "but in order for him to love me I have to have his child to prove I love him. Why can't he just love me anyway? I am tired of proving my love to someone else. How come he can't prove his love to me first?" Nikki was crying more.

Feather agreed with her too.

"Do you love him Nikki?"

"Yes."

"If there was no past and this was your start would you keep his child?"

"Yes."

"Why not now?"

"'Cause I'm scared…I'm afraid of waking up one morning four babies in the hole and alone. Daddy's can go…Phil can go…Mama's can't. I'm a Mama Feather, 'cause in reality it's all on me." Nikki was crying harder.

"I know baby—but not all Daddy's leave. I think Phillip is in for the long haul, what do you think?"

"I can't think Feather, I need to know. You know what makes me doubtful? I finally started to look at life through my eyes instead of my heart. I'm concerned because Phil has not asked me to marry him. He asked me to live with him. I got pregnant and he asked me to have his baby. The only thing he has not asked me is to spend the rest of my life with him. Yeah he's a good man and all, but I have my concerns. I gotta think about what's best for me too. I don't need another baby daddy—I need a husband, some stability for the kids I have. A partner for life, hell a commitment, Phil hasn't mentioned that!"

Feather had not looked at it that way. She had to admit that Nikki's point was valid.

"Do you think if you told him how you feel he'd marry you?"

"Oh yes, but I don't want to get married to keep a baby or prove a point or to satisfy myself. I want him to *want* to marry me too. I mean actually want to grow old with me. Watch my hair turn gray, watch me lose my rhythm, my teeth…all that."

Nikki smiled in spite of herself.

Feather thought back to her argument with Black about marriage that's exactly how she felt. Then she remembered his feelings.

"Maybe he's scared Nikk?"

"Ok. I'll give him that, but so am I. I'm supposed to swallow my fear, pick a name and push so he can feel better. I can't do that anymore. I'm tired of sacrificing." She was crying again.

The door opened and closed. She had no time to gain her composure.

The boys turned and went to their room like they had been instructed to go to bed.

Phil leaned into her and whispered in her free ear. "Are you ok?"

All she could do was nod.

"Feather, Phil just walked in so, I'll call you back. Kiss Mikey for me and tell my brother hello for us. And thank you."

"Ok. Tell everyone we said hello too. Talk to you later."

"Ok bye."

Phillip sat next to her.

"Babe, I talked to my Dad tonight about our situation and he had some interesting insight."

Nikki was slightly annoyed.

"When I got there I was a mess. I was hurt that you didn't want my baby, but my Dad made me see that it wasn't that you didn't want *my* baby you didn't want to repeat the same mistake."

Nikki was pleased. Her fondness of Mr. Bordeaux grew.

"He said that you had already been through a lot and you probably just wanted to relax in love before producing another member of the family. We talked about how I was feeling and my fears too. I know I might make this father thing look easy, but I'm scared all the time. Everyday I wonder if the day will come when the boys say to me 'You ain't my Daddy' Can I handle that? I confessed these and many more things to Pops. He diagnosed my problem to be love. He suggested that I come home, to my family, and make this thing work. So here I am."

Nikki started to cry again. Suddenly she felt real bad about her feelings on this pregnancy. Still she hadn't changed her mind.

"He told me to do whatever it took to make me happy. And I decided that I would be most happy if I could remain in your life forever…may I?"

He looked adorable. He was so damn fine. That eyebrow raised, head tilted, the pleading tint of sincerity in his stare and the slight quiver of fear on his lower lip.

Nikki wanted to get excited, but she was in shock. She didn't want to keep the baby still, but yes she wanted to be his wife.

"Nicole will you marry me?"

"Yes." She leaned into his arms and he held on as if to grab hold of the actual moment. Nicole was the happiest woman alive. Neither of them thought about the pregnancy for a moment.

First they called Feather and Black. Feather was ecstatic. Black was surprised and happy.

"Nikki, I'll call you later, my baby's crying. Congratulations girl. You too Phil."

The women hung up. Black talked to Phil a little more. Nikki went to help the boys get to bed too.

Phil told his Dad next.

"Daddy I asked her to marry me…she said yes."

"Did she change her mind about the baby?"

"I didn't bring that up. I don't want her to feel like it has anything to do with that. I love her even if we have to get through this without the baby. Next time we'll plan which is what she wants anyway. I still want the baby though."

"Well son give it some time. You wanna tell your mother or you want me to tell her?"

Phil didn't really feel like being bothered with his mother, but it was time he started standing up for his wife. That's what husbands do. "I can tell her. I'll stop by tomorrow."

"Alright. Let me talk to Nikki."

Nikki accepted the phone with a puzzled look.

"Hi baby. This is Grandpa B, congratulations. Welcome to the family."

"Thank you." Nikki was warmed over with love. She knew whom Phil had gotten his ways from.

"Well, I'm gonna let y'all get back to the kids."

"Thanks again. Bye-bye."

♣♣♣

After talking to Mr. Bordeaux Nikki lost some of the joy of becoming Mrs. Phillip Bordeaux because Colleen came to mind. Nikki understood her issues as a mother not wanting her only son to marry a woman with such responsibilities. It would be different if Nikki was a bad person, but she was not. Her decision to have three babies had no bearing on her ability to love Phillip. Nikki knew Colleen considered her worth far less than what Phillip deserved.

It took all of Nikki's reasoning to bring her to the logic that despite what Colleen thought she would make him a good wife…it's what she lived for. Some people were created to sing, write, draw—she was created to nurture and guide.

Phillip ate dinner tonight. He had not had a normal appetite since Nikki announced that she wasn't keeping the baby. He sat there thinking about telling his mother that they were getting married.

The scent of puppies tickled Nikki's nose.

"Are those my babies smelling like little puppies?" She stood in the doorway with her hands on her hips.

Johnny crept past her. He knew it was bath time.

"Don't make it too hot, Justin's getting in too."

Johnny was mad. He wanted to take a bath by himself sometimes.

Nikki knew his problems, but it was a weeknight they needed to get to bed. She needed to iron clothes for tomorrow, fix lunches and clean the kitchen. While Johnny and Justin bathed she cleaned the kitchen. Phil bathed Joshua while she prepared the lunches. Finally with all the boys in bed she began ironing. Phil showered and ran her a tub of bath water. After she was done she stepped into the tub.

He came into the bathroom.

"Hey Babe." Often he sat on the toilet and talked to her while she bathed.

"Hey." Nicole smiled.

"I can't believe we're getting married." He smiled. (Nikki's smile faded some) "Don't worry about Mom she'll get over it. You know my mother is really a good person. She will come around. It's not that she doesn't like you, it's that she feels she knows what's best for me. The problem is her desires for me are always socially correct. Our marriage is going to flaw her "family" portrait. She believes that every mantle should have a family portrait. Once she figures out what the word "family" means she'll be ok."

Nikki was touched by his consultation, however she didn't consider her children to be flaws of any kind. "Thank you, but I am not at all concerned about your mother's feelings for me. I hate that we can't be friends, but I ain't gonna lose any sleep over it."

Phillip was speechless, he also understood. He couldn't ask her to accept his mother if she wouldn't accept her. He leaned over the tub and kissed her forehead. "Babe I'm going to bed. It's my turn to take the boys."

Nikki may have been last to get to bed, but in the morning the men would be up and out of there while she slept. She smiled thinking about the weekend. They were going to buy Phil's SUV.

Entering the room Phil was already sleep. Nikki lay awake for hours watching him. Loving him. She smiled at remembering the days she didn't believe he existed. He didn't have a face then. He was just a prayer. Now he was soon to be her husband. And he was worth fighting Colleen to the death for.

♣♣♣

The SUV brought some temporary distraction to the home. Phil was like a kid with a new toy.

The excitement disappeared the morning of Nikki's appointment. Feather picked her up.

Phil took Mikey to Big Mama's too since he had to drop Joshua there anyway. Then took Johnny and Justin to school.

Feather was uncomfortable in his presence. She felt like she was stabbing him in the back. Before this moment she had not realized she was playing a role of any type, giving Nikki a ride. Her intention was to support Nikki that's it.

Phillip sensed Feather's fear. He walked over to her. After taking Mikey from her arms he kissed her cheek. "Sis, thank you for going with Nicole. I just couldn't do it."

"No problem."

There really were no hard feelings. He was sincere.

"Bye Nicole, see you this evening." Phillip did not make eye contact with her nor did he kiss her.

It stabbed her in the heart when he left without giving her a kiss, looking at her or willing her anything that resembled support. He stepped out the door, Mikey in his arms and the three others in tow. It did her no good to see him dressed in his fatherly manner on this morning.

"Are you ready."

"Yes."

They walked out shortly behind Phil and the kids.

Nikki was silent on the way there. Wondering if her and Phil's relationship could handle this dilemma.

They walked into the hospital. The waiting room was filled with young girls. Nikki felt stupid instantly. The names were being called one after another. The young women rose. Some excited to be there, some confused and some afraid.

Nikki remembered promising God that she would do the 'right' thing if he helped her out of her situation. She thought of Phil, his desire was haunting her.

"Nicole Collier."

"Nicole Collier."

Feather was tempted to nudge Nikki, but when she looked into her face she saw tears rolling down her cheeks.

"Nicole Collier." Nikki stood. Feather stood with her. Then Nikki turned and walked out of the hospital. Feather followed. There was relief exuding from both of them.

"Let's hope for a girl this time." Feather teased.

"It's a girl. I just kept a promise."

Phillip tried all day to dissolve his pain and was unsuccessful. By the time he and the boys arrived home he had a fully developed attitude. He was still marrying Nicole…still loved her, but oh was he hurt by her actions.

"Babe, I'm sorry I didn't cook…this pregnancy is making me so lazy. You're gonna have to really help out now."

Phil walked past her pretending not to see her sitting there. When the words registered he turned around…"You didn't do it?"

"No, I couldn't do it. I got to thinking about babies being gifts from God and thinking about you and all you've given me—and, well, I think I can push one last time, but I'm having my tubes tied, burnt, removed, severed, and buried." She smiled.

Phil smiled too.

"And one last thing." She was crying a little. "You can never leave even if you stop loving me you betta keep it a secret. You can never leave."

"I won't. I promise." He looked deep into her eyes.

"Thank you." He whispered.

The phone rang.

"Hello?" Johnathan answered.

"Hey boy where's yo' Daddy?"

"He here…Daddy."

"Hello?"

"Hey man. I heard you're gonna be a Daddy. Congratulations."

"Yeah…Again."

Black liked the fact that he still counted Johnny, Justin and Joshua as his. 'Again' was a good sign. Some people changed after their own babies came into the picture. Not Phillip. He was glad to be a father. Like Nikki it's what he was created to do.

"Man we need to celebrate."

"Aw…right. Saturday. Y'all working?"

"I don't know. I'll check with Nicole."

"Feather does until 2:30-3:00 o'clock I'm gonna have Mikey."

"I know if Nikki does, I'll have the boys until she gets home. Why don't y'all come over here after Nikki gets off? Tell Big Mama and everybody too."

"OK. Saturday."

They hung up without exchanging a farewell.

♣♣♣

Colleen was highly upset about the news. "A BABY??!! HAVE YOU LOST YOUR DAMN MIND??"

"No. I have chose a wi—"

Colleen cut him off. "Phillip, out of all the women in the WORLD you had to go out and find a pretty, stereotypical little conniving hussy and bring her home with three of some other man's kids in tow and you expect me to be happy? Oh, yeah you done lost all of your mind if you think I'm supporting some shit like that!"

Phillip opened his mouth to speak. Colleen raised her voice just enough to silence him.

"It's yo' life you can throw it away if you want to. Just don't think I'm standing here and watching you be a fool.

(She threatened.) I ain't biting my tongue and I ain't pretendin' like this is ok with me, 'cause it ain't and ain't never gon' be." Colleen stomped out of her kitchen into her bedroom. Slamming the door behind her. Phil never got a word in.

Phillip knew she wasn't going to be pleased, however he didn't expect her reaction. He left with a heavy heart. He was no longer sure that she would come around. He wanted her to, part of him needed her to she was his mother. The other part of him needed to love Nikki and her children. He needed the love Nikki gave, her way. Colleen could not give him that. It was time for Phillip to do what was best for Phillip.

From the porch he smelled food, distinctly, fried chicken. It was Nikki's day off so, he knew she was Suzy Homemaker today. The house was immaculate. The lights were out. The table was set to candlelight. She served fried chicken, scalloped potatoes and green beans. He had never known candlelight to be so casual, but when she sat down and Nikki rested her foot across his lap while they ate he loved her.

Nikki put her finger to her lips requesting his silence. Her hair was styled the way he liked it. And she wore only, a T-shirt and underwear.

He crept the rest of the way in closing the door gently behind him.

"I just put the boys to sleep."

It was amazing the peace he felt in her presence. No matter what his occurrences once he got to her he was all right.

Jimmy stomped into the bedroom.

"Where's Phillip, Colleen?"

"He left."

"I guess so. You know I was outback and I heard the way you spoke to him. You oughta be ashamed of yourself."

"Ashamed for what? I don't like her and I ain't never gonna like her."

"Well, that just shows how stupid you are. Babies ain't no reason to dislike someone. You so hung up on what people think you ain't thinking at all. That's stupid. If Phillip's happy you should be too. That girl ain't using him; ain't mistreating him. The only thing Nikki's doing is loving him. She's loving him a lot better than any of them other childless women he brought home."

"She ain't sincere. Hell I'd be nice too if I had three babies and no Daddy for them."

"You're so busy looking at her kids you haven't looked at your own."

"If you wanna deal with your daughter-in-law you can. I don't have to deal if I don't want to."

"So does this mean you gon' half-ass love the baby too. Loving just the half that's Phil's?"

"Jimmy I don't need this from you. I am a woman…I know when another woman is trying to get over and when she's not."

"Well, I'm a wise old man and I can spot a fool a million miles away."

This time, it was Colleen that was walked out on.

Jimmy knew he had set Colleen to thinking. Also that she was going to come around. He didn't know when because he had not seen her this angry before. When Colleen thought she was right about anything she wouldn't let go. And if she changed sides it was with such subtle grace that the transition was not noticed.

In bed that night Colleen was prepared to sleep on the edge, but Jimmy crawled in and pulled her into him as usual.

"You know I can't sleep unless you put all that butt on me." Jimmy was aware that regardless to whether they agreed he wasn't going anywhere. Nothing had changed between them; the changes were between her and Phillip.

♣♣♣

Phillip lay in Nikki's arms releasing his pain silently. Not mentioning his encounter with his mother at all. Nicole knew that he was going by there to tell her, so he simply informed Nikki that she knew. Nothing else was said.

Nikki lay in the comfort of his arms hoping that telling Colleen wasn't too hard on him. Like him she kept her conversation with Colleen a secret not wanting to hurt him. Justin slept in his on bed, but thoughts of Colleen slept with them in his absence.

Nikki and Phillip both stayed away from Colleen's house for the next couple of months.

Colleen had not seen her pregnant. Had not called to check on her. Had not asked about her. Mr. Bordeaux had come by the house sometimes. He spent time with the kids. He inquired about the wedding planning, talked to the baby via Nicole's stomach. He was a good father-in-law.

Nikki was seven months pregnant when the wedding took place.

Feather dressed Mikey, then dropped her off at Big Mama's. She and Big Mama had planned a reception for Nikki and Phillip at Big Mama's after the wedding. She lied and told Nikki that she made dinner reservations for afterwards, knowing that the entire family including some of Phillip's were gathering at Big Mama's in celebration of their union. Mr. Bordeaux was helping with that part. Colleen had not come around yet, but Mr. Bordeaux said that he and the family would be there whether she came or not.

"Nikki I'm on my way. Is Phillip bringing the kids to Big Mama?"

"Yes. He should be there any minute. They were dragging this morning."

"Ok."

Feather showed Big Mama and Tee the clothes that the boys were to wear later.

While they were at the courthouse Pat, Lillian, Tee, Carl, Bo and Jimmy were going to set everything up, decorate and spread the food out.

Mr. Bordeaux hired a photographer and videographer.

Feather had Nikki and Phillip believing that Big Mama wanted to see them before they went to dinner.

Nikki wasn't having the wedding that she dreamed of, so Feather and Big Mama were planning her a celebration she would never forget.

Feather arrived at Nikki's and Phillip arrived at Black's about the same time. He was getting dressed there and Feather was getting dressed at Nikki's.

"Are you going to a funeral before we go to the courthouse?"

"No."

"Then why the long face? You're getting married."

Nikki felt like her dreams, all of them, were gone. Nothing she set out to do had been accomplished. Here she was about to marry someone whose mother couldn't stand the sight of her. She had already birthed three babies with no Grandmother now this one had a grandmother that didn't want it. There was no train on her dress. No veil on her head. No flock of loving guest.

"It's just…well, my wedding…hell my life ain't what I wanted it to be."

"Girl, come off that. It ain't never what you want it to be. You better appreciate what it is. It could always be worst. What if there was no Phillip to love you, in spite of. What if you couldn't have any kids? What if you had no one in the world to love you?"

Nikki smiled. "I hear you, but it's so different from what I wanted. I feel like I've been pregnant all of my adult life and crying in between that." She started laughing. Feather joined her.

After getting dressed Feather pulled Nikki's hair into a French roll and added baby's breath to the crown. She wore a light pink dress with pearl accessories. The sleeves were short and lace on top of chiffon; it came above her knees in mini fashion. The body of the dress was flared and ruffled at the bottom in chiffon material only.

Feather wore pink too. An after fiveish style dress, but she wore it with such elegance it was appropriate. Her hair was styled into a bun on top and a Frenchroll in the back.

Phillip and Black walked in.

"Babe, y'all ready."

Nikki walked into the living room. Everything about her was beautiful. Her dress was picked so well that her stomach was not noticeably visible. Only on a profile could her pregnancy be seen.

Her beauty took Phillip.

"You look great."

"You too." Nikki was trying to hold her tears.

Feather walked to Black and whispered, "Did you get the bouquet?"

"I couldn't he was there before I could leave. I called Big Mama. She said she'd have Carl or somebody run and get it."

"Good. You look good too baby." She kissed his cheek.

Feather smiled. She had a secret too. After Nikki's day was over she would share it until then she would enjoy it all by herself.

Phillip circled the courthouse three times looking for a park, finally he decided to pull over to let the girls out. Then the car in front of him pulled out to leave. As he looked over his shoulder to parallel park he made eye contact with

Champ. The moment was frozen in time. No one else in the truck noticed Champ.

Phil got out and helped Feather out. Black got out and helped Nikki out. Nikki raised her head and looked into the face of Champ.

He walked away as fast as his feet could carry him. Phil and Feather was walking around from the other side of the vehicle to join them. Phillip felt sorry for Champ; he was a pitiful sight. Neither Black nor Feather saw him.

It did Nikki's heart some good to see him. She was glad to be rid of him. Her blessing came into view.

Phillip surprised Nicole during the ceremony. He purchased the baguette solitaire that she looked at the day they bought their bands. Since, she wasn't having the wedding she wanted, the pregnancy was mainly for him, and she was deserving of her hearts desire, he decided to give her something special.

Nikki cried at the sight of it. Feather cried too. Black felt good too.

"We need to stop by Big Mama's, don't forget." Black reminded Phillip in the car.

"Ok." Phillip looked over at his wife. He felt good knowing that he had made her happy.

At Big Mama's they walked into balloons and wedding bell streamers. The house was filled with people. Nikki cried some more when she started recognizing Phillip's family members. A photographer snapped a shot of them. (Phillip smiled at Black. Their friendship was the best he'd ever had.)

The best photo taken was the one of Phillip when he looked into the face of his mother. Colleen Bordeaux was present, without her attitude. Oh, she had brought it, but after meeting Big Mama and all of these wonderful people who weren't even Nikki's blood family she warmed up to the idea of accepting her. *She must be a decent woman to* win *the hearts of all these people.*

It was difficult to tell that Nikki was not Big Mama's biological grandchild or that Pat and Lillian were her surrogate mothers. Even though they looked nothing alike it was hard to tell that Feather and Nikki were not true sisters.

"Congratulations Nicole. You look beautiful." Colleen offered through her embrace.

The evening was pleasant. (Nikki laughed aloud when she saw Big Mama place Feather's hand to the soft spot of her throat and then pull her into her.)

That night Colleen and Jimmy took their grandsons home with them. And despite how they cried all the other babies were sent home with their parents. Big Mama was off duty. Black promised to come back in the morning and help her put her house back together.

Nikki fell asleep in the car. Phil fell as soon as the lights were out. The newlyweds were too tired to make love, but then …they had a lifetime to do that.

47

Feather announced her pregnancy the day after Nikki's reception. Black was ecstatic. Nikki was too.

"Phil, man guess whose pregnant?"

"Man, congratulations!...hold-on." He looked at Johnny. "You know better than that don't you? Ok, then don't let me see you do that anymore." Phil returned to his conversation with Black. "What y'all trying to do, catch up with me and Nicole?"

Black laughed. "That will take some doing."

"She's almost four months. This time she's considered high risk since Mikey's complications."

"Well at least now y'all know she need to take it easy."

"Yeah. I'm trying to go fishing. We need to hook up soon."

"Ok. I'll call Pops and see if he wants to go."

"Cool. I'm off next weekend."

"Ok, I'll trade or something."

"Man congratulations on the baby. I need to go see about these knuckleheads of mine. Johnny's getting beside himself. He don't want nobody on his bed or in his stuff. Yeah we need to go fishing his brothers are working on him too." Phillip smiled. "I gotta explain to Johnny that his brothers look up to him".

"Well, give me a call after you talk to Pops."

They didn't get to go fishing for two months. First, Feather had some difficulty, and then Nikki had a false alarm. Then Big Mama took ill and they were juggling kids from Nikki to Feather since they were both off on maternity leave. Feather was seven months and afraid the same thing was going to happen as did with Mikey, especially since the doctor relieved her from work.

While the men were fishing Colleen called to check on Nikki, since Phillip wasn't home. Nikki treated her as if things were always pleasant between them. Colleen appreciated that. She was aware that she had behaved poorly. The small talk was laboring, but they managed. It was a start anyway.

At 2:38 am Phil woke up to warmth running down his leg. Nikki woke too. Phil looked at her. It was time. He recognized the look.

"Mama. Nikki's in labor we are on our way to the hospital."

"Ok. We'll meet you there."

"Big Mama, Nikki's in labor can you come. The kids are asleep."

"Yes baby, I'll get Tee to bring me right now."

"Our bed is wet, her water broke."

"Don't worry about it."

Nikki changed her clothes. Phillip called the hospital and dressed himself.

The doorbell rang. It was Big Mama and Tee.

Tee helped Nikki to the car. Phillip told Big Mama which hospital and his cellular number.

♣♣♣

Nikki was taken straight to a birthing room.

"You don't mess around do you baby?" Phil teased. The nurse came in and checked her. Another nurse appeared with Colleen and Jimmy.

"It's time." The examining nurse informed. "I'll get the doctor."

Nikki's eyes fell on her in-laws. Their eyes held pity for Nikki. Her pain was felt. The doctor entered the room.

Nikki began pushing immediately. Two pushes and a little girl plopped from her womb. Phillip cut the cord. He was speechless. Making eye contact with Jimmy he shared a masculine sort of pride. There was not a strand of hair on her head, which made her look more like him. When they showed Nikki her baby she said 'Hey you...You look just like somebody else I know.'

Phillip looked on... "Hi Monique. It's Daddy." He spoke to her softly.

The nurse took the baby, weighed her, cleaned her and offered her to whoever was carrying her to the nursery.

Phillip and Nicole looked at Colleen as if it were preplanned.

Colleen accepted her granddaughter.

Monique and her grandparents walked out of the room to the nursery.

Phillip kissed Nikki. "Thank you baby."

"Thank you."

"Babe I wanna name her Monique Nicole Bordeaux."

"That's fine."

Nikki was pleased. She knew what Phillip was doing. He was trying to combine all the women in his life into this one little girl. She remembered their pillow talks and the time he'd told her that had he been a girl his name would've been Monique.

Colleen and Jimmy walked into the waiting room to find Lillian, Pat, Feather and Black. Each of them peeked through the nursery glass at Monique.

48

On Wednesday Mikey turned two years old. This morning while Black was running around picking up balloons, tablecloths and disposable eating utensils Feather and Mikey lay in bed just looking at each other. Last night Feather was up 'til midnight cleaning and preparing her side dishes while Black and Mikey were resting. Now it was her turn to rest. Looking closely at her baby she smiled. Mikey was the kind of baby that looked like everyone in her family. When Pat was holding her she looked like Pat. When Lillian was holding her she looked like her. She was a beautiful baby.

♣♣♣

Lillian and Bo were at her house getting ready for the party. They had bought Mikey a rocking horse.

Bo was happier than he remembered being in a long time, but he was getting impatient on the decision of whether or not Lillian was going to marry him. He was at that stage in life where he wanted to commit and be about living. Living and loving…it went well together. He was ready to come home from work to a house with someone in it. Ready to stop at the store and pick up something nice for someone special. He was ready to smile on someone and be smiled on. Bo was ready for love, and although he loved Lillian he wasn't going to spend the rest of his life trying to convince her that he did.

Lillian was happier than she had ever been. Bo was exactly whom she had waited for. He had touched her life so gently that she didn't even realize that she was a different woman. She was thinner, healthier, glowing, relaxed and open. She was the woman she wanted to be simply because he loved her. She wasn't alone anymore. She could fall and know she'd be helped up. She could jump foolishly and maintain that same confidence. Love was a wonderful thing.

Then she reflected back to her life with Michael. It was never what it appeared to be. She was terrified of that happening again. She simply wanted to rush home to someone. Have to stop shopping to get home and cook. To hear roaring laughter in the living room from the guys hanging out at their place. She needed someone to share her secrets and opinions with. Bo had become that person. Bo had become her everything, but Bo had not dissolved her insecurities.

Tee and Carl were trying to conceal their pregnancy too. Big Mama and Pat had preached that there would be no babies coming there. Not to live anyway. Black had not done it, which meant she better not try it. So they were looking for an apartment. Hopefully the one they looked at yesterday would work out. It was only a matter of time before she started to show. She was already entering into her fourth month. Wearing her tops on the outside was about to draw attention to herself, especially since it was out of her character.

♣♣♣

Pat was first to arrive. Mikey was getting her hair combed, she cried at the sight of her grandmother.

"Feather hurry up. Can't you see we're trying to get to each other?" Pat joked.

"Yeah I see. Just give me a minute."

Mikey stretched out her arms as Black entered the room. So much for Pat. Mikey loved her Daddy. He couldn't be anywhere around and not pick her up.

Feather finally gave up and let them have her.

Pat was holding the wiggling Mikey it was no use now, she wanted her Daddy. Black hated to do this to his mother, but he hated to hear his baby cry. He took her from Pat. Mikey turned in his arms facing the two women as if to say "now" in a sassy lil' way. Black leaned down and Feather fastened the hair bow.

"Mama, where's Big Mama?" Black asked.

"She'll be here with Tee and Carl, they're suppose to swing by and pick her up."

"Swing by?"

"Yeah, they stayed out last night."

"Stayed out??" Black couldn't believe Tee was out all night with a man. And Pat and Big Mama knew.

"Yeah. All night with Carl."

Pat tried to get Mikey back. Mikey only smiled. She wasn't leaving her Daddy until he put her down and then she was going to act a fool about it.

"I think they're about to get a place together. She's been buying house stuff. Sometimes I see her with the classified section of the paper."

"Move out? Man, y'all ain't even watching my sister."

"We ain't watching her? Boy, Tee is almost twenty-five years old. You're married with a child, pleeease!"

Black had to think about it. She was right. He was married and was working on his second child. Tee just always seemed so much younger than he did.

The doorbell rang. It was Bo and Lillian. Feather was so happy for them. It was evident that they were in love.

Nikki and Monique could be seen getting out of their car from the doorway. Feather went to help Nikki.

Sometimes when Lillian looked at Nikki she admired her. The girl had been through the ringer, visited hell and came back, yet she found the courage to love again. Lillian begrudged her that, secretly.

♣♣♣

Nikki dressed Monique in a cute little frilly dress. She was glad she had kept her baby. Unlike the boys this baby looked just like her Daddy. Phillip should have done the pushing, because that was truly his reflection. It was also his heart. He called Monique, Nicole also. Her grand parents called her Gumdrop.

Pride filled Nikki every time she looked at her baby. Monique had given her everything she had ever hoped for. Love.

Even Colleen had embraced her at the last family get-together and called her, her daughter-in-law instead of Phillip's wife. Monique was the only baby of Nikki's that was born into normalcy. No yelling. No crying. No fighting. Just love. All day long she had three little men and one big one in her face.

Sometimes, Nikki gave her a bath just so she could have some time alone with her.

Justin and Joshua had gone with Phil to pick up Johnathan from Grandpa B's. They were going to meet them at the party.

Astro Jump had the attention of the kids. Bob the Builder was on his way to the party. Big Mama, Pat, Lil and Bo were out there with the kids. Most of the others were in the house. Tee had taken on the role of Disc Jockey.

Feather and Nikki were in the kitchen as usual. Their wedding rings flickering in the sunlight. Each woman was in the exact place in life that they always wanted to be dead center of joy. The beauty is they had the good sense to know it.

Black and Phil were standing over the grill trying to discreetly smoke a joint, cook the meat and drink a beer. They were fanning like crazy on the exhale trying to keep the scent of marijuana from dancing under Big Mama's nose.

Black accepted the joint with his chest stuck out. They were happy men. If Life weathered a storm at this moment their happiness would umbrella it.

Bo and Lil had made eye contact from across the yard. Lil mad her decision about marrying Bo.

Carl was sitting next to Tee just glad to be a part of such loving family. Tee sat next to him, loving him back. She slipped on the next song. Carl's love for her had increased the wealth of the song tremendously.

"It's soooo...good loving somebody. When that somebody loves you back."

In her heart Big Mama was remembering love and Pat was craving it. By the time he got to....*'talking 'bout a 50/50 looove,'* they were all shamelessly singing.

Big Mama was first to laugh the contagious laughter of life and love. They all began to laugh. They were laughing at each other.

To order

When Somebody Loves You Back

Send $21.31* Check or Money Order to:

Pressin On Publications
P.O. Box 2304
Oakland, Ca 94614

Or Call:

(510) 213~4525
(510) 213~4526

Or order on-line at:
www.Amazon.com

*Amount includes Shipping and Handling and California Sales Tax, $5 S&H, and 8.75% CA sales tax